WALTER AND THE RAVEN

A.J. PRUFROCK

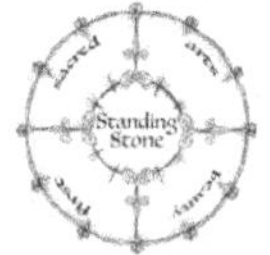

ISBN 978-1-7362968-4-4 (Paperback Edition)

ISBN 978-1-7362968-5-1 (Ebook)

Illustrations by Molly Kantz

Editing and book design by Lucy Marsh

Published by Standing Stone Press

P.O. Box 677

Alvarado, TX, 7600

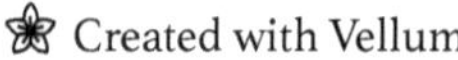 Created with Vellum

For Jill and Lucy

ALSO BY A.J. PRUFROCK

In Light of the New Moon

The Forging of Finnian Ludwell

A Circle of Dragons | Babiola

CONTENTS

PREFACE

Of all MacDonald's fantasies, *Lilith* has always been my favorite. *Walter and the Raven* is a daring (perhaps foolish) attempt to burn away the dross from the darkest and most troubling of his stories—one hundred and twenty-six years after *Lilith's* publication. MacDonald declared when he penned the work that he felt he was writing a transcript from God.[1] I think, like many artists, he took himself too seriously. And, while I have taken quite seriously the task of not harming his original magic, I believe it is counterproductive to consider the text sacrosanct. If Lewis's *Screwtape Letters* can been adapted as a play and turned into a graphic novel, why not a retelling of MacDonald's *Lilith*? As it is, it sits in the boneyard of the public domain, for the most part unheard-of.

MacDonald's final work of fantasy hovers somewhere between the romantic and the spiritual, living right along the border of the fantastical and the real. I hope this reworking allows modern audiences to be drawn in to wrestle with the groundbreaking author's take on the ultimate mystery of evil and the profound and painstaking work of repentance.

Sincerely,
A. J. Prufrock

1

———

A FAMILIAR SPIRIT

WALTER F. LUDWELL WAS AS ALONE IN THE WORLD AS A MAN MIGHT FIND HIMSELF. The funeral of his grandfather, Arthur McVeigh, had overshadowed his university commencement and all plans for the future. Grandpa Arthur had taken Walter in as a child of twelve when both of his parents had died from the same illness. Now twenty-two, Walter had just begun to realize the depths to which he and his grandfather had eased each other's pain from losses they never spoke of.

Arthur had never remarried after the passing of his beloved Olivia. Walter, having now loved and lost himself, began to understand in some small way the trials of grief. He had been befuddled by how Grandpa—a man who debated and won every argument with a half-mile of his brilliance—had shown silent respect for beliefs he did not hold when it came to Olivia. Walter had very few of his own memories of his grandmother but, looking back, her religious mysticism seemed to jar against her sharp intelligence.

The extended family attending the graveside had just exited

the Ludwell estate, and, though loyal and dutiful, they felt like strangers to Walter. Most guests, in his cursory estimation, shared his parents' spiritual view of the world, of which he had retained very little. Many had been kind in their attempts to comfort him. Walter was thankful both that they were gone and that they were not the sort of folk who became interested in a man's belongings after his passing.

To be all at once the sole inheritor of both the Ludwell and McVeigh estates was a sorrowful and weighty business. Walter also felt an accompanying guilt. Becoming the owner of Grandpa Arthur's expansive library was both comforting and exhilarating.

The exquisite literary collection had begun before the invention of the printing press and had never stopped expanding. A new volume, in fact, had arrived during the funeral. Wrapped in brown postal paper, it greeted Walter from the entrance table in the foyer. Tenderly, as an act of homage to Grandpa, he found it a place on the bookshelves that encroached into one room after another. The library occupied the greater part of the ground floor. Its chief room was large and well-designed with shelves rising almost to the ceiling. The adjoining rooms that housed the overflow beckoned readers to explore through open arches, short passages, steps up, and steps down.

Walter had possessed a half-hearted approach to his formal schooling, but he had never been lukewarm towards Grandpa and his books. Every college holiday he could manage, the grandson hurried home hoping he had garnered some bits of knowledge unknown to the old man. Grandpa and his collection always outclassed the dry intellect of the lecture halls.

A solitary Walter now stood among the volumes wondering how a man might explore and not lose himself in the maze of unfathomable riches.

A WEEK AFTER THE FUNERAL, Walter was reading in his usual place in the main room of the library, slouched and dispirited. His low mood was not helped by the fact that it had rained the greater part of the day. Just as the sun began to set, the clouds parted allowing evening sunshine to fill the room. Walter rose, stretched, and looked out the wide picture window noting how the light filtered through the feathering spray of the fountain in the center of the wide lawn. Prisms danced upon the grass. As he turned back to his reading, an invading beam of sunlight caught his eye. It seemed to bend and touch a portrait tucked within a niche on the eastern wall.

Walter crossed the room and found a little shrine sunk within the great expanse of bookshelves. Why did the portrait hang there alone? The work seemed more icon than realistic art. Should it not be displayed in Grandma Olivia's chapel on the floor above? Walter decided he would have it moved, though he did admit that the direct sunlight brought out the colors wonderfully.

The more Walter studied the oddly drawn face, the more he felt it was somehow looking back. It seemed to respond to his attention, to throw off a little light. The more he looked, the more he doubted that the source of illumination came from the evening sun. He had the sensation that his own eyes were slowly filling up with the same light.

A soft movement from the farthest end of the room made him glance up. A tall figure stood reaching a hand to a crowded bookshelf. Walter blinked, allowing his pupils to adjust, but looking again saw no one. He shook his head. Patting his cheeks roughly, he returned to his window seat. He knew no response but to continue reading.

WALTER LUDWELL WOULD HAVE FORGOTTEN the strange vague impression of the tall figure and the dancing light had he not had occasion, less than an hour later, to consult the new arrival: the volume on Byzantium unpackaged and shelved a week before. But when he went to fetch it, there was a gap in the row where it ought to have stood. The empty space was right where he had seen—or thought he had seen—the tall man reaching. Walter looked all about the spot for several minutes but in vain.

The next morning, however, there was no gap. The book had been returned. Walter scratched his head, for no servant or recent houseguest was likely to be interested in the ancient city on the Bosphorus.

Three days later, an even odder event took place.

Along the library wall opposite the grand entrance of the house was a low, narrow, thickset closet door. The closet contained the oldest and rarest of the volumes but it was the door itself that fascinated Walter. Some quirky ancestor had cut shallow shelves no more than an inch deep into the solid wood. Upon these faux shelves had been affixed old book spines. Some of the titles on the sham bindings were homemade and humorously original. Some were actual bindings of books beyond hope of repair. To complete the illusion, some inventive workman had shoved in, on the top of the second row of spines, part of a thin volume. The handwritten manuscript lay horizontally across the fake spines with one of its dogeared corners projecting out. A considerable portion of the book had been cut away to achieve the effect, and the mutilated volume's limp parchment was the finishing touch in the humorous deception. Walter loved it.

Returning to his couch, he glanced, as was his habit, down at the whimsical door. The mutilated manuscript was gone.

Livid, Walter rang the bell to the servants' quarters for the first time since becoming master of the estate. Percival the butler appeared. When asked about the volume, he turned pale and assured Walter he knew nothing of its whereabouts. Because Mr. Percival had earned the implicit trust of generations of McVeighs, Walter did not doubt his word, but he was left with the impression that the servant knew more.

That afternoon, Walter sat trying to finish a passage that demanded reflection. Pondering, he lowered his book and let his eyes go wandering about the shelves. Once again he caught sight of a tall figure, the back of a slender old man in a long dark coat, frayed from much wear. This time he was not reaching for a volume, but disappearing into the closet. Walter darted across the room, pulled the door open, peered in, and saw exactly nobody.

He glanced around to make sure he was indeed alone. He peered around every shelf and even scrutinized the ceiling. Perched again on the edge of his reading couch, he found he could not settle upon a single word. Looking about, he was on his feet again running to the little door. The mutilated volume was back in its place! He laid hold of it and pulled but found it firmly fixed as usual.

Walter, utterly bewildered, again rang the bell. Percival came and was told everything his master had observed. This time the butler told all.

2

PERCIVAL SPILLS THE TEA

"I HAD HOPED, SIR," Percival began, "that the old gentleman in the black coat was going to be forever forgotten. I heard a good deal about him when I first came to serve, but by degrees the specter ceased to be mentioned."

"The place was—rather, is—haunted by an old gentleman?" Walter inquired.

"There was a time that all the residents believed so," Percival conceded, "but I had thought the thing had come to an end."

"What have *you* seen?"

"Nothing at all firsthand, Sir, in spite of my long service to the family. Your grandfather would never hear a word on the matter, declaring that whoever alluded to it should be dismissed without warning. He claimed it was nothing but an excuse for the maids to run into the arms of the men. Then again, your grandfather believed in nothing he could not lay hold of."

"Was anyone dismissed for speaking of it?" asked Walter.

"No. One footman did leave the place of his own free will, having caught sight of the phantom."

Percival shifted his weight from foot to foot hoping to be dismissed. Walter caught his eye and stared.

"Sir, I have told you all I know first- and second hand. To say more would be gossip and conjecture."

"I'll keep that in mind," said Walter. "Please continue."

"As you wish, Sir. When I was a boy, an ancient woman in the village told me a legend concerning our haunting spirit—a Mr. Raven. How she learned so much about him I do not know, but the description she gave corresponds exactly with the figure you have just seen. Mr. Raven was hired as both secretary and librarian to Sir Alban, your great-great-grandfather, whose portrait hangs there among the books. The woman held the strong opinion that Mr. Raven led Sir Alban astray by encouraging him to read unwholesome publications—strange, forbidden books. She believed that the librarian was probably the devil himself and many became sure of it when both men disappeared without warning. Sir Alban was never seen again, but Mr. Raven continued to show himself sporadically in the library."

Percival paused and raised an eyebrow, then lowered his voice to almost a whisper, "There were some who believe he is no specter. I find it easier to think that a dead man might revisit the world he has left than that a man might go on living well past one hundred and fifty years."

The butler straightened himself and attempted a more professional tone. "In any case, Sir, I have never heard of Mr. Raven meddling with anything in the house, but he might consider himself privileged in regard to the books. It was most likely a friendly call on the part of an old gentleman."

"I have no objection to any number of friendly calls from Mr. Raven," answered Walter, "but it would be best, Percival, that we continue on with your wise resolution of saying nothing about him to the other servants."

Percival nodded and turned to go.

"One more thing."

"Yes sir?"

"Have you ever seen the mutilated volume attached to the closet door out of its place?"

"No sir, never. I have always thought it a fixture."

Percival crossed the room and gave it a pull.

It was immovable.

SOME DAYS PASSED without noteworthy events. Each evening, Walter tried to discover a way of releasing the manuscript fragment in the faux shelf, but in vain. The closet became a fixation. Grand intentions were birthed for its thorough reorganization. One morning after coffee, intention became resolution. Walter rose from his breakfast chair and rolled up his sleeves.

Entering into the grand library with firm determination, Walter beheld, flickering in the morning light, the old librarian. Mr. Raven—or at least a shadow of a slight, stooping man in a shabby dress coat—was exiting the closet. The tails of the scruffy coat reached almost to his heels and parted a little as he walked, revealing thin legs in black stockings and large feet in slipper-like shoes.

Without hesitation, Walter trailed after. I might be following a shadow, he thought to himself, but I'm definitely following something. The shadow went out of the library, into the entrance hall and began to climb the great staircase. Walter followed. Up both went to the first floor, where lay the chief rooms. They continued through the wide corridor past every door and ascended a narrower stair to the third floor.

The third story was a region unfamiliar to Walter. He had never shared the house with siblings or cousins. Romping games of hide-and-seek that make children familiar with every nook and cranny of an abode were outside his experience. Now he found himself in a different game of chase altogether.

Through several passages Walter's pursuit led him to a door at the bottom of a spiraling wooden stair, rising upward in a corkscrew. Every step creaked under his weight as he ascended, but he heard no sound ahead of him from the steps of his guide. Somewhere in the middle of the climb, Walter lost sight of his quarry, and when he reached the top, the shape of the old librarian was nowhere visible. The huge attic was full of shadows, but Mr. Raven was not one of them.

3

A MIRROR IN THE HIGHEST ATTIC

HEAVY BEAMS stretched before him underfoot and long rafters arched overhead. Doors peeked out from the west along an unfinished hallway, and here and there the gloom was thinned by windows curtained in cobwebs. A strange mingling of awe and pleasure washed over Walter, feelings untapped since his adventurous boyhood when he encountered wide expanses of forest in need of unsupervised exploration.

In the middle of the garret stood an unpainted inclosure of rough planks. The door hung loosely on its hinges and was slightly ajar. Thinking Mr. Raven might have entered there, Walter approached and pushed open the door.

Unlike the wider attic, the small chamber was full of light, but the sun's rays took on a dull, remorseful look as they bounced off the walls. It was as if they regretted having come, finding no use for themselves in the deserted space. A few beams fell upon a tall mirror with a dusty face, old-fashioned and narrow. On top of the frame perched a black eagle with outstretched wings. In his beak he held a golden chain meant for use in hanging, but the links sagged limply as the mirror leaned against the eastern wall.

Walter at first looked *at* rather than *into* the mirror, and was puzzled that the glass reflected neither the chamber nor his own person. He thought perhaps it was not a looking glass after all but a well-painted countryside. Leaning to inspect it he saw within the ebony frame a wild landscape, broken up with desolate hills of no great height. Along the horizon stretched the tops of far-off mountains. In the foreground lay a tract of moorland, flat and melancholy.

Being short-sighted, Walter stepped even closer to examine the texture of a prominent stone. In doing so, he saw hopping towards him, with great solemnity, a large and ancient raven, purply black yet softened with gray. The bird seemed to be looking for worms as he came closer. Astonished at the appearance of a living creature in a painting, Walter took yet another step forward to see him better. As he lifted his foot, he tripped over the frame and fell forward, landing on hard ground with a shocking thud. When he regained his senses, he found himself in the open air on a houseless plain, staring nose to beak with a large unflappable bird.

Walter leapt to his feet and spun from the piercing beady gaze. He glanced about trying to take in the uncertain boundaries between fog, field, cloud, and mountainside. Nothing made sense. All he knew with certainty was that he could not see anything he remembered ever seeing before.

Imagining himself caught up in a visual illusion, he assumed touch would correct sight. Stretching his arms out he walked first in one direction and then another. Nothing changed. He turned about again, bewildered as fear crept in. Could a man at any moment step beyond the realm of order and become the sport of an illusion?

The raven stood a little way off, regarding him with an expression both respectful and quizzical. Walter was struck by the absurdity of seeking counsel from a bird, but it was the only living thing nearby. He did not *know*, but he felt confident that he *saw* the Raven. He knew he *felt* the ground under his feet. He was quite certain he *heard* a sound of wind.

"How did I get here?" he said—apparently aloud—for the question was immediately answered.

"You came through the door," replied an odd, rather harsh voice.

Walter looked about for a human shape to go with the crackly tone. A terror that he might be descending into madness choked his heart. Could his senses be trusted? Had he wandered into a region where the material relations of the natural world ceased to hold?

But in the same instance he knew that the Raven had spoken, for the bird had hopped round to face him and stood looking at him with an air of waiting.

Walter supposed that a bird capable of addressing a man had the right to a civil answer—perhaps more than a right. "I did not come through any door," he replied.

"I saw you come through with my own ancient eyes," asserted the Raven firmly.

The bird's tone, although edged with roughness, was not disagreeable, and what he said (although conveying very little enlightenment) was not rude.

"I never *saw* any door," Walter persisted.

"Of course not," returned the bird. "All the doors you have yet seen—and you have not seen many—were doors in. In this instance, you passed through a door out."

Walter could think of nothing to say in return. The bird went on, "Even stranger, you will find that the more doors you go out of, the farther you get in."

Walter, since he could not follow, changed the line of inquiry. "Oblige me by telling me where I am."

"The only way to discern where you are," answered the Raven, "is to begin to make yourself at home."

"How?"

"By doing something."

"Doing what?"

"Anything worth doing. And the sooner you begin, the better. For until you are at home, you will find it as difficult to get out as it is to get in."

"I have, unfortunately, found it too easy to get in," said Walter, his voice rising. "Once I am out I shall not try again!"

"You have stumbled in, and may possibly stumble out," countered the Raven, "Whether you have got in *unfortunately* remains to be seen."

The black bird cocked his head to one side. "I think it is now my turn to ask you a question."

"The fact that you *can* ask gives you the best of rights," Walter agreed.

"Well answered!" said the Raven and Walter felt the bird would have broken into a grin if his beak allowed for it.

"Tell me, then," the Raven continued, "*Who* are you? If you happen to know."[1]

"How should I help knowing? I am myself."

"How do you know you are yourself?" shot back the Raven. "Did you ask your father or mother? Did they know? And if you come from them, are you therefore them? Are you your own fool? *Who* are you?"

Walter was suddenly aware he could not answer. Indeed, who was he? He had no grounds upon which to determine his identity. As for his name, "Walter," he had forgotten it. To recall it would have been pointless, for his name held no meaning here. In fact, he had almost forgotten that it was a custom for everyone to have a name.

"Look at me," said the Raven, "and tell me who *I* am."

As the bird spoke he turned his back, and instantly Walter knew him. He was no longer a Raven, but a tall man, very thin, and wearing a long black tailcoat.

The man turned to face him, and again Walter saw a bird.

"I *do* know you, sir," Walter said, feeling more foolish than surprised.

"How can you say so from seeing me from behind?" the bird asked. "You never saw yourself from behind. Tell me then, *who* I am."

"I humbly beg your pardon," Walter answered. "I believe you were once the librarian of our estate, but more of *who* you are I do not know."

"Why do you beg my pardon?"

"Because I took you for a Raven," Walter said.

"You did me no wrong," Mr. Raven said. "Calling me a Raven, or thinking me one. You allowed me existence, which all that one can demand of his fellow beings."

"Forgive the question but it begs asking," Walter ventured.

"Have I been wrong my whole life in presuming that a man is superior to a bird?"

"To generalize is a waste of intellect," answered the Raven. "Let us take each man or bird as we find him."

Walter returned again to a previous subject. "I suspect, sir, that whatever 'in' and 'out' mean, you do either as you please."

The bird nodded. "But I do not go out often or for long. Your world is such a half-baked sort of place. It is simultaneously infantile and self-satisfied. It is no place for an old Raven like me."

Here the Raven trailed off, then picked back up, saying, "I fear you have gotten into this region too soon. Nonetheless you must get to be at home here, at least a little. For home is the only place where you can go both out and in."

The bird turned to walk away, appearing again as the librarian. Walter gazed after him until he saw him no more.

4

WALTER DOUBLES DOWN

NOW ALONE, WALTER LOOKED ABOUT AND WONDERED IF HE WERE DEAD. Perhaps this was the world beyond the grave. Perhaps he must wander about and seek his place in it. Perhaps he should "do something" like Mr. Raven instructed.

While Walter thought, he began to amble along in the direction Mr. Raven had gone. What could he do here? And what action would make him somebody? Most pressing, he wondered why he had not asked the old bird how to get back to his warm bed while the feathered sage stood before him. Soon he saw a grove of tall slender pine trees. The pleasant odor made him hurry his steps and a strange desire to be enveloped caused him to plunge like an eager child into the shadowy gloom.

In fewer than a dozen steps he spied two trunks, almost identical in their straightness and circumference. A translucent span trembled between them like the vibrating strings of a musical instrument.

"Another door!" Walter cried, quickening his pace. Close

up, the colors beyond the opening became uncertain and strange. Passing through, he stumbled and fell. Down he came on rough-hewn flooring with a shocking thud. When he regained his senses, the master of the manor found himself on his back looking upward at the black-framed, eagle-topped mirror.

Terror at once seized Walter; towards the comfort of the library couch he fled. His trek from top to ground floor felt bizarre. The whole house had grown strange. The wide attic space had an uncanny look, like it had been waiting for him to come back "out" and was enlivened by his appearance. Hurrying past beam and rafter, Walter shuddered and rushed down the winding stair as if something were about to leap upon him from behind. Striking a door jamb he fell and rose and and ran on. He lost his way on the second floor, going through several passages more than once before finding the head of the grand stairway.

By the time he reached the foyer he needed to sit on the lowest step to recover his wits. Light pierced the Tiffany glass crowning the entranceway and he beheld it, noting the elegant workmanship for the first time. By the time he reached the library his breathing and heart rate had returned to normal. Still, he confessed to himself he could not think of anything that would ever again make him go up that last terrible corkscrew stair to the attic.

From the comfort of his couch Walter looked at the ceiling. He measured out how the space above stretched the whole length of the house. Nowhere was he out from under the brooding attic. Its mysterious inhabitants could invade the safety of his library at any moment. He would rent the dreadful place out. No, he would *sell* it and purchase a house in Switzerland. There, atop a high peak, he would build a one-story hut open to the rafters. Avalanches were preferable to living under a fantastical portal.

If I have no understanding of my own attic, Walter thought, what is there to secure me against my own mind? What is it even now generating? What thought might present itself to me in the next moment, the next month, or the next year? What is behind my thinking? *Who* am I? Walter could no more answer the question now than when the Raven put it to him. What did he know of himself or of the universe?

Less than an hour later, a dozing Walter started up and onto his feet. He hurried across the room straight to the closet door, where the mutilated volume protruded. There it was as usual, sticking out from the flat pageless non-existent books. He went down on his knees and opened the fragmented manuscript as far as its position would permit, but could read nothing. He lit a taper and held it as close as possible without setting the volume on fire.

Peering like a dentist into a pair of reluctant jaws, Walter finally managed to perceive lines of poetry. Beginnings of couplets were visible on the left-hand page, and each ended on the right, but connecting a beginning and an end of a single line was impossible. He could make no sense of it, but the mere words aroused in him an impossible strangeness. A dream? A song? A lyric? A description? Sensations unfamiliar to him fashioned themselves around the aroma of an idea, awakening in him a great longing to know the meaning of the stanzas. He copied out a few of the readable shreds and struggled to complete some of the lines with words of his own—but with no success. All he gained in his efforts was so much weariness that when at last he went to bed, he fell asleep at once.

In the morning all the horror of the empty attic space had left him.

Dawn was bright and glorious, but Walter doubted the fine weather would hold. He dressed and deliberately put a sapphire ring on his right pinky, a piece given to him by his grandmother. It reminded him somehow of the Tiffany window in the entryway, but he did not think about why. At breakfast he noticed the gem's center star was milky, more like the cream in his coffee than the clear brilliance he had remembered in his bedroom.

Before settling in to read the morning news, he stood staring out the library window. There had been heavy rain the night before. On the lawn a sparrow was breaking his way into the shell of a snail. Glancing away from the bird, Walter turned his ring to catch the sun, and all at once he spied a keen black eye gazing at him out of the misty blue jewel. Startled, he dropped it. When he reached to pick it up again from where it had clattered beneath a nearby sofa, the eye was gone.

As he had predicted, the fine weather did not hold. Dark clouds obscured the sun even as it climbed the morning sky. The air became sultry and the heavens turned gray. There came a wind and a flash of lightning. After a single sharp thunder-clap, the rain fell in torrents.

Walter opened the dormer window and welcomed the storm. Motionless, he stared out at the deluge. A raven with a solemn gait, showing utter disregard for the downpour, began walking across the lawn towards the house. Walter watched the bird closely, taking comfort in the fact he stood safely on the ground floor. He was well aware that if he were not careful, anything could happen.

5

WILD HYACINTH AMONG THE STRINGS

THE RAVEN CAME EVER NEARER. Ten yards from the house he paused and made a profound bow towards Walter, then with a sudden winged leap stood on the window-sill. The feathered guest stepped over the ledge, jumped down into the room, and walked across the thick carpet. Walter, guessing the bird was on his way to the library closet, followed. As he trailed, he made an inner vow not to take so much as a single step upward upon the stairway.

The Raven turned neither towards the bookshelves, the little closet, nor the stair. He approached instead an exterior door that led to a short breezeway between two portions of the rambling house. Walter made haste to open the door for his guest. The bird ambled out onto a grass patch under a screened-in roof covered in creeper vines and stood looking at the rain. Walter remained in the doorway behind him.

Another flash of lightning came, and a lengthy roll of distant thunder. The Raven swiveled his head over his shoulder, looking at Walter, as if to say, "Do you hear that?" His posture and mannerisms were so human that Walter remarked without thought, "Fine weather for the worms, Mr. Raven!"

"Yes," the Raven answered in his rather croaky voice. "The ground will be nice for them to get out and get in, but the shower is nearly over. After the next thunderclap, it will stop ... There it is!" A flash came with his words. The storm turned to drizzle and then ceased.

"Now we should be going!" said the Raven, stepping out.

"Going where?" Walter asked.

"Going where we have to go," he answered.

"I do not want to go," Walter said.

"That does not make any difference—at least not much."

"I am quite content where I am."

"You may think so, but you are not. Come along."

The Raven hopped onto the grass and turned, waiting. Walter noted a white patch on his feathered throat wrapping round, much like a white-collared swift's.

"I will not leave the house today," Walter said with obstinacy.

"Come into the garden!" quoth the Raven.

"I will give in that far since it is my property after all," Walter muttered.

The sun broke through the clouds. Raindrops flashed and sparkled on the grass.

"You will wet your feet!" Walter said playfully.

"And mire my beak," the Raven answered, immediately plunging his face deep into the sod and drawing out a great wriggling red worm. Throwing back his head, he tossed the worm into the air where it spread great wings, red and black, and soared aloft.

Walter watched with wonder and laughed like an astonished child. Then he remembered himself, and in an attempt to recover some dignity, said, "Mr. Raven, you made a mistake. Worms are not the larva of butterflies."

"I'm a sexton by trade," croaked the Raven. He added with a wink, "I am more used to burying than digging up. My mistake."

He turned and bowed.

"I see!" said Walter. "Your white feathered collar makes sense now. Well, you should check what you dig up before you make it fly. No creature should be allowed to forget what it is and where it came from."

"Why?" asked the Raven.

"Because it will grow proud, and cease to recognize its superiors," answered Walter, quoting a college professor he had forgotten he had no real liking for.

"No man knows it when he is making an idiot of himself," said the Raven under his breath. Then to Walter, "Is it not good for a creature sometimes to forget his origin and rise higher? I only teach them to find their way."

"Would you have the air full of worms?"

"That is the business of a sexton," answered the Raven. He dug again with his beak in the soft turf and released another worm into the air. "If only the rest of the clergy understood how to dig up as well. Instead, they continually tamp down."

Walter looked back towards his house and gave a cry of dismay. He was once again a stranger in a strange land. His home was nowhere in view.

"What right do you have to trick me, Mr. Raven?" he demanded. "Am I, or am I not, a free agent?"

"A man is as free as he chooses to make himself, never an atom freer," answered the Raven.

Walter looked all about and saw only scattered pines along the horizon. Did all the doors of his house open into a another world and he could not stay inside? He accused the bird again, "You have no right to make me do things against my will!"

"When you *have* a will," the Raven shot back, "you will find that no one can. Perhaps it may comfort you to be told that you have not yet left your house." He fluttered his tail.

"I do not understand you," Walter said. "Where am I?"

The Raven drew a deep breath. "You'd better follow me carefully for now, lest you should run a person over."

"There is nobody to run over but yourself, Mr. Raven!" Walter answered testily through tight lips, "and I must confess I feel tempted to do just that!"

"That you see nobody is where the danger lies. Look at that large tree over to your left, about thirty yards away."

Walter nodded at the obvious.

"That tree stands on the hearth of your kitchen, and grows straight up its chimney."

"Don't play games with me," Walter said with a touch of scorn.

"Was I playing games with you yesterday when you discovered me looking out of your star sapphire?"

"That was this morning—not an hour ago!"

"I have been widening your horizon longer than that, Mr. Ludwell."

"You mean you have been making a fool of me!"

"Excuse me, no one can do that but yourself."

"Then ... if you are to be believed," continued Walter ignoring the comment, "if I walk to the other side of *that* tree, I shall walk through my kitchen?"

"Yes. But first you would walk through the lady at the piano in the breakfast-room and that would frighten her terribly."

"There is no lady in my house!"

"Indeed, is your housekeeper not a lady?"

"Well, I suppose, if the term is applied to character and not bloodline ... but she cannot play the piano, anyhow."

"How do you know? She does so often when you are not around."

Walter softened. "Excuse me, Mr. Raven, but what you say seems sheer nonsense."

"If you could only hear the music!" cried the Raven, lost in the melody, "Those long stems of wild hyacinth are inside the piano among the strings, and give a peculiar sweetness to her playing!" Raven checked himself. "Pardon me. I forgot your deafness."

Walter said frowning and determined, "Two objects cannot exist in the same place at the same time."

"Can they not? Ah yes, I remember now they do teach that to you. It is a great mistake."

"You—a librarian—and talk such rubbish!" Walter cried, "Did you even read the books you were in charge of?!"

"Yes," answered the Raven pointedly, "I read through all your library in my time, and came out the other side not much the wiser. I was a bookworm but then woke up among the butterflies. I've given up reading for years now ... ever since I was made Sexton."

The Raven cocked his head and exclaimed "There! I smell Beethoven's "Alla Turca" in the quiver of those rose petals!"

Walter walked to the rosebush nearby and strained his ears, but could not hear the thinnest ghost of a sound. He did smell something he had never before smelled in any rose. It was still rose-odor, but with a touch—he supposed—of what must be Beethoven.

"Mr. Raven," Walter began again, "forgive me for being so rude. I was irritated. Will you kindly show me my way home? I must go, for I have an appointment with my foreman and a man must keep his word."

"You cannot break now what was broken days ago. Here, time does not pass like you think it does."

"Please show me the way," Walter implored, steadying himself from the shock of his missed appointment.

"I cannot," the Raven said. "To go back, you must go through yourself, and that way no man can show another."

Walter, finding all entreaty useless, went silent and tried to adjust to the bewildering situation. He told himself he was on an adventure, that he was being given the rare advantage of knowing two worlds.

"There is no hurry," said the Raven, scrutinizing his companion. "We do not go much by the clock in this region. Still, the sooner one begins to do what has to be done, the better.

Walter knew he had yet to justify his existence in his former world. How would he establish himself in this one? Then an idea came. He knew that he was not to blame for being *here* any more than he had anything to do with being *there*.

"*There* I found myself heir to two large properties," Walter mused aloud. "Perhaps *this* world will be just as generous."

The Raven interrupted him. "I will take you to my wife."

Walter nodded and Mr. Raven led the way.

6

———————

THE SEXTON'S WIFE

W ALTER FOLLOWED MR. RAVEN deep into the pine forest. Neither said much for awhile. A sacred gloom closed round as they encountered larger, older trees. Groves thinned to individual trunks, some of them gnarled with age. The two stopped a moment to admire an ancient hawthorn.

"That tree is in the ruins of the church on your home farm." said the Raven, "You were going to give some instructions concerning the area to the foreman, were you not, the morning of the thunder?"

"Yes," Walter said. "I was going to tell him I wanted wild rosebushes planted in the churchyard, but that the soil should be dug with a spade with care. I would have given orders that the plow should not ever come within three yards of of the cemetery."

The Raven nodded in seeming approval. "They go there still, you know."

"Who goes there?" asked Walter.

"Some of the people who used to pray at the church go to

the ruins still."

"Whatever for?"

"So that their prayers may join all the prayers ever offered in that space. Look! Look! There goes one!"

Mr. Raven pointed and right up into the air fluttered a snow-white dove as if mounting an unseen spiral stair. The evening light flashed on its quivering wings.

Walter stared and confessed, "I did see a dove."

"Of course you saw a dove," rejoined the Raven, "for there *was* a dove. It was also a prayer on its way." He then added to himself, "I wonder from whose heart it came. Someone may have come awake in my cemetery ... "

"How can a dove be a prayer?" Walter asked. "I understand, of course, how it might be a fit symbol or represent one, but you speak as if a live pigeon came out of a heart! A prayer is a thought, a thing spiritual."

"There is very little separation between what is real and visible and what is real and invisible."

"How do you know for sure when a dove is a prayer?" Walter asked. "Can you teach me how to properly identify one when I see it?"

"I cannot. If I could, how would that help you? You would only know the *name* of the thing which is not the same as knowing *the thing*."

Walter, for all his slowness, could at least see that the beautiful flight of the dove had been different from any before he had encountered. A great awe came over him. Perhaps, he thought, if I understand another world besides my own, I just might understand my own much better.

The companions walked for some time over a rocky moorland. Walter spied a little wood framed house in the farthest distance, enrapt in a gray cloud emitting a paltry light that shone over a stubby landscape. The wind blew bitter as though it came from a place where it was always night.

"It feels like winter," shivered Walter.

"It is."

"But it seems half a day since we left home!"

"The day in this region contains—in its own way—all the seasons," quoth the Raven, breaking into verse—

Winter in his winding-sheet of ice rules dark of night,
Spring awakes with the glimmering dawn and sinking modest moon,
Summer blazes noontime beauty setting all alight,
Autumn's glory permeates slow-changing afternoon.

The Raven sighed at the beauty of his own poetry.

THE TWO HAD DRAWN QUITE near to the house and the Raven bowed and lifted a wing in introduction, "Welcome to the Sexton's cottage."

Seeing nothing but a surrounding flat horizon, Walter was puzzled. "But where is your churchyard and cemetery? Where do you dig your graves?"

The Raven stretched out his neck, held his beak parallel to the ground, and turned it slowly round to all the points of the compass. Walter followed with his eyes as he realized the Raven was the Sexton of all he surveyed! They stood on the burial ground of the universe.

The two neared the house just as the clouded sun was gliding down the steep slope of the west. A wind swelled up the moor and rushed to the door with an assailing cold that seemed a material presence. Walter struggled across the threshold and closed the door with difficulty.

A candle burned on a three-legged table in the middle of the room. Its light flickered against the lid of a coffin set upright against the back wall. The lid turned upon a silent hinge, revealing that it was a door. Through it entered a woman. She was dressed all in white, bright like new-fallen snow.

Her face was warm, her features perfect, but her eyes made one forget everything else. The life of her whole person gathered and concentrated in them. Large and dark, a whole night-heaven seemed to lay condensed therein.

"Mr. Ludwell, may I present the fine lady who is good enough to let me call her wife," said the Raven. "Dear wife, may I present Sir Walter Ludwell."

"He is welcome," she said in a low, rich, gentle voice. Treasures of immortal sound seemed to be buried in it. She stood in front of the door by which she had entered and did not come nearer.

Walter gazed, and could not speak.

"Will he sleep, husband?" she asked.

"I fear not," replied the Raven. "He is neither weary nor heavy laden."

"Then why have you brought him?"

"Because it may prove to expedite his journey."

"I do not quite understand either of you," Walter broke in, filled with an uneasy foreboding. He gazed into the white face of the woman and his heart shivered. She returned his gaze in silence. "Surely a man must do a day's work before he accepts the hospitality of a place to rest. Let me first go home and I will come again after I have found, or made, or invented, or at least discovered something!"

"He has not learned much yet," said the lady.

"A man must learn to rest before he can do anything," said Mr. Raven. "Most think too much of having done, and turn themselves into empty shells just for the sake of activity."

At these words, Walter saw no longer a raven, but the librarian—the slender elderly man in a rusty black coat. For the first time, Walter could see his face. It was so gaunt that it showed the shape of the bones under the skin, but Walter had never before seen a face so ardent and perceptive. His pale green eyes had a haze about them, like a father who had done much weeping.

7
____

AN INVITATION TO SLEEP OVER

"YOU KNEW I WAS NOT A RAVEN," the Sexton said with a smile.

"I knew you were man," Walter replied, "but somehow I thought you were a bird as well."

"Sexton and librarian too," was his answer. "Technically, I am still the librarian in your house, for I was neither dismissed, nor did I resign. I am a sort of librarian here too, for whether it be books or bodies, it is the same profession. A library is nothing but a catacomb."

All three went silent. The woman, motionless as a statue, stood against the back wall by the door leading further in. Walter considered Mr. Raven more closely. He was above the ordinary height, and stood more erect than before. His nose handsomely encased the beak that had retired within it. His lips were very thin but their curves were beautiful, and about them quivered a shadowy smile that mixed humor, love, and pity.

The Sexton broke the quiet. "Mr. Ludwell and I are in need

of something to eat and drink, dear wife," he said. "We have come a long way!"

"You know, husband," she said, "we can give only to him that asks."

She turned her unchanging face and radiant eyes upon Walter.

"Please give me something to eat, and something to quench my thirst," Walter said.

"Your thirst must be greater before you can have what will quench it," she replied, "but what I can give you, I will gladly."

She went to a cupboard in the wall, brought from it bread and wine, and set them on the table.

As Walter ate, the bread and wine ran deeper into him than his hunger and thirst. Anxiety and discomfort vanished and expectation took their place.

"I have earned nothing, my lady," he said, "but you have given me this meal freely. Perhaps it would be good to rest a little while I am here, but do let me do something for you first. How else how could I accept your generosity in good conscience?"

The lady remained silent but the Sexton offered an answer. "Sleep is too fine a thing ever to be earned. It must be accepted in full."

"What do you mean by *in full*?"

"In this house, a man must give himself over completely, in full knowledge that no one awakens of himself."

"Perhaps you or your lady would kindly call and wake me?" Walter said, not at all understanding, but feeling a fresh foreboding.

"We cannot."

"Then h-how could I dare go to sleep?" Walter stuttered.

"If you would have rest under our roof," answered the

Sexton, "you must not trouble yourself about waking. You must go to sleep heartily, altogether, and outright."

Walter's soul sank within him.

The Sexton sat studying his face. His eyes seemed to say, "Will you not trust me?"

Walter returned Mr. Raven's gaze, with a silent "I will."

"Then come," the Sexton said. "I will show you your couch."

The two men rose. The woman took up the candle and turned to the inward door to guide them. Walter went close behind her and the Sexton followed.

AIR as from an icehouse met Walter as he crossed through the casket doorway. The door fell closed behind them. The lady turned to see it shut and Walter caught sight of a transformation. All the splendor of her eyes had grown too much for them to hold, and her countenance shone with Life itself, immortality streaming like unbroken lightning. Her beauty was overpowering and Walter was glad when she turned from him to once again lead the way.

The candlelight reached such a little way that at first Walter could see nothing of his surroundings, but soon he noticed a glimmer of objects raised a little from the floor, each the size of a slender cot. How can any living thing sleep in such cold? he wondered. No wonder no one wakens by themselves!

Walter's soul grew silent with dread as they passed aisles of couches innumerable, almost every one of them occupied. In the light of the dim flame, row after row vanished into the shrouded darkness. Nearest to him Walter could discern the shape of human forms draped over, straight and still.

Was it here he was expected to lay his head? Was this the

Sexton's library? Were these his books? Must he go to sleep among the unwaking with no one to rouse him? His mouth kept silent but his mind screamed, "Call the place what it is! This is the chamber of the dead!"

"The moon is rising. She will soon be here," said Mrs. Raven with a clear voice, low and sweet.

Even as she spoke the moon looked in at an opening in the wall, and a thousand gleams of supine whiteness responded to her shine. The wall should have marked a boundary of the dwelling, but Walter could see no beginning or end of the couches. They stretched beyond and away, as if for all the departed world to sleep upon. Each couch held a lonely sleeper but Walter now hesitated to deem it death. Their state was something deeper—a something he did not know.

The moon was colder than any moon in the frostiest night of his other world, rising higher and shining through every gap. Walter could not fathom the shape or character of the structure but it most resembled a long cathedral nave arching over the dwelling of tombs. Walter thought perhaps it was the forms in the chamber that made the moon so cold and not the other way round.

8

SOME RISE AND GO

THEY CAME AT LAST to three empty couches. Just beyond these were two more, one occupied and one with its covers mussed as if just exited. The inhabited bed held a stalwart figure of a man of middle age. One of his arms was outside the sheet with a strong hand almost closed, as if it gripped a sword. Walter thought he must be a king who died fighting for truth.

"Will you hold the candle nearer, my lady?" whispered the Sexton, bending down to examine the empty couch. "She has not been gone long," he murmured. "All is healed and she is up and away."

Walter ventured to speak. "Are they not ... dead?"

"I cannot answer you," the Sexton replied in a subdued voice, "for I almost forget what folks in the other world mean by *dead*. This is but one of my many treasure vaults."

"But why leave your treasures out in the open?" Walter asked.

"In your world, a sexton lays huge stones upon the graves,

as if to keep the bodies down. Here the sexton watches for his charges to wake up unto true life."

It was at this moment that Walter concluded Mr. Raven was mad. The whole situation was preposterous, but how was he to get away? In this world of the dead—in which two or more things could occupy the same space—the Raven and his lady were the only living he had yet seen. Who could he turn to for help?

"You see among your treasured dead differences beyond my perception," Walter ventured to remark.

The Sexton took a deep breath and tried again, "When you say a person is dead you understand one thing while we mean quite another. None of these before you, in truth, are dead. Some have but just begun to die and come alive. When anyone is indeed dead, that instant they wake and leave us. Almost every night some rise and go."

Walter stared ahead numbly. The Sexton apologized, "I will say no more for I only mislead you." He pointed to a nearby bed. "This is the couch that has been waiting for you."

"Why now this fate?" Walter stammered, beginning to tremble, casting about for a way to delay.

"For reasons that one day—when you awake—you will be glad to know," the Sexton answered.

"Why not know them now?"

"That answer will come when you awake."

"But everyone here is dead, and I am alive!" Walter objected, shuddering.

"Not much," said the Sexton with a smile.

"The place is too cold to let one sleep," Walter mumbled.

"Do these find it so? All around you all sleep well—or will soon. Do not be a coward, Mr. Ludwell. Turn your back on fear, and face to whatever may come. Harm will not come to you, but a good you cannot foreknow."

The Sexton and Walter stood on each side of the couch. The lady, with the candle in her hand, stood at the foot of it. Her eyes were full of light, but her face had returned to its former stillness.

"Would you have me make a mortuary my bedchamber?!" Walter cried aghast. "I will *not!*"

Neither host answered him. Each stood still and sad, looking at the other.

Mrs. Raven spoke to her husband softly, "He does not understand."

"You were right, wife," the Sexton said. "I brought him too soon."

He turned to Walter. "Did you not find the air of this place pure and sweet when you entered it?"

"Yes, but not so now!" Walter answered, voice rising.

"Then know," said the Sexton, his tone becoming stern, "that you, who call yourself alive, have brought into this chamber the odors of death. Until you are gone, its air will not heal but become unwholesome for the sleepers. Go."

Mr. Raven and his wife turned and began walking yet farther in, leaving Walter all alone in the moonlight in the midst of a myriad of couches. Walter turned back the way they had come, thinking only of escape.

It was a long way back through endless aisles. At first he was too angry to be afraid, but as his temper abated, the still shapes grew terrifying to him. In a loud affront to the gracious silence about him, Walter fled with tramping feet and wild cries.

Bursting out, he flung open the coffin door, and attempted to slam it behind him.

It closed slowly with an awful silence.

Walter stood in pitch-darkness. Feeling about, he found yet another door. Opening it he discovered himself back in his own library. In his fingers he clenched the cold brass handle of his own closet door.

ONCE AGAIN BEFORE his couch Walter threw himself down, relieved but exhausted. This time he found no peace. Which world was the real one? What he saw now? Or the one he had just ceased to see? Had he come to himself out of a vision? Or lost himself back into one?

His eyes fell once again upon the closet door.

He was sure that behind that door, the boundless graves under the vaulted ceiling still lay. He sprang to his feet, crossed the room and opened it. Light from the room shot before him into the closet, but instead of a moonlit sky, it pounced upon the gilded pages of an oversized book.

"What idiot," Walter shouted, "has put a book in the shelf the wrong way!?"

The golden edges of the volume flung the light further in and onto a chest sitting in a dark corner. A drawer gaped half-open.

"More meddling!" Walter cried, and went to shut it.

The drawer containing old papers was overfull and would not close. Taking up the topmost manuscript, Walter perceived his father's writing. The first line caught his eye—

I am filled with awe at what I write.

Spellbound, he carried the document out of the cramped closet and back with him to the couch.

Settled once more, Walter read with fascination what followed next.

9

FATHER FINNIAN'S MANUSCRIPT

I am filled with awe at what I write. The golden sun shines above me, the blue sea lies beneath, birds wing across the sky, and flowers stretch their petals upward. It is the same world I've always known, but I have been reminded it is all a passing shadow.

Shortly after my father's death, I was seated at the library desk sorting family papers. Fascinated by the discovery that the icon hanging among the books was a distant ancestor, I had been pondering exactly what the man did to distinguish himself spiritually, and wondered what reverberations, if any, resonate down our family tree.

I was interrupted by a thin pale man in rusty black coming towards me from the direction of that very icon. He looked sharp and eager and his notable nose reminded me at once of a certain peddler my sisters used to call Mr. Crow.

"Sir Ludwell," the visitor said, "I was in your vicinity and have given myself the pleasure of calling."

His voice was peculiar but agreeable. "Your honored grandfather *knew me from his childhood and treated me as a respected friend. I worked at the time as the family's librarian."*

The age of my visitor, if what he said were true, did not strike me at the time. I replied, "Pleased to make your acquaintance ... Mr. Crow?"

He smiled an amused smile saying, "You nearly hit upon my name. We met, you and I, long ago when you were quite small."

"Where was that?"

"In this very room."

As we shook hands, I could not decide if I remembered him. However, vague and marvelous tales associated with him floated through my mind.

"Please set me right on your name, sir."

"Well, one of my names you have guessed near enough: Mr. Raven."

"It is very kind of you to come and see me, Mr. Raven. Will you not sit down?"

He seated himself at once.

"Did you know my father as well, sir?" I inquired.

"I knew him," he answered, eyes twinkling, "but he did not care to know me. No, your father did not extend to me the friendship his father before him did. However," and here Mr. Raven's face lit up as he pointed towards the icon, "Old Sir Alban was a close intimate."

As Mr. Raven continued to talk, it began to dawn on me how old my visitor claimed to be. Sir Alban, according to the papers scattered upon the desk, was my great-grandfather.

"I owe Sir Alban much," my guest continued. "Although I had read many more books than he, he brought me into knowledge that does not come through sheer study."

A flash of memory from my early twenties lit up a small corner of my mind. I leaned in to absorb every word.

"I will try to convey this knowledge, at least as much as I am able," Mr. Raven said. He pointed to a small door standing ajar.

"*That closet held Alban's entire library; a hundred manuscripts or so.*"

"*Yes, many of those manuscripts are still there.*" I said proudly.

"*I attempted to catalog them, but felt it to be an impossible task. In fact, I was at that very work when Sir Alban looked in at the door and said, 'Come.'*

"*I at once laid down my pen and followed him across the great hall, down a steep rough descent behind a seldom-used door into an underground passage. We came to a tower he had lately built consisting of a spiral stair and a single room at the top.*

"*I had scarcely crossed the threshold after him, when he began to shrink. I rubbed my eyes and realized Sir Alban was not dwindling, but moving swiftly away. He was now but a speck in the distance with only the tops of blue mountains beyond him. I recognized the country, but I had never known this way to it.*"

Mr. Raven paused, lost in thought. I supposed he was reminiscing. He looked at me again. "*The tower has long since been pulled down but the permeability—the thinness—of your family estate remains.*"

I nodded, attempting to absorb all he asserted. He went on, "*I ask your pardon after the fact that I, from time to time, have used your house when I want to go home the quickest way. It is also nice to find that another of Alban's descendants might have interest in all he taught me.*"

"*Do I understand, Mr. Raven,*" I said, "*that you go through my house into another world, heedless of time and space?*"

"*There is in your house a door, and one step through carries me into a world very much other than this.*"

"*A better world?*"

"*Not throughout. Most of its physical as well as intellectual laws differ from those of this world. As for moral laws, they are everywhere fundamentally the same.*"

What Mr. Raven said might try a man's powers of belief, but in truth it all reawakened much I had forgotten for a long time.

"Do you take me for a madman?" asked Mr. Raven

"No, sir. In fact, once in my youth I traveled similarly, but since then slow plodding duties and practical matters clouded all from my consciousness."

"You went by way of a book, did you not?" he inquired.

I nodded and smiled.

"Ah, books … " he sighed, "some are doors in, and therefore doors out. Most are quite useless."

Mr. Raven sat silent for a moment. His head rested on his hand, his elbow on the table, and his eyes wandered over the rows of volumes before him. His gaze came to rest on the icon again, "I see old Sir Alban and my heart swells with love for him. What world is he in, I wonder?"

"I have no experience with icons," I confessed. "I was considering Sir Alban myself for the first time actually, when you came to visit."

Mr. Raven hardly heard my words, but he broke his reverent gaze as if returning to me reluctantly. "I tell you there are many more worlds, and many more doors to them, than we two could imagine in many years."

With these words, the old librarian rose, crossed the hall, and went straight up the main staircase, evidently familiar with every turn. Flight upon flight, up he went and I followed, studying his back. His hair hung down long and dark, straight and glossy. His coat was so wide and long it reached to his heels. His shoes seemed too large for his feet.

In the attic, light seeped through the great slate shingles where the roof butted against the eaves. By its soft shine we made our way from joist to joist until we reached a partition with a curtained opening. I followed Mr. Raven into the small chamber, whose top narrowed with the slope of the roof.

"That is the door I first used with Sir Alban," Mr. Raven announced, pointing to an oblong looking glass. A black-framed mirror stood on the floor leaning against the attic wall. An ebony eagle perched on top. I went in front of it to see our figures dimly reflected in its dusty face. Something about it made me uneasy.

"As a mirror," said the librarian, "it has grown dingy with age, but its clearness depends only on the light."

"Light?" I questioned, "there is not much light here."

Mr. Raven said nothing but began to pull at a little chain on the opposite wall. I heard rotating shutters yawning above. He stopped, looked at his watch for several minutes, and then began to pull again.

"We arrive almost to the moment," he said, "the very stroke of noon!"

The circular opening went creaking and revolving for a few seconds more until a patch of sunlight fell down. In the dust, a path formed, tunneling its way towards the glass, but from the mirror no patch of light was reflected anywhere in the tiny room.

"Where have the sun rays gone?" I cried.

"I am sure you know," he answered, one brow raised, "that there are many, many more dimensions than three."

His words took little hold for I was suddenly aware that our reflections had been displaced by a white mist and, beyond the mist, the tops of a mountain range began to appear. Soon the mist vanished entirely, uncovering the face of a wide meadow. I recognized that country, for I had been there before, but I had never known this way to it. Next, I saw Mr. Raven moving swiftly away from me into the frame, and in a flash he became the merest speck in the distance. His wide coat was flying and his black hair lifting in a wind.

The breeze that blew the coattails of Mr. Raven never touched me, for I rushed, greatly shaken, down from the attic heights. It took some time to calm myself, to pick up a pen and write this account.

I am changed. Nature's beauty still enraptures me but now I know that outspread splendor at any moment could, like the drop-scene of a stage, be lifted to reveal even more wondrous things; even within, especially within, this thin place I call home.

10

MILES TO GO BEFORE I SLEEP

WALTER LAID THE MANUSCRIPT DOWN, amazed to find that his father had also peeked into the mysterious world of Mr. Raven. He thought about the strange circumstances of his parents' death and began to wonder whether one or both of them had followed the Sexton too far. He wished Grandpa Arthur were here to give counsel. What a lively discussion they would have!

Walter grew ashamed. He had run away in the face of discovery. What wondrous mysteries might he have unearthed concerning life and death, and human perception if he had stayed the course? Assuredly the Ravens were good people and a night in their house would not have hurt him. Yes, they were strange, but no more than many artists he knew. He had treated them as undeserving of his confidence and was now embarrassed by his behavior. An inexplicable longing came over him as he recalled his time in the moonlit chamber, especially for the stately stillness of the warrior laying with his arm exposed. Unsought tears fell on the library couch, and suddenly, he was asleep.

An hour later, Walter awoke as if someone had called him. The house was as still as an empty church. A robin was singing on the lawn. He sat up, earnestly thinking, I will go and tell the Ravens I am ashamed, then do whatever they ask.

He washed his face and went straight up the stair to the attic. The mirror dimly reflected all before it but, since it was nearly noon, he tilted the glass a little towards the ceiling as he had seen Mr. Raven do. He pulled the chain and a patch of sunlight fell upon the mirror. Within the glass lay a tremulous landscape like a pool ruffled by a puff of wind. Walter touched the mirror and found it impenetrable. He reached and pulled the eagle slightly forward to sharpen the angle of refraction and saw that the mountains became blue and the surrounding country, steady and clear. When he stepped forward, his feet were in the heather.

All Walter knew of the way to Raven's cottage was that one must travel through a pine forest. He passed thickets and several small fir groves, imagining again and again that he recognized something familiar. Yet as the sun sank and the air chilled with the coming winter night, the groves and undergrowth did not thicken into woods.

To his relief, he saw a little black figure coming closer. It was the Raven. Walter hastened to meet him.

"I beg your pardon, sir, for my rudeness last night," Walter said in greeting. "Is there any way you might take me again to your home, though I in no way deserve it?"

The bird kept his pace as if to pass him so Walter turned to join him. Without a glance in Walter's direction, the Raven gave answer, "Our lady does not expect you tonight. In fact, she regrets that I encouraged you to stay before."

"Take me to her that I may tell her how sorry I am," Walter begged.

"It is of no use. Your night had not yet come, or you would

not have left us. It has not come now, and I cannot show you the way." He croaked out a little tune like a Greek chorus—

> *Daisies rejoice above the dead*
> *Who lay below the roots of flowers*
> *You left them shivering in their beds*
> *Not caring for the winter hours.*
> *When the universe's spring arrives*
> *In a hundred thousand years or so*
> *It's for your sake, my handsome lad*
> *That final dawn comes oh so slow.*

Before the Raven could begin the next verse, which was his favorite, Walter interrupted. "Tell me one thing more about your graveyard, please, Mr. Raven."

The Raven nodded but did not slow.

"Is my father with you? Have you seen him since he left my world?"

"Yes. He is with us, fast asleep. He was the man you saw with his arm uncovered and hand half closed."

"Why did you not tell me!?" cried Walter, hardly able to contain his disappointment. "I was so near him and did not know!"

"And turned your back on him," admonished the Raven.

"I would have lain down at once had I known!"

"I doubt it. Had you been ready to lie down, you would have known it was your father."

"What of my mother?"

"Oh, your mother hardly laid down a moment before she was awake again, arisen, and gone," said Raven dreamily, as if talking more to a memory than to Walter. "She had learned to sleep long before coming to us."

Mr. Raven's answers were incomprehensible to Walter, but

this did not slow his stream of questions in the least. "And what of my grandfather?"

"Old Sir Alban, your twice great-grandfather, was up and away long long ago. Your great-grandfathers—both of them—have been with us for some time, but I think each will stir quite soon."

"I want to know about my *grand*father, Arthur McVeigh. Is *he* with you?" persisted Walter.

"No," came the blunt reply. "He is in the Evil Wood, fighting the dead."

"Where and what is the Evil Wood?"

"The Evil Wood is easy to find but people within it are nearly impossible to locate. There the dead fight, kill, and bury their own dead. Those who will not sleep, can never wake."

"I cannot understand you!" yelled Walter, nearly out of his mind with desperation.

Mr. Raven picked up his pace, mumbling to himself, "I am so often unable to tell people what they *need* to know, because they *want* to know something else."

"Will you not in pity tell me what I am to do? Walter called after him, hurrying to catch up.

"How can I tell you *your* to-do, or the way to it? *Your* work, to open *your* eyes, is your own."

"Enigma treading on enigma!" Walter said. "I did not come here to be asked riddles and made a fool of!"

"The universe is a riddle trying to get out, and you are holding the door hard against it. Its business is to make such a fool of you that you will know yourself for one, and so begin to be wise."

"So *I* am to blame?!" Walter cried, completely vanquished. "If I cannot stay with you at your cottage, where can I go? Will you be so good as show me the nearest way home? I know there are more ways than one, for I have gone back by two already."

"There are indeed many ways. How to get there, it is of no use to tell you. But you *will* get there. You *must* get there."

Walter looked down at his feet. "May I get directions of *some* kind?"

"I do not know of any, but the beings most like you are in *that* direction."

The bird pointed with his beak.

Walter could see nothing but the setting sun, which blinded him. "Well," he said bitterly. "I cannot help feeling misused—taken from my home, abandoned in a strange world, and refused instruction as to where I am to go, or what I am to do."

"You forget," said the Raven, "that, when I brought you to my home, *you* declined my hospitality. Afterward, you reached what you call home in safety. Now you have come back again by your own doing! I must go now. Goodnight."

Without another word, the Raven turned and walked steadily away.

Walter stood dazed and heartsore. He gazed after the Raven, and would have followed him, but felt the effort useless.

It was true he had come by his own doing, but had he not come with intent of atonement?

In the near distance, the Raven pounced on a spot in the turf, throwing the whole weight of his body on his bill, digging vigorously. With a flutter of his wings, he threw back his head and, just as the sun set, something shot upward.

High in the air a creature opened into a soft radiance. Like a firefly, it came pulsing towards Walter with bright, large wings more birdlike than insect. As it flew over his head, Walter turned and followed it.

11

IN THE LIGHT OF THE SILVERY MOON

THE AIR GREW BLACK, winter closed swiftly around, and the fluttering creature, part prism and part phoenix, blazed, soared, and then hovered in flight. The longer it lingered suspended, the more luminous the prisnix (for so Walter named it) grew.

Walter took a few strides and came under the umbrella of its radiance. He continued to walk and it continued to shelter him with its beams, flying only as fast as his pace allowed. The creature would pause and linger over difficult rocky spots that might cause Walter to lose footing, and every time he glanced up, it seemed to be larger and brighter. The prisnix's wings were now the size of a swallow's. Squarish in shape, they flashed a wonderful splendor of color.

Walter—absorbed in the beauty—stumbled, fell, and lay stunned. When he revived, he found his companion hovering over his head, unperturbed and waiting. Wings radiated light, a full chord in multiple octaves, and in them Walter saw colors he had never known before. Unable to look away, somehow he rose and went on. Again he stumbled. Fearing another fall, Walter sat down. He would take in the beatific display of his guide in the safety of stillness. A longing awoke in him and the longer he sat the stronger it grew. He must have the blessed beacon in his grasp. To his unspeakable delight, the prisnix began to sink towards him, wafting back and forth and downward. When the creature began to free-fall, Walter felt as if a treasure of the universe were giving itself to him.

He put out his hand and possessed it.

The instant Walter took hold, the light went out. All around went pitch dark. The creature lay cold and heavy in his palm, like the binding of a dead book with cover splayed open. Desperate, he threw it into the air again—only to hear it fall among the heather with a thud.

Burying his face in his hands, Walter sat in motionless misery, but the growing bitterness of the cold made him fear. He arose to his feet to move on. The moment he stood upright, a faint glow appeared around him. "Is it coming back to life?" he cried. A great pang of hope shot through his heart, but it was only the edge of the moon cutting over a level horizon.

Downcast, Walter felt the brunt of his loss. The Moon would not hover over him, waiting on his every faltering step. She would only show him all his ignorant choices as she did for every creature below. She would bring light—but no guidance. In her soft glow, he looked westward and saw a range of low hills breaking the horizon line. Toward these he set out with the moon staring down. Walter felt intruded upon by her attentive curiosity and irked by her wondering, pitying gaze which seemed to ask, "Why is this creature out in my night?"

In the hours he was used to sleeping, Walter came awake to the sense he was alone in a wide awful universe.

PLODDING ALONG, Walter did not notice that the terrain had become dry and powdery under his footfalls. He was conscious of nothing until the ground trembled under his feet. Pulsing like a bright blue vein, a narrow earthquake ran along the path before him, heaving and rippling. He stared after the tunneling wave, watching with wide eyes as it curved round and turned back. A few yards from his feet the mound burst open. Out bound a great feline whose eyes shot flame and white teeth formed a soundless snarl. It lunged an inch from taking Walter's face into its great jaws, but turned its head downward and plunged back into the hole from which it had sprung.

Walter—sure the moon was affecting his brain—did not flinch. In his certainty that what he had witnessed was phantasmic, he felt neither courage nor fear. In truth, what he took for phantoms were realities and the light of the moon, which he resented, was his only defense against multiple monsters brooding below. As he plodded along, he was being stalked.

Ten steps more and the head of a worm as big as a grizzly bear protruded from the earth. A white mane flowed from its red neck. It drew itself out, wriggling huge and monstrous. Walter could not take his gaze from the horrible thrashing exiting of naked flesh. Yet, the moment it pulled free, it lay under the moonlight as if exhausted, wallowing in feeble effort to bury itself once again. Walter began to think himself brave. He would not be appalled by that which only seemed to be!

And so the night continued. Walter traveled on and hideous creatures, no two alike, emerged again and again from the burrow to threaten him. Beauty of color clashed against hideous forms, initial horror fading each time into harmlessness. Smirking, Walter began to imagine what fanciful monstrosity might come next. He gave himself over to impetuous creativity, never suspecting that he owed each moment to the staring moon whose reflected light paralyzed and defanged. Walter's feet would have scampered with highest speed over the undulating, restless soil, had he known that the moment the moon ceased to shine on that cursed plain, he would be at the mercy of such that have no mercy.

Walter did not pay much attention the descent of the solemn, anxious moon down the dome above him. His only uneasiness was the dread of losing his way, though, in truth, he had no way to lose. Drawing near the hills, his chosen goal, he at last took note that the moon was brushing the horizon.

As he reached the slope of the range, the moon sank behind one of the summits. With her sinking, there arose behind him the screeching moan of frustrated desire. The hair-raising sound was the first Walter had heard since the thud of the lifeless prisnix. His heart shook like a flag in the wind as he turned to look back. Dark shadows bound up the slope after him and among the forms he swore he saw the shape of a willowy woman with long dark hair streaming behind. Walter scrambled into a gap in the ridge where the moon still offered light and where neither tooth nor claw dared come. He understood somehow the moon had lingered, waiting for him.

The first rays of dawn pierced the eastern sky and the weary moon at last sank down. Walter rubbed his eyes and yawned. Sitting upon the ridge, he breathed in the pure, strong morning air, and, in the face of the coming day, fell fast asleep.

12

____

A COMMOTION IN THE FOREST

THE SUN WAS SHINING FULL AND BRIGHT when Walter awoke. From the crest of the hill he looked back down upon the hollow he had crossed under the moonlight. It lay still without a sign of life. In front of him was a wide desert. Not a cloud floated, nor the thinnest haze curtain any segment of the encircling blue rim. A patch of a different color lay in the distance slightly to the right. He thought it might be a group of trees.

Walter descended and set out for the hoped-for forest. Something alive might be there. The wide plain he crossed was a dry pockmarked river bed. Now-vanished water runs scored the dry channel, scratchy bits of moss clinging here and there. A few lichens as hard as river stone dotted his path. The air was as silent as Mr. Raven's bedchamber.

It took the whole day to reach the woodsy patch. Along the way Walter did not cross a rudiment of brook or stream that might nurture the forest's growth. It grew dark as he left the dry riverbed and entered among the trees.

As the light sunk below the treetops, rays shot between the

pillar-like trunks and a world of blessed shadows received him. He threw himself beneath the boughs of what seemed a eucalyptus in blossom. From beneath its broad curved leaves, his eyes peered into the deep forest. The sharp cold of night was upon him.

The trunk under which he lay rose high from the forest floor before it shot out mighty branches that bent back downward, so low they came near to brushing the ground. A light wind began to blow and all the boughs of the trees rocked. In the twilight he noticed that every offshoot, every twig, and every leaf blended its motion with the sway of the others. His pupils dilated and contracted in the changing light. Roving clusters of foliage began to assume or suggest shapes other than simple vegetation.

One clump of leafy branches was a pack of wolves struggling to break from a wizard's leash. Walter watched them strain savagely as the wind gathered force. Another mass of leafage, larger and more compact, presented a group of horses' heads projecting from their stalls. Their necks moved up and down with impatience until a gust of wind broke their vertical rhythm and they swayed wildly from side to side. The heads became gaunt and strange, several just bare skulls, one with the skin tight on its bones, another missing its lower jaw, and yet another looking unutterably weary, rearing high as if to ease the bit.

Walter, pushed to the edge of wonder, began to doubt his discernment between dream and reality. The twilight became darkness, the wind ceased, and every shape was folded into the night.

In the pitch dark, Walter became aware of a far-off rushing noise mingled with faint cries. The confusion grew into a tumult and gathering multitudes came crashing through the woods from all sides. The spot where Walter lay seemed the center of a commotion that radiated throughout the forest. He dared not move hand or foot lest he should betray his position.

The din increased to an uproar and dim shapes became clearer. A furious battle raged just outside the weave of the eucalyptus boughs. Skeletons and phantoms fought in mad confusion. Wild cries of rage and the shock of onset mingled with inarticulate snarls and sneers. Laughter and mockery, sacred names and howls of hate surged in Walter's ears.

Swords swept through wraiths and they shivered. Maces crashed on skeletons and they shattered, but none ceased to fight so long as a single joint held two bones together. Bones of men and horses lay scattered and heaped, ground and crunched under foot. Wind-blown battle horses and bone-gaunt steeds reeled; weapons and hoofs clashed and crushed. Skeleton jaws and phantom throats swelled in deafening war cries of any opinion that might breed strife: "Injustice! Cruelty!" Lie-distorted truths flew hurtling in the wind of javelins and bones. With the holiest words came the most hating blows.

At every moment a fighter would turn against his comrades, and fight more wildly than before. "THE TRUTH! THE TRUTH!" was both a curse and a call to arms. One wheeled his sword ever spinning in a circle and smote on all sides. A pair would sit, worn out, side by side to rest a moment from the melee, then rise and renew fierce combat. None stooped to comfort the fallen. None stepped wide or swerved to spare the wounded.

All the night long above the strife-tormented multitude Walter glimpsed a woman moving on this front then on the opposite. One arm was pressed to her side, the other outstretched, urging, "Ye are men! Ye are men! Arise and slay one another!"

Her beautiful countenance was consumed by pride and misery. The eyes in the ravishing face were dead. Long hair hung nearly to her feet and mixed indistinguishably in the windy mist that formed her garment.

For a moment the full moon shone a single beam through the canopy. The woman, now illumined, pressed both hands on her chest and fell to the ground. The mist rose from where she lay and melted into the air. Walter ran to her aid, only to see her writhe in such torture that he stepped back aghast. Her legs convulsed and broke from her body, writhing in the dirt like serpents. Her shoulders and arms followed with the snap of bone. Her body dismantled, dispersing itself like a frightened nest of centipedes.

Walter retreated back to the trunk of the tree and hid his face in his hands, wishing to see no more.

Minutes before sunrise, a breeze went through the forest, and a voice from beyond its borders called out, "Let the dead bury their dead!" In fatigued obedience, the contending thousands dropped noiselessly to the forest floor. Walter then remembered the Sexton's answer when he had asked about his grandfather, "He is in the Evil Wood, fighting the dead." A sliver of hope brought a moment of desire. Walter rose to search about, but the sun peeped in revealing that not a single bone remained, only piles here and there of withered branches.

In the daylight, the forest was wrapped in a holy silence. The wind in the trees was still. No bird sang. Not a squirrel, mouse, or weasel showed itself. Not a moth flew across his wandering path.

Walter feared the ten thousand phantoms awaited only his consent to appear. He kept careful watch over himself, lest his imaginative eye rest on any of the many forest shapes and re-enliven that which he did not wish to see. He could not stop, though, from hearing faint sounds of pickax, spade, and hurtling bones.

At last, in the middle of the afternoon, Walter exited the wood and found before him a second dry watercourse—another branch of the same forgotten riverbed. By sunset, he made it to the bottom of a wide channel. Exhausted, he stretched himself out upon the moss. The moment his head touched earth, he heard the sounds of rushing streams. Sweet watery noises below sang him into a dreamless sleep.

When he awoke, the sun was already up making the wrinkled, speckled country visible for miles.

13

BIGS AND SMALLS

Before his adventures with Mr. Raven, Walter had loved—more than any soul in the world—his Arabian mare and his books. Even his attachment to Grandpa Arthur was so interwoven with the great and powerful library that Walter could not have separated the affections. Now, alone in a strange land, he began to thirst for any human presence. He wondered what Mr. Raven meant by "beings most like you."

He rose to travel on, doubting whether he was going in any direction at all. By noon, began to encounter small shrubs that looked cultivated rather than the wild plants he had seen so far. He knelt to examine a bush and found it bearing a small purple fruit. The plants increased in number and size until he found he was passing small rows of dwarf fruit trees. All the adjoining channels of the riverbed gradually became so full of them that it was difficult to cross through without treading upon the work of unknown gardeners.

In a hollow that looked to have once been the basin of a lake, Walter came to the edge of a full-sized orchard. Unlike the sweet berries and citrus on the smaller trees, the large branches bore prickly fruit that emanated an odd odor like the mix of vinegar and dishwater. Repulsed, Walter continued down the slope to where the trees shortened again to chest height. Here, grass mingled with moss comforted the soles of his feet. Walter lay his whole weary body down and turned to face the sky.

A slender branch dipped down towards him, full of rosy apples no bigger than cherries. The delicacies offered themselves and Walter reached up, plucked, and ate. The fruit's sweet richness broke open upon his tastebuds in surprising delight. He was in the act of taking another when a sudden shouting of childlike voices broke in. The noise, mingled with laughter, was clear and sweet like the music of the underground brook.

"He likes our apples! He likes our apples! He's a Good Giant! He's a Good Giant!" cried a multitude of tiny voices.

"But he *is* a giant!" objected one.

"Well, true, he is rather big," said another, "but littleness isn't everything! *You* will keep growing and become big and stupid too unless you take care!"

Walter rose on his elbows and stared. Standing in the grass and hanging from the branches swarmed children ranging from toddler to preteen. Only three or four seemed older and these stood apart in a cluster. The air was filled with chattering, declaring, and contradicting, like a gathering of grown-ups at a convention, but with merriment.

Walter understood that by reaching for a second apple that the children knew he liked the first one. But how, from this act, did they conclude he was *good*? What was their basis for sudden celebration? He said nothing, for he did not want to frighten them, and felt he would learn more by just listening. He comprehended little of what was said in the avalanche of banter, but understood he was receiving a joyful welcome. It felt no less wonderful than love.

A path was made in the crowd and a roguish little fellow came forward. He walked straight up and handed Walter a huge green prickly apple. Silence fell on the noisy throng. All waited, expectant.

"Well eat, Good Giant," the boy said.

Walter sat up, took the apple in both palms, smiled in thanks, and in good faith sank his teeth deep into the green flesh. He gagged as soon as the juices hit his tongue. Out the bitten fruit was spewed and the rest flung as far away from him as possible.

A shout of delight roared from the children and they flung themselves upon him. Walter was nearly smothered in kisses. His hands, face, feet, and legs were bound in embraces. Little ones clambered about his arms and shoulders, hugging his head and neck. Down he came to the ground at last, overwhelmed by lovely little imps.

"Good, Good Giant!" they cried. "We knew you would come! Oh you dear, good, strong giant!" Their babble sprang up afresh with jubilant shouts.

Then a hush fell over the happy chaos. Those around Walter drew back. Those atop him hopped off and tried to pull him to his feet. Concern displaced merriment on every sweet face.

"Get up, Good Giant!" said a little girl. "Make haste! Be quick! He saw you throw his apple away!"

Before her little speech ended, Walter was on his feet looking where she pointed up the slope.

Over the brow of the hill came the hostile face of an oaf. He was few inches taller than Walter but unarmed. Walter was glad his little friends had vanished.

As the brute began to descend, Walter found the higher ground. The lummox growled like a bear as he closed in.

Walter found a level spot, stood wide-stanced, and waited for him.

As the lumbering lout came near, he held out his hand as if expecting for it to be filled. Walter at first thought it was offered in greeting but, when Walter moved to reach back, his opponent's hand had become a fist. Walter stepped out of range. The thick fingers were thrust out again, palm open in expectation, the face grimacing as if offended by some rejection.

Walter now understood what was being demanded of him —the return of the spurned green apple.

A howl burst forth. "Do you dare tell me my apple was not fit to eat!?"

Walter attempted an answer. "One bad apple may grow on the best of trees."

No answer came, nor sign of comprehension. With great strides he came nearer. Walter, on his guard, raised both of his fists in front of his face.

There was no question who would have out-maneuvered whom in a fair fight, but the fight was not fair. A second oaf had been stealing up from behind and the two struck together. Walter received a sharp blow in the back of the head one moment before he took a punch to the face. Overpowered and unconscious, he was dragged away.

The two hauled Walter out of the valley and into the wood where their tribe lived in a village of wretched huts. After boxing his ears and kicking him, they threw him into an outbuilding. A woman—at least Walter thought it might be a woman—looked on with indifference.

Through gaps in the hovel Walter observed his captors. They seemed to have just enough intelligence to produce locomotion and an emotional range that expressed only anger and greed. Their food consisted of tubers, bulbs, and sour fruit. When offered a share, Walter refused, but learned quickly and painfully that there was nothing that angered his jailers more than to show dislike for the menu. He was cuffed by the women —at least Walter thought they might be women—and kicked by the men whenever he did not show pleasure in what was offered.

The next morning, Walter was taken back down to the orchard, tied to a tree by a long rope, and given a flat stone with a saw-like edge. Through signs and grunts he was made to understand his task: to scrape the bark off every branch that had no fruit. Kicked once more in parting, he was left to his tedious work.

Walter was glad when he was once again alone and equally pleased that dwarf trees grew within reach. Plucking and eating, he was not only delighted but wonderfully refreshed.

14

LONA TRIES TO EXPLAIN

WALTER HAD BEEN AT WORK IN THE ORCHARD mere minutes when the sound of small voices joined the noise of his scraping. Little ones crept out from among the small trees that filled the spaces between the big ones and in no time, scores of children were all about.

He placed a finger to his lips and made signs that the giants had only just left. The little ones laughed. "They cannot see us. They are too blind!"

Their chortles sounded like birds in the trees mixed with a multitude of sheep-bells.

"Do you *like* that rope about your ankle?" asked one.

"I want them to think I cannot take it off," Walter replied.

"They can scarcely see their own feet, much less yours. If you walk with short shuffling steps, they will think the rope remains."

As the young informants spoke, they danced about in merriment.

One of the bigger girls got down on her knees to untie the clumsy knot and the children made Walter sit down so they could fill his mouth with delicious little fruits. When he could not eat another bite, the smallest toddlers began to play with him in the wildest fashion. It was impossible to resume work. When one wave of playmates grew tired, others took their place, causing the hours to speed by.

As darkness fell, heavy steps approached. The little ones hastily replaced the ankle rope.

"We must take care," said the girl who had untied him. "They are blind and they are stupid, but one stomp of their horrid feet might kill the smallest among us."

"Can they not see you at all then?" Walter asked, incredulous.

"They see nothing really, other than themselves."

"Nothing at all of this movement and laughter?"

"We are too alive for those who barely are."

The girl whistled like a bird and, in the next instant, not one of them was to be seen or heard.

Walter's master dragged him home, threw him on the bare ground of the hut, retied his feet, and gave him a swift kick goodnight.

Each night it was the same, for the giants were too stupid to be inventive even in their cruelties. Walter found he could avoid a bad kick by catching the foot and causing its owner to fall. After such a consequence, the attempt was never renewed. One giant at a time, the kicks subsided as did the boxing of his ears.

Walter hardly noticed the giants. All his attention was on the children. He would drift off towards sleep, thinking of the happy greeting he would receive the next day. There was no account kept of his progress in their orchard and so, at the very beginning and very end of his day, Walter made a show of work. The rest of his time and energy was spent in playful revelry. He had no memory of such a joy of soul and began to love the little ones more than he had ever given his heart to horse or library.

Walter was in a quandary. Escape would be easy. Leaving was not.

EACH MORNING before the sun rose and awakened his captors, the little ones brought their Good Giant plenty to eat. One, morning instead of a mass of little berry-stained hands, soft footsteps approached. Lona, the girl with the commanding whistle, approached from the woods. She held an infant in her arms and left behind a crowd of shushed little ones. Each little mouth was covered by its own little hand lest they awaken the sleeping giants.

Lona came and laid the infant in Walter's arms. The baby opened his eyes and looked up, closed them again, and fell asleep.

"He loves you already!" Lona exclaimed.

"Where did you find him?" Walter asked. He knew that before now a little girl about a year old had been the youngest in her care.

Her eyes beamed with delight. "In the woods, of course, where we always find them. Isn't he a beauty? We've been out all night looking for him. Sometimes the searching takes much longer."

"How do you know when there is one to find?" Walter inquired.

"I do not know," Lona replied, crinkling her forehead having never thought of the question before. "Happy news invades and each excitedly tells the next. We never find out who spoke the tidings first." She paused to ponder. "When there is a baby in the woods there is no time to ask questions.

After we have found the infant, it is too late to find out from where the news sprung."

Walter, seeing the question was vexing, tried another line of inquiry. "Do more boy or girl babies come from the woods?"

"They don't come from the woods, Good Giant. We go to the woods and find them."

"Where do the babies come from *before* the woods?"

"From the woods—always," answered Lona, both eyebrows raised.

Walter saw that in her mind there was no other place babies came from and there was nothing else to know.

"Are there more boys or girls among you now?"

"I do not know," she said. "We shouldn't like to be counted. The joyful happening of a baby takes all the glad we've got and we forget the last time."

So many questions crowded Walter's mind but he doubted it useful to ask any of them.

She gestured towards the sleeping infant in Walter's arms. "You are glad to have him—are you not, Good Giant?"

"Yes, indeed, I am," Walter said. "Will you show me how feed him?"

Lona took from her pocket two ripe little plums. She squeezed a drop of juice to the fruit's surface and held it to the baby's lips. Without waking, he began to suckle. Lona went on slowly squeezing until nothing was left but skin and stone.

In hushed tones Lona spoke to the infant, "The giants would have it be a big-apple world with nothing for the babies! We wouldn't stay in it—would we, darling? We would leave it all to the bad giants!"

Walter pondered what a lovely woman Lona would grow to be. What would become of her when she grew up? Who had gone into the woods to find *her*? Who would have left her there?

"Will you tell me where you lived before?" he asked.

"Here," she replied.

"Have you *never* lived anywhere else?"

"Never. We all came from the woods."

"You are all so young."

"I do not understand. Some are smaller and some are bigger. I am very big."

"This baby will grow bigger, won't he?"

"Of course he will!"

"And will you grow bigger?"

"I don't think so. I hope not. I am the biggest. It frightens me sometimes."

"Why should it frighten you?"

She gave him no answer and looked down.

"How big will the baby grow?" Walter said as gently as he knew how.

"I cannot tell," answered Lona, still staring down. "Some begin to grow after we think they have stopped. That is a frightful thing. We don't talk about it."

"What makes it frightful?"

She was silent for a moment then stammered, "We fear some may begin to grow into giants. It is t-t-terrible. I don't want to speak about it any more."

"How old are you, Lona?" Walter said.

"I do not know what you mean."

She pressed the baby to her bosom with such an anxious look that Walter dared no further questions.

15

HOW HIGDEN GREW

AFTER HIS CONVERSATION WITH LONA, Walter began to perceive the small differences in the characters of the little ones. Although most freely doled out loving encouragement, a few showed traces of greed and self-ishness. None would lend a hand to Walter's work—for they would do nothing for the giants—but some would sing to him for hours. Others climb ed trees to reach his mouth and popped fruit into it with their chubby fingers. Still others appointed themselves lookouts for the approach of the enemy.

Often they would sit and tell him stories—childish ones with not much meaning. Tales would become plays, and plays, musicals. One moody little fellow would pipe up and sing strange crooning lullabies. During one of his performances, the jumbled, unintelligible refrain was so full of pathos that it caused tears to run down Walter's face. The show of emotion perplexed all who saw it.

One little one, alarmed at Walter's tears, cried out against the singer, "Stop! Juice is skeeezed out of da Good Giant's see-berries! Stop the moo-zick!"

Walter wiped his face and apologized, wondering at the fact that his young friends had never before seen tears. They possessed hearts in perpetual unbroken innocence while his giant captors had hearts that were either unbreakable or missing altogether. Considering this brought a strange connection: Nowhere in the area was there any water to be seen—neither falling nor puddling nor running—and yet the terrain showed that water had once been abundant. The fruitful orchards attested that underground aquifers were bountiful enough to sustain life, but brooks and streams and pools and lakes were as foreign to the land's inhabitants as were tears of mourning.

LATER THAT DAY Walter found Lona as she sat with the baby in her arms at the foot of the tree whose bark he had been scraping. He sat down beside her. "How is it that I never see any children among the giants?"

Lona stared a little, struggling to find some sense in the question. "They are giants. There are no little ones."

"Have they no children ever?" he pressed.

"No. There are never any babies in the woods for those who do not love them. If the giants were able to see our babies, they would stamp them out."

"Is there always the same number of the giants then?" Water said. "I thought—before I had time to know better—that they might be your fathers and mothers."

Lona burst into merry laughter. "No, Good silly Giant. *We* are *their* firsters."

But as she spoke, the merriment died out of her, and a worried look took its place. Walter gazed at her, bewildered. "Firsters? What does that mean?"

"I cannot say," she answered. "But they go from us, not us from them. *We* cannot help our being. *They* could have helped it."

Walter returned to his scraping.

Lona saw he did not understand."If a little one doesn't care," she began in a hesitant tone, "he grows greedy, then lazy, then big, then stupid, then bad."

Walter stopped to listen. Lona continued, "The dull big creatures don't know that they come from us. Very few of them believe we even exist."

Lona pointed across the orchard, "Look at little Higden. He is eating one of *their* apples and will be the next. I held him when he was an infant and fed him of our nectar myself, but he will soon be big and bad and ugly ... and not know it."

Higden stood by himself a little way off from the others, eating an apple as big as his head. His eyes were as full of greed as Walter's were of disgust.

Walter kicked off his rope. "I will take the horrid thing from him."

Lona put her hand on his arm. "It is no use."

Walter retook his seat as she went on. "We have done all we can. He no longer believes anything we tell him. I knew we had lost him some time ago when he refused to share his berries, saying he had gathered them for himself."

"Could not some of the boys watch over him, and prevent him from touching the poisonous things?" asked Walter.

"To eat the apples and to be a boy who *would* eat the apples is all one and the same," Lona sighed. "He must go to the giants, for his actions show he belongs to them. You can see how much bigger he is even since yesterday."

Walter noted that Higden looked as much like the hideous green lump of an apple in his hand as a boy could look.

"Does he *want* to be a giant?"

"He hates the giants, but he is making himself one all the same." Lona's voice cracked, "Oh, sweet baby, he was just such a little darling when we found him!"

"He will be very miserable when he finds himself a giant," Walter said.

"Oh, no," Lona shook her head. "He will like it very well! That is the worst of it."

"Will he hate his former family of little ones?"

"He will forget us and come to believe we are imaginary."

"I understand your world so little," Walter sighed. "I come from a world where everything is arranged differently."

"I do not know what you mean by *world*. What is that word besides a sound in your big kind mouth?"

"Never mind about the word. Tell me what will happen next to Higden."

"He will wake one morning and find himself a giant—not

like you, Good Giant, but like any other Bad Giant. He will think he has been a giant always. You will hardly know him and he will not know you, or any of us. The giants have lost themselves."

"What an existence," moaned Walter.

"I wonder whether they are not glad because they are bad, or bad because they are not glad. But how *can* they be glad? They have no babies!" She stared at Walter. "What makes you big *and* good, dear Giant?"

"I am not good," Walter looked away. "I only try to be good, and mean to keep on trying."

"So do I—and that is how I know you are good."

A long pause between them followed.

Lona rose to go, not wishing to look upon Higden any longer. "I wish none ever grew bad and big. When they begin to grow big they care for nothing but bigness. When they cannot grow any bigger, they try to grow fatter and care for nothing but fatness."

"It is the same in my world," Walter said, "only they do not say *fat* there. They say *rich*."

THE NEXT DAY the rumor reached Walter's ears that Higden had vanished. He saw a few grave faces among the bigger children, but, in truth, Higden was not much missed.

A day later Lona found Walter and whispered, "Look there by that apple tree. There sits the giant that was once Higden! Would you have known him?"

"Never," Walter said, "but now that you tell me, it does look like Higden staring through a thick, stupid fog."

"He is forever eating those apples now," she said. "It is what comes of little ones that refuse to be little."

If only Lona could teach me to grow the other direction,

Walter thought to himself. What joy it might be to release all big adult considerations and to lie down as a child and sleep, not worrying about the morrow. How wonderful it would be to rest among the little ones with no thought of rising to face another day of pointless servitude.

16

THE CHRISTMAS GOOSE TAKES FLIGHT

ONE MORNING WALTER AWOKE to the vague sense that he ought to be doing something. He was not meant to be pampered and fattened like a Christmas goose. Having come into a marvelous world, it was his business to discover and learn. He wanted to do something in return for the children's goodness. What, he wondered, was interfering with their proper growth?

Lona seemed the eldest and she looked no more more than fifteen. Full of wisdom yet with little knowledge, she ruled by gentle love. Her only anxiety was that her little ones should not grow and change into bad giants. She knew what they should *not* become but did not know what they *should* become.

Their "good giant" took comfort in the idea that the little ones had in no way become dependent on him. If he left, his ripple in their peaceful waters would grow still in a matter of days. He had not become their protector. In fact, his presence could potentially bring them more danger from their idiotic neighbors.

Should he impart knowledge? Knowledge, no doubt, made

bad people worse, but it made good people better. He could teach them reading, writing, and mathematics, even musical notation. They could learn to record all the dainty melodies they murmured and then forgot.

One day while working, Walter causally mentioned to his companions that he would long ago have escaped the bad giants and continued his journey, except that he loved the little ones so much. In response, the children came rushing and crowding. In a blink Walter had three little ones in his arms, one on each shoulder clinging to his neck, one standing straight up on his head, and five holding him fast by the legs. Still others grappled his torso. He was nearly smothered.

Absorbed in the merry struggle, neither Walter nor any of the children saw his tyrant-keeper coming. With just one cry, "Take care, Good Giant!" the little ones ran from him, flying up the trees like squirrels. Walter was not so fortunate. A sharp round switch came down and dealt him such a blow on the head that he collapsed to the ground.

When Walter came to himself, it was night. Above were a few pale stars that shimmered waiting for the moon. His head ached and he was terribly thirsty. Turning wearily on his side, his ear touched the ground. Again he could hear the gushing and gurgling of the aquifer below. The noise made him groan with longing, and by that groan he found he was not alone but amid a multitude of silent children.

Delicious little fruits began to visit his lips. Again and again they came and came until his thirst was gone. One whispered in his ear while she fed him. "We gave the Bad Giant many bumps of his own, throwing big apples and stones. He was frightened and ran blundering home." She patted Walter adding, "Good, good, poor Good Giant."

Walter sat up, and with much pushing and pulling the littles helped him struggle to his feet.

"You must go away, Good Giant," they said in unison. "When the bad giants see that you are hurt, they will all surround and trample you."

Walter nodded, his countenance growing sad.

"Go and grow strong, and come again," a chorus called out.

"I will," he replied, but sat down again, head throbbing.

"Indeed you must go at once!" said Lona, who now knelt beside him.

One of the bigger boys came forward and explained. "I spied on the giant village last night. They think you are an idler, spending your days talking nonsense to moles, mice, and squirrels. They want to kill you. There is no use talking to them. They will kill you for disturbing the trudging sameness of their lives."

"Then I will go at once," Walter said, staggering to his feet again. He looked around forlornly and added, "I shall come back as soon as I have found out how to make you bigger and stronger."

"We don't want to be bigger," the littles cried together, looking very serious. "We will *not* grow into bad giants! We are strong now. You don't know how much strong!"

Little boys strutted and flexed to convince him. Walter said nothing more, knowing it was no use holding out a prospect that had no attraction.

Walter rose and tottered up the slope of the valley. The children formed themselves into a long procession, both spectators and participants in a long sad parade. All, but especially the girls, kept feeding him as he went. "You are broken," they said. "Much red juice has run out of you. Put some back in."

Traveling away from the heart of their home territory caused the children to talk in hushed tones that Walter had not heard from them before. Hints of anxiety infused innocent conjecture. As they walked, Walter heard whispers that his departure was the work of the evil giant-queen. He began to question those nearest him. When he asked where she lived, they said they did not know. When he asked if the place were near or far, they said they did not know. When he asked in what direction her palace lay, they said they did not know. Did they know the girl giant's name? Not that they could remember. All that the little ones knew was that she hated little ones, and would kill them if they did not hide. Walter wondered if anything at all separated this particular giant from those he had already seen.

"I will go to the giant queen," he announced off-handedly, "and ask why she hates my lovely little ones."

The children cried out together, "No, no! She will kill you, Good Giant. She will kill you! She is an awful Bad Giant witch!"

As the procession made its way up the second branch of the riverbed, all saw that the moon was lifting her forehead over the rim of the horizon, greeting them at the edge of the valley.

"We must return," Lona announced, "for we have never gone so far from our trees before. Please watch how you go, that you may see inside your mind how to come back to us." She pointed at the moon. "She has come to take care of you, and show you the way."

"But beware," inserted one of the bigger girls, "of the leopard lady that lives in the desert! You know about her, do you not?"

"No," Walter answered.

"Well, take care. She is ugly and she scratches."

The others looked at Walter gravely before shuffling forward to kiss his cheeks and walk away with somber steps.

Last to leave was Lona. She held up the baby to be kissed, gazed into Walter's eyes, and whispered, "The leopard lady will not hurt *you*." She turned and left without another word.

Walter stood a while, gazing after them in the moonlight. With a heavy heart he turned to continue his solitary journey. The laughter of the little ones overtook him, rippling the air, and echoing against the rocks. Walter looked back again and saw them all romping as they went along, not a single care in any of their sweet souls.

But Lona walked apart with her baby.

WALTER PONDERED AS HE WENT, recalling the fragments of conversations with his little friends.

When he had suggested that they should leave the country of the bad giants, and go with him to find another, they had answered, "But then we would not be ourselves! And who would gather the babies?" They had no ambition or fear, discomfort or greed, no motive or desire for change. For them, nothing was amiss. How were they to grow? Why should they grow? Their fear of growth as the possible beginning of giant-hood might be blessedly self-protective.

17

WHAT'S IN A NAME?

WALTER TRAVELLED ON ACROSS A SUCCESSION of small ravines, attended only by the moon. As she sank, he thought he perceived something like a face and a smile. Finding a place where the sand was soft, he resolved to remain there until morning. He made his supper from the fruit the children had given him, stretched out, and was soon asleep.

Near midnight, Walter awoke to constellations unknown. He lay a great while gazing at the twinkling majesty before becoming aware of a figure seated on the ground a few yards off. Startled, he sat up. It was a human outline. Walter discerned by the way it moved its head that its back was towards him.

A sweet, mellow, unmistakably feminine voice spoke. "Will you come with me?"

"I thank you, but I am comfortable here," Walter answered warily. "I like sleeping in the open air."

"The air will not hurt you," she replied. "However, the creatures that roam here are dangerous company for a man asleep."

"I have not as yet been disturbed," Walter argued.

"No. Because I have been sitting by you ever since you lay down."

"How did you know I was here? And why do you show me such favor?"

"I am often out in the wilds. I saw you lay down in this hollow when I was still a ways off. You fell asleep before I could reach you and I did not want to disturb your rest. Besides, people are frightened if I come upon them unaware. They call me the leopard-lady, though that is not my name."

Walter remembered what the children had told him—that she was dangerous, and scratched—but her voice was tender and Lona had believed he had nothing to fear from her.

"You shall not hear *leopard-lady* from me," Walter said. "What may I call you instead?"

"When you know me, call me by the name that you feel fits best," she said. "That will tell me what sort of man you are."

Her voice entered into him, stilling all restlessness.

"I will accompany you, Madam," Walter said, rising.

She was already on her feet, and, without a glance behind, led the way. Walter could see her just well enough to follow. She was tall and slender, but never turned her face towards him. Though this caused no apprehension, it made him curious. How could he fit a name to his guide without first seeing her face? He strove to walk alongside her, but when he quickened his pace, she quickened hers—always keeping ahead with ease.

In a short space, the quiet between them unraveled Walter's calm. Dread crept in as he followed her through the dark. Did she hide her countenance due to extraordinary ugliness? Did she fear terrifying him? A slow horror of an inconceivable monstrosity crept in and he began to regret accepting her hospitality.

The silence grew unbearable and Walter, trying to keep his voice steady, called out, "I am hoping you might help guide me in my journey."

"I will do my best to direct you." The sound of her gentle voice allayed all his fears. To Walter's delight, she continued, "I have taken notice of your wanderings. The stupid Hoons know nothing, and the careless little Dearlings forget almost everything."

"What? ... Who?"

"You just came from them."

"I'm sorry. I never heard those names before: Dearlings? Hoons?"

"There was no way for you to hear. Neither society knows its own name."

"How odd."

"Perhaps so. Unless you realize that hardly anyone anywhere knows his own name. What people call names are just sounds rolling off the tongue. Labels come from the lips of parents long before a child is known—if he is ever known."

Walter held his peace, beginning to wonder what his own name might be.

"What do you think your name is?" the woman asked, guessing his thoughts. Walter opened his mouth to answer, but his own name had escaped him. He could not even remember the first letter of it and recalled the same forgetting had happened in the presence of Mr. Raven.

"Never mind," she said, "it is of no consequence. Your real name swirls about you and cannot be read, but I will do my part to steady it, and in the end it will settle."

Mystified, Walter was silent.

THE TRAVELERS LEFT the dry channels and walked a long time towards the shining moon. The lady said nothing of their intended destination, and no abode appeared on the near horizon.

"The little ones," Walter said at length, "spoke sometimes of a smooth green country, pleasant to the feet. They told me too of a girl-giantess who is queen. Is the green country her territory?"

"There is a city on a grassy land, where a woman, not a girl, reigns unquestioned. She is older than this world. She and her terrible history came in from yours and with her came great change. The country once called the *Land of Waters* is now, as you have seen, channel after channel gone dry."

"Did she ... *does* she control the weather and seasons?" questioned Walter.

"She has influence with the Prince of the Power of the Air. He lent her his authority and with it she gathered what water she could to herself. The rest fled underground."

"And what of the citizens? What terror to live under!"

"Yes, terror binds them," the woman sighed, "but they are blind and believe themselves free and prosperous."

Walter was now not so sure he wanted to visit the smooth green country. He changed the subject. "Tell, me, if you please, something more about the little ones—the Dearlings. Who are they? Why don't they grow?"

Her answer reminded Walter of the last time he followed a guide with no idea of the destination—

> *The Dearlings, the darlings by means of great pain*
> *By sorrow and suffering will learn of their name*
> *Rising up they will cause all to see and to fear*
> *And showers will come, made way by their tears.*

"Am I to understand that when the littles are grown, their land will have water again?" Walter asked.

"No. When the Dearlings are thirsty enough, they will have water again, and when they have water, they will grow."

"Beneath the ground, the water is still flowing. I have heard it twice."

Walter saw a hesitation in the woman's step as if she might turn.

"How will tears make a way?" Walter asked.

"To cry, they will have to grow ... and to grow, they will have to cry."

"But they fear growth," objected Walter.

"But grow they must."

"They are right to fear," said Walter.

She nodded yet continued her unflagging pace, always several unreachable steps ahead.

18

A VIEW FROM THE SECOND FLOOR

THOUGH THE WOMAN WHO WALKED AHEAD OF HIM never turned round, Walter missed not a single word that left her lips. Her voice reminded him of the Sexton's wife, and though he did not understand much of what she said, he forgot that he had ever been, for even one moment, afraid of her.

On and on they traveled, crossing wide dunes. At last a cottage came into view. Its foundation sunk deep into the sand before striking impermeable rock. Its ancient look was similar to Mr. Raven's house, but its walls were thicker. Two glassless windows were cut out opposite from one another. The heavy door opened into a large bare room. Walter's hostess walked in and straight to the farthest corner. Still without turning, she took a long white cloth from the floor and wound it about her head and face. Only then did she return to close the heavy door, move to trim a small horn lantern by the hearth, and bow to receive her guest.

"You are quite welcome here, Walter Ludwell," she said,

calling him by the name he had quite forgotten. "My quarters are meagre, but I am comforted to have you at last indoors."

"I thank you, Madam," Walter replied, "both for the shelter and for reminding me of my name. May I now know yours?"

"Some people take me for Lot's wife, lamenting over Sodom," she answered. "Some think I am Rachel, weeping for her children. I am neither. My name is Mara."

"Lady Mara," Walter said. "Where would you have me lie down? I am ready to sleep heartily, altogether, and outright."

"Go to the top of that stair and you will find a bed. Some who lay upon it sleep better than they expected. Others remain awake on it all the night long. It is not soft but it is better than the sand, and there will be no beasts sniffing about."

The stair, narrow and steep, led straight up to an unfinished attic. A single low dormer window provided a view across the wide sparkling sands. Under the sloping roof stood a oblong bed, the sight of which, with its white coverlet, made Walter shiver. On the table was a dry loaf and a cup of cold water. For one who had tasted nothing but fruit for weeks, it was a feast.

"I must leave you in the dark," Mara called from the bottom of the stair. "I have but one lantern, and there is work I must do tonight."

"Please do not worry, and thank you, ma'am," Walter called back. "Eating, drinking, and lying down to sleep are things I can do in the dark."

"Rest in peace," Mara said, and went out.

Walter ate up the loaf, drank every drop of water, and laid himself down. The bed was hard, the covering thin, and the night cold, but in the womb of Mara's attic the thought of a dozen creatures scratching at the door and a hundred more hunting for him out in the desert did not disturb his sense of safety. When he at last closed his eyes, Walter dreamt that he lay in the Sexton's chamber beside his father.

Walter woke in the middle of the night, thinking he heard the low growls of wild animals. Turning over he would have fallen straight back into slumber, but a rough purring rose to a loud bellow under his window. He left his bed to peer out.

Before the door of the cottage, in the full radiance of the moon, the figure of a tall woman draped in white stooped over a large lion-like animal. She patted and stroked the pure white fur with one hand and with the other pointed halfway up the heaven in the direction of the moon. She drew her finger down in a line perpendicular to the horizon. Without hesitation, the creature darted off with amazing swiftness.

For a moment Walter's eyes followed its graceful stride then looked back down to find the woman. She was gone. He looked back after the animal. The monster-cat had disappeared as well. Wondering what possible errand the feline was sent out to accomplish, Walter went back to bed and slept undisturbed, dreaming now of the pale face of the moon.

Coming down in the morning, Walter found more bread and water waiting. His hostess sat with shrouded face beside him at the table while he ate. Except for greeting him as he entered, she held her silence. The loaf was so large that he could only eat half.

Once sated, Walter looked into her eyes for advice and she gave it. Of all the wisdom offered, he comprehended but two ideas: the cold wind will do you no harm, and always sleep with your face to the rising moon.

Hoping to discover more, Walter confessed all he had observed from his window during the night. "Your feline messenger understands you so well. If only I had an animal like that to guide me ... "

"She goes before to prepare your way," Mara answered.

"Have you many messengers like her?"

"As many as I require."

"Are they hard to train?"

"If I say more, it will only seem unbelievable to you."

"May I take what is left of the loaf?" Walter asked.

"You will want no more today."

"Tomorrow I may."

"Take it with you if you wish."

Mara held open the door, waiting for him to exit. He took up the bread but lingered, wishing so to see her face.

"Must I go?" he asked.

"It is a great burden to sleep in my house two nights in a row," she answered.

"I thank you for your hospitality then, and farewell," Walter said.

"The time will come when you must stay with me many days and many nights," she murmured through her muffling.

"Willingly," he replied.

"I'm afraid, *not* willingly," she said.

As Walter crossed the threshold, he turned back. Lady Mara stood in the middle of the room. Her white garments lay like rolling waves at her feet. Her face was lovely as a night of stars. Her dark gray eyes looked up and tears flowed down her pale cheeks as if she were weeping for the first time in a thousands of years.

Overawed by the beautiful, hopeful face, Walter prostrated himself, forehead to the ground. He begged forgiveness for his intrusion only to look up and find himself alone again, outside a doorless house. Around and around he walked, but could find no entrance. Stopping under one of the windows, Walter took a deep breath to cry out in contrition. Before he made a sound, he heard from within the gentle sobbing of one who suffered much and could not be comforted.

19

LEAF AND STEM

WALTER WALKED MANY A DESERTED MILE and began to long for a mountain, or a hill, or even a tall rock. His heart cast about for some goal upon which to set his sights. If only there was a summit to climb from which to take in the wide expanse of the dismal plain, he would find a measure of comfort. He did not notice that he was climbing every time he took a step forward, for the gradual incline of the rugged rocky ascent was imperceivable. Instead he was disheartened. The sun was only halfway to the horizon and all he could think of was rest.

Toward evening, he saw in the long shadows the height to which he had climbed. Not many yards ahead a crevasse plunged to a dark valley floor. Underneath his feet a carpet of soft green moss appeared, inviting him to lay down and enjoy the comfort of a royal couch. Accepting, his weariness at once began to ebb. With his head pressed against the green pillow, Walter heard for a third time the noise of many waters. Ethereal harmonies within the stones of long-buried channels came to his ears. A lovely cacophony ran round and down in chaotic mingling, gurgling, dripping in a common refrain.

Walter lay listening and noted the gradual slope he had just ascended. A cataract had once rushed down, filling the channels he had left behind. His heart swelled at the thought of the splendid tumult—waves dancing, reveling, helpless in their fall, crashing into the thirsty valley below.

As the hidden brooks beneath lulled him to sleep, Walter remembered Mara's words: "the rest fled underground ... " All other thoughts fell away as the watery lullabies mingled with his dreams.

HE WOKE before the sun and saw the drop ahead of him was indeed deep, but the daylight showed its width to be no wider than the height of a man. On the other side of the plummeting space lay a desert of finest sand. He sat and sought in his pocket the half-loaf, but the bread was no use. Shrunk and hard as stone, he dropped it on the powdery sand and set out across the wasteland.

In the late afternoon he came to some tamarisk trees, and then to a few stunted firs. Going on, thickets and larger junipers met him and he began to feel as if he were back in the forest where the Dearlings searched for babies. Was the story repeating? Was he walking in circles? Was he making any headway at all? Self-examining, he tore at his own uselessness. It seemed no matter where he was, he was not a man who did anything. He moved in dreams—a consciousness with a viewpoint, nothing more. He had merely existed in the world he left and did little more in the world in which he now found himself.

The idea of sliding back into his half-baked existence sent tremors through his soul. If the black eagle mirror suddenly appeared before him in the woods—offering a way back to the time and space of his origin—he would turn and run. It was *here* his change would occur or nowhere.

The trees were now large and stood tall in regular intervals. Their placement was almost geometric and the lack of undergrowth gave Walter the feeling of standing in a great cathedral, solemn, silent, and empty. Though he could see a long way in every direction, he saw no sign of life, though on occasion he sensed in the far distance a swift rushing by.

Deeper in, Walter at last heard a few birds. To their songs many butterflies danced in marvelous combinations of colors. Moths flitted by in pure dazzling whiteness. Coming to a spot where the pines stood far enough apart to give room for flowering shrubs, he began to hope that some human dwelling might be nearby. Again and again he chose the direction where more and more roses grew, hoping for civilization of any sort.

How was it he had always preferred books over men? In his home world, the author of his most worn volume could have popped in for tea, and he would have kept his nose in the text. Now an ever-deepening hunger craved the company of another living soul. Even a simpleton for a companion would suffice.

The wood thinned yet more, and the pines grew yet larger with columns eager to support the very heavens. Rosebushes rich in variety increased in size to compete with the trees. Their blooms vied with the butterflies in marvelous hues. Walter now yearned for even a dog at his heels with whom to share the beauty.

The shape and form of the trees, their spatial elegance and uniformity, suggested he had entered a palace. A ruined chateau, overgrown with ivy and roses, had crumbled, stone by stone leaving behind its shape in leaf and stem. Only a ghost of what was once brick and mortar hinted at a former edifice.

Walter stepped through the impression of a doorway and

found himself in an open space like a great hall. The floor was covered with grass and wild flowers. Walls and roof were all climbing vine mingled with roses. Knowing he would find no better place to pass the night, he gathered a pile of withered leaves into a corner and collapsed.

Gazing up at the live ceiling, his eyes went wading through the tangle. A warm crimson sunset filled the hall. The red roses went dark, but the yellows and whites remained shining until replaced by starlight that hung in between the leaves like live topazes, throbbing and flashing.

The roof was laden with little nests; tiny heads popped in and out once, then twice, before becoming still. Walter became still as well. An owl sailing across on silent wing was the last thing Walter remembered before passing into unconsciousness.

20

A NIGHT OUT DANCING

L ONG BEFORE DAWN, Walter was startled awake by the noise of nearby revelry. Branches above criss-crossed, forming a trellised roof. The moon shone through and wove shadows with her shafts of light. As his eyes adjusted, Walter found his bed of withered leaves was now tucked in the corner of a checkered marble floor. Before him, a crowd of gorgeously dressed men and gracefully robed women danced together. None seemed to see or sense him. Besides their otherworldliness, there was a great oddness about them. The rhythmic steps each took vaguely embodied the story of their lives—meetings, passions, partings.

It was difficult to catch sight of faces as the figures moved passed. Walter sat up and rubbed his eyes. He leaned in and squinted. When he focused at last, he was shocked to find each head was a skull—hard, gleaming bones, bare jaws, truncated noses, and lipless teeth. Some jaws were set, white and murder-ous. Others were decayed, broken and gapped. More fright-ening than the teeth were the lidless living eyes still set in each socket. Glowing, flashing, sparkling eyes of every color, shape, and expression; beautiful and proud, lustrous and condescending, languishing and repulsive, dim and sad. Some eyes were so lost in melancholy that they drew Walter's heart in spite of the horror of the surrounding personage.

Walter rose and moved among the dancers. Still, neither by look, nor by gesture, nor by the slightest break in measured step, did they show themselves aware of him. Neither was he an obstacle to them. They passed through him without a single change in motion, making Walter wonder if *he* were a body and *they* spirits, or the other way round. Were they souls? Or was this a phantasmic reenactment of something that happened long ago in this place? Since he was not present to them, were they fully present to one another? Did they see each other as he saw them? Did each know how he appeared? Did they see each other as they once were—fully enfleshed? If not, did they find one skull beautiful and another plain?"

Walter neither saw a single movement of one naked mouth, nor heard one word of speech, but their eyes spoke as if longing to be understood. Were they bereft of speech by a curse as punishment for lying? Did their eyes now speak truth? They *seemed* to know one another. Had they used their faces, not for communication, not to utter thoughts and feelings, not to share existence with their neighbors, but to show what they wished to appear and conceal what they wished to conceal? Having made their faces into masks, were they now deprived of those masks, and condemned to go faceless until they repented?

On many of the skulls the hair held in place, dressed and coiffed, adorned, powdered, ribboned, clipped, braided, sprayed, perfumed, wound, and curled. All appeared to Walter as ridiculous—wigs upon frightful skulls. In some the outer ear lobe remained and from these hung gleaming pearls, opals, and diamonds, the gems abutting naked bone.

The music became wilder and the dance faster. Eyes flared and flashed, jewels twinkled and sparkled, casting color and fire on the pallid grins that glided through the hall. Ghastly rhythms wove an intricate maze of motion, and suddenly there came a pause. Every eye turned to the same spot—an arching doorway where rose vines embraced the stately pine.

On the threshold stood a woman, fully enfleshed, perfect in form, surveying the ongoing dance.

"Dead things, I live!" said her scornful glare.

Her disdain only invigorated the dancers. They broke afresh into cavorting across the floor, a new expression in their eyes. Their silent answer to her was a fellowship of triumph. They seemed to shout, "You also will soon become as we! You will be just like us!"

Walter watched the woman's haughty look change into a dead stare. She grimaced and looked down and pressed both hands against a small dark shadow on her side. She looked up again, and Walter knew she understood the talking eyes. She gave a smothered cry, and fled into the night. In that moment, a flash of joy lit up the lidless orbs in the skulls of every dancer.

A warm wind, growing in strength, began to blow. The low moon ducked behind a cloud, half-hiding its murky radiance. The wind moaned and as it blew upon the dancers, garments and hair pieces fell fluttering in rags and strips. Bits of remaining flesh peeled from bones and dropped like soiled snow losing its grip from under the spring-warmed eaves. In minutes, whole white skeletons stood exposed and bare, ankle-deep in the decay that littered the floor. As the wind continued to sweep through, a faint rattling shivered the naked company. Pair after pair of lamping eyes went out. Every shape began to fall to pieces in papery flakes. The leaves fluttered all south-ward. The owl floated back into the silent hall. Darkness grew, and deep solitude resettled itself upon the lonesome watcher.

Not for a moment had Walter felt fear. Neither had he felt any particular courage. He simply was not afraid. The skele-tons, somehow, were fellow sojourners, nothing more. He went out into the wood, turned his face towards the moon, and, in the dead of night, resumed his journey.

21

BARE BONES

WALTER HAD GONE BUT TEN PACES when he caught sight of a hulking object in the dim moonlight and turned to investigate. A carriage, decaying beyond repair, sat upright on its heavy wheels. On each side of the pole lay a skeleton of a horse and from their two grim white heads ascended shriveled leather reins, ending in a bony hand. It was all, he assumed, that was left of a skeleton-coachman. Both side doors had fallen off the coach and within sat two complete skeletons, leaning back in opposite corners.

As Walter was inspecting the wreckage, the two passengers awakened. With a cracking rattle of bones, they stepped out of opposite doors. One fell in a heap. The other stood a moment shaking, then crept on stiff joints around the back of the carriage, holding on to the vehicle for support. Though its thin leg bones barely carried its own weight, it knelt and sought to raise its companion up, almost falling in the endeavor.

The heap rose with concerted effort into a sitting position, turning its yellowish skull side to side. Heedless of its neighbor, it grasped the spokes of the back wheel and raised itself half erect. Both hands held one of its knee-joints.

"Have you hurt yourself, my lord?" asked the kneeling one, now rising. Its voice sounded far-off as if borrowing breath from a cross-breeze.

"Yes, I have," answered the other, in a rough tone. "You sit doing nothing, and this cursed knee is out!"

"I did my best, my lord."

The lord looked at his companion. "Bless my soul, madam! Are you out in your bones?"

The female skeleton looked down. "I have nothing else to be out in." She looked up again to stare at him. "As if *you* should point a bony finger. " She gazed back and forth. "How did this come to be ? Am I dreaming?"

"*You* may be dreaming, Madam, but the pain in my knee prevents my having that illusion." He looked to himself and exclaimed, "Good God! I, too, have nothing to walk about in but my bones. How did this come to be?! Did I collapse again drunk upon the parlor floor?"

"Probably so," she hissed fiercely, "my *Lord Cocaine.*"

"What! what!—How do you know the title my gambling mates gave me? I do not know you. How dare you take liberties! My name is ... I am Lord ... what do people call me when I am ... I mean when they are sober? I must have been very drunk when I went to bed! I often am."

"You come so seldom to *my* bed that I would not know, my lord. I believe it when you say you were drunk, though I will take your word for nothing else."

"What the—I never told you a lie in my life!"

"You never told me anything *but* lies."

"Upon my honor! I have never seen you before, woman!"

"You knew me well enough to lie to me, my lord."

"Perhaps I *have* met you ... but upon my oath, there is

nothing to know you by! Out of your clothes, who is to tell you from anyone else? One thing I *do* swear—I never saw you so much undressed before! By heaven, I have no recollection of you!"

"That is a comfort to me. My recollections of you are now slightly less distasteful! Good day, my lord!"

She turned away, hobbled a few paces, and stood still.

"You are just as heartless as—as—any other woman, madam! Where in this hell of a place shall I find my valet? What was the cursed name I used to call that fool?" He turned his bare skull this way and that on its creaking pivot, still holding his knee with both hands.

"I will be your valet just once, my lord," said the lady, turning again. "What can I do for you? It is not easy to tell."

"Tie my leg on, of course, you fool! Can't you see it is all but off?"

She examined the surrounding brush with her eyeless sockets, found a piece of fibrous grass, and proceeded to bind together the adjoining parts that had once formed a knee. When done, he gave one or two careful tentative stamps.

"Your dancing days are over," she said, getting up from her knees.

"Now I look at you again, it seems to me I used to hate you ..."

"Naturally, my lord! You hated many people. Your wife, of course, among the rest."

"Ah, I begin to recall ... but ... have I been gone a long time away somewhere? I really do not remember."

He grabbed at his knee again. "Look! Your damned miserable bit of grass is breaking!"

She answered him not a word and he added in a softer curious tone, "We used to get on well together—eh?"

"Not that I remember, my lord. The only happy moments I

had in your company were scattered over the first week of our marriage."

"Was that the way of it? Well, it's over now, thank goodness!"

"I wish, how I wish we were done. But *why* did we sit in that carriage together? It makes me dreadfully nervous."

"I think we were divorced, my lady."

"Hardly. We are still together."

"A sad truth, but capable of remedy. The forest seems large."

"Not large enough."

"My lady, I am sorry. I cannot think of a parting compliment to pay you without lying. To judge by your figure and complexion you have lived long and hard since I last saw you." He clanked his teeth in an attempted smile. "Take no offense, madam. It is all just a dream, a jest of no consequence. All is appearances and you can be certain of nothing. Life can teach any fool that."

"It taught me I was a fool to love *you*!"

"You were not the only fool to do that. Women were always falling in love with me. I had forgotten that you were one of them."

"I did love you, my lord—a little—at one time."

"Ah, there was your mistake, my lady. You should have loved me much, loved me devotedly, loved me savagely, loved me eternally! Then I should have tired of you the sooner, and not hated you so much afterward. But let bygones be bygones. Locality is the real question! *Where* are we?"

"In the other world, I presume."

"Granted. But in which or what sort of other world? This can't be hell."

"It must. There's marriage in it. You and I are damned to each other."

"Then I'm not like Othello, damned with a *fair* wife! Oh

glory, I remember my Shakespeare, madam! It is not hell completely."

She picked up a broken branch that had fallen into a bush, steadied herself with it, and walked away, tossing her little bare skull.

"Give that stick to me!" cried her late husband. "I want it more than you do!"

She returned him no answer.

"You mean to make me beg for it?"

"Not at all, my lord. I mean to keep it," she replied, continuing her slow departure.

"Give it to me at once! I mean to have it! I require it!"

"Unfortunately, I think I require it myself," returned the lady, picking up her step with a sharp cracking of joints and clinking of bones.

Her husband started to follow her, but nearly fell. His knee-grass tore again, and with a curse he stopped, grasping his leg. He would have thundered, "Come and tie it up properly!" but his voice only piped and whistled.

She turned to look at him, turned back, and walked a step or two farther.

"I swear I will not touch you!" he cried.

"Swear on and on, my lord! There is no one here to believe you, but do not lose your temper or you will shake yourself to pieces, and where will you find enough string to tie up all your joints?"

To Walter's surprise, the skeleton lady came back. Before kneeling again at her husband's side, she lay the staff beyond his reach, though within her own.

The instant she had finished retying the joint, he made a grab at her, thinking to seize her by the hair. His hard fingers slipped on the smooth skull.

"Disgusting!" he muttered, and laid hold instead of her upper arm-bone.

"You will break it," she hissed, looking straight into his empty sockets.

"So be it!" he returned through clenched teeth, and began to squeeze ever tighter, bone on bone.

"*Who* will tie your leg again the next time it comes loose?" she threatened.

He gave her arm a vicious twist, but her bones were in better condition than his and his smallest finger snapped. She stretched her other hand towards the walking staff.

"That's right, good girl," he grinned, "fetch me the stick!"

She brought it round and struck him with such a swing that one of the bones of his sound leg snapped. He fell, choking with curses.

The lady laughed.

"Now you will have to wear splints always!" she said. "Bones so dry never mend!"

"You devil!" he cried.

"At your service, my lord! Shall I fetch you a couple of wheel-spokes? Rounded, smoothly sanded, but heavy I fear."

He turned his bone face away and groaned.

22

———

FLY BY NIGHT

ALTER MARVELED that the skeleton lord had not gone all to pieces when he fell. He watched his bony lady rise and walk away from her sprawling husband—not at all ungracefully.

"What can be accomplished in this?" Walter asked himself aloud. "They are too wretched for any world, and this cannot be hell, for the Dearlings are in it, and the beautiful sleepers under the Sexton's watchful eye. What can it all mean? What can ever come right for the bones of the living dead?"

"There are words too big for you and me," said a voice near him that he knew. "*All* is one of them, and *ever* is another."

Walter looked about, but could not find the speaker.

"You are not in hell," it said. "Neither am I in hell, but the lord and his lady *are* in hell."

Before he ended his sentence, Walter caught sight of the Raven overhead, on the bough of a nearby beech. The same moment the bird alighted on the ground and there stood the thin librarian with his long nose and black coat.

"The male was never a gentleman, though he was called

one." the Sexton went on, "Now having his skeleton free of his skin, and his character outside his manners, he no longer appears as one. The female is less vulgar and has a little heart. With the restraints of society removed you see both just as they are and always were."

"Can you tell me, Mr. Raven, what will become of them?" Walter asked.

"We shall see," the Sexton replied. "In their day they were the handsomest couple at court. Now even in their dry bones they seem to regard their former reputation as an inalienable right. They felt themselves rich while they had pockets, but without them they have begun to feel rather poor.

"The lord used to regard his lady as a worthless encumbrance, for he was tired of her beauty and had spent her money. Now he needs her to cobble his joints for him. The lady grew despondent when her beauty no longer held power. Though hateful, she has now begun to serve. These changes have roots of hope in them."

"Mr. Raven," Walter interrupted, "I saw many more of their kind an hour ago, in the hall close by."

"Of their kind, but not of their sort," Raven said. "It is providential that they are left alone together, so that they need each other. In time they may grow weary of their mutual repugnance and begin to love—even a little. A long time will pass before these two have become as advanced as those you saw dancing. Those can now dress themselves a little, have eyes, and will by and by develop faces. Every grain of truthfulness adds a fiber to the fabric of their humanity."

"By your hope I feel a small amount of unexpected optimism myself," said Walter. "Do the skeletons themselves sense any hope?"

"By hope they move and have their being, but they have no idea where their hope lies or what to hope for. That knowledge is still immeasurably beyond them," said the Raven.

Walter felt that more knowledge of the progress of skeletons was beyond him. He dropped the line of questioning. He noted that the Sexton's unexpected appearance had caused him no astonishment. He supposed his time among the Dearlings had taught him to be constantly wondering and surprised at nothing. His next question was almost childlike in tone. "Did you come to find and fetch me, sir?"

"Find you? Not at all," Mr. Raven answered. "I have no anxiety about you. Folks like you always come back to us."

"Tell me, please, what folks am I like?" begged Walter.

"I have a strict policy not to talk about my friends," answered the Sexton with a cheeky smile.

"Even when that *friend* is present?"

"I decline even the more strongly."

"Even when that friend *asks* you?" Walter persisted.

"Then most positively I refuse."

"Why?"

"Because he and I would be talking of two persons as if they were one and the same. Your consciousness of yourself and my knowledge of you are far apart."

The lapels of Mr. Raven's coat flew out, and the points of his collar lifted. Walter thought the metamorphosis of man to bird was about to take place before his eyes, but the coat closed again and Mr. Raven added as an afterthought, "By the way, my friend, in this world never trust a person who has deceived you, even once. Above all, never do anything such a person requests."

"I will try to remember," Walter answered, "but I may forget."

"Then some evil that is good for you will follow."

"And if I remember?"

"Some evil that is *not* good for you will *not* follow."

The thin man seemed to sink into the ground, and immediately Walter saw the Raven several yards from him, flying low and fast.

Remembering Mara's words, he turned towards the moon. She was not yet high and stared straight down into the forest. Something ailed her. She looked dark and dented, like a battered disc of old copper, dispirited and weary. Not a cloud drew near to keep her company, and the stars seemed too bright. Her disconsolate look asked, "Is this going to go on forever?"

23

OF WOUNDED BIRDS AND FALLEN ANGELS

WALTER HAD TRAVELED LESS THAN AN HOUR since the Sexton had taken flight when a whiteness in the underbrush of a spreading tree caught his eye. Its form was vague in the shadow of the foliage, but as Walter drew nearer it appeared to be a human body.

Another skeleton? he asked himself. He knelt for a closer look. Though it was no skeleton, it was as near to one as an emaciated body could be. He wondered if perhaps one of the wild dancers had lost her way. Cold and quite naked, the body was so gaunt that every rib could be counted through the tight, elastic skin. Terrible yet perfect teeth showed between retracted lips. Hair, long and thick and very fine, flowed black as night itself. How had this woman, so tall and graceful, come there? Had she fallen and died of hunger? How did the mass of skin and bone become naked? Wild beasts did not steal garments and leave prey unmarred by tooth and claw.

Walter rose to his feet and considered. He could not leave a human body exposed, forsaken, and unburied. He feared brutal claws might yet come and toss her about well before rain and dew would wash her body into the soil. The ground was hard, burial impossible between interlacing roots, and he had only his bare hands. There was no sign of decay. Might she still be alive? This was a strange world after all.

All Walter had in his pockets were a few grapes gathered from vines outside the dancers' hall. In a world where skeletons could dance, might grapes revive a corpse? Her mouth was a little open, but her head was in such an awkward position that he had to pass his arm under her shoulder to move her slightly. In doing so, Walter discovered the pine needles beneath her were warm. If she were dead, she had not been dead very long. He put his ear to her chest but could discern no heartbeat or indication of breath. Her right hand was clenched hard, around something small but apparently valuable to her. He squeezed a grape into her mouth, but no swallowing followed.

Walter found himself committed. Until his charge was clearly dead or restored, there was no moving on. He gathered a thick layer of pine needles and dry leaves on the ground. On top of this he laid one of his garments still warm from his body. He lifted the lady upon it, and covered her with a another great heap of leaves. So tight was the skin upon her bones that he dared not use friction. He would save the little warmth left in her and hope to increase it when the sun rose. He tried another grape but to no avail.

Walter crept into the heap of leaves and got as close as he could, repeating to himself, "This is no corpse. This is no corpse." He had not much heat left, but what he had he gave, spending the night sleepless and shivering. He pondered how he had fled from the beautiful sleepers, each on a dim, glim-mering silver couch, only to lie alone in a dirty pile of leaves with a ghostly bedfellow.

Walter lay with the dead, or mostly dead, longing for the dawn. At last the eastern horizon grew clearer. Mother birds awoke overhead reminding him of the guileless Dearlings. The body felt a trifle warmer, and the light of the morning revealed a drawn and hollow face. Sharp bones lay under the skin and the shape of every tooth pressed through the lips. If life remained, it did so hidden under a human garment worn down to its threads.

Walter rose and followed a beaten track where forest life made its way through the trees. As he progressed, the forest retreated and the grass grew thicker. Half a mile further, a wide expanse of meadow stretched away towards the horizon. Along the meadow's edge flowed a small rivulet. The stream was deep, full to the brim, but nowhere more than a few yards wide. A bluish mist rose from the water and vanished towards the tree-tops. Tasting it, Walter found that the water had a strange mineral flavor, and its temperature better suited a hot spring than a flowing river.

Walter leapt to his feet ecstatic and sped back to his helpless charge. Here was the warmth he sought!

Exulting in hope, Walter bore the invalid to the stream. Tall as she was, she was marvelously light. Her bones were delicate and so little covered them. She was far from stiff, so flexible in fact that he could carry her on one arm like a sleeping child. The water was too hot to lay her all at once in, so to avoid shocking away the flutter of possible life, he laid her on the bank and bathed her by dipping one of his garments in and out of the stream. Loneliness drove him on.

In time, the body became warm enough that he ventured to submerge it. He first entered and drew her in after him, holding her face above the stream and letting the swift, steady current flow over her. Watching for any flicker of life, he noted that her shut right hand never relaxed its hold. Her body was so wasted that besides the plentiful black hair, there was no way to guess whether she was young or old. Would she ever again be clothed with strength? Would her eyelids ever lift and a soul look out?

After several minutes, Walter lifted his patient and laid her again on the bank. There he dried her, covered her as well as he could, and ran to the forest for leaves. Three times he went and then a fourth to ensure a warm, thick covering of foliage. She was now retaining heat, giving him more freedom to explore.

Walter ran up the rocky hills searching for the stream's source, and found the warm water issued from a bubbling spring inside a cave overlooking the valley. Back down he strode to see how his patient fared. She was neither better nor worse. He pulled large warm rocks from the stream to place beside her, and returned to the cave.

Into the shelter Walter carried branches. These he arranged to lie across the channel within. Crosswise he placed smaller woven branches of beech. Upon these he created a comfortable couch of leaves and moss. The stream flowing underneath would keep his patient warm. Back down he went, fearing he might behold a skeleton, but she had not deteriorated in the least. To the cave he carried her, placed her on the bed that bridged the current, and again covered her body with a thick layer of leaves. Once more he tried feeding her with a grape, but the juice lay in her mouth unheeded.

Day after day, night after night, Walter sat or lay within the cave, always watching. Every morning he went out and bathed himself in the hot stream. Daily he bathed his patient and, in one of those bathings, the shadow of discoloration on her left side vanished. Every morning he put fresh leaves upon her and a fresh grape in her mouth. He too ate of the grapes and other berries he found in the forest, but it was the daily bath in that river that brought true sustenance.

Often when Walter slept, he dreamed he found a wounded angel who, unable to fly, remained within his care. At the end of each dream the angel, fully restored, loved him and refused to leave. When he awoke, he sighed to see instead the white, motionless, wasted face upon the couch. Walter was no longer dutifully committed, but obsessed. If this one wasted shred of womanhood disappeared, he would have nothing in him but a consuming hunger for a second self to love. He even forgot the Dearlings.

24

THE SLEEPER AWAKENS

W ALTER WOKE ONE MORNING FROM A PROFOUND SLEEP to find his left hand swollen and painful. In the center just below the knuckles was a triangular wound like the bite of a leech. As the day went on, the swelling subsided. By the evening the hurt was all but healed. He searched the cave, turning over every stone, but discovered nothing.

There was neither clear progress nor regression in his patient, but Walter thought perhaps the sharp angles of her bones had begun to disappear and the skin had less of a parchment look. Twenty times a day he looked for evidence of improvement, and twenty times a day he doubted.

One night, after several weeks of vigilance, Walter could not sleep. He rose to escape the oppressive heat of the cave and breathe the cool night air. The moon was full, allowing him to glance back and look upon his treasure. Great orbs, dark as if cut from the sphere of a starless night, offset the whiteness of her face. "Bliss eternal! Her eyes!" he cried aloud and stole nearer. His heart beat so hard he feared the noise would startle her. Bending, he found her eyelids closed. He turned in despair stifling sobs that threatened to overwhelm all composure. Turning back again, he was certain he caught a glimpse of an open lid. Walter was now certain eyes had indeed opened—though only for a moment before being overtaken again by sleep. Walter exulted and gave himself over to slumber as well.

That night he was bitten again, and awoke with a burning thirst. The wound was of the same character, but was again well by evening, thanks to the healing stream. He searched the cave even more thoroughly, but in vain. He comforted himself with the fact that he himself had been its only victim. There were no marks on the lady. Out of habit, he peeled a grape and put it in her mouth. This time her lips made a slight movement of reception. She lived!! Hope soared.

Inspired, he began to think of clothing for his sleeping patient. She must be able to rise and move about the moment she wished. He scoured the forest, investigating materials that might be of use. He gathered leaves of the puntina ficus, laid them in the sun to dry, and pulled them apart. From these he was able to form two loose garments, one to hang from her waist, another from her shoulders. He wove layers of the left-over fibers into sandals, using the soles of his own worn-out shoes.

During the week that followed, she more eagerly took the grapes and seemed slightly plumper, though she did not open her eyes. Again Walter was bitten, and again—then in regular intervals of every three days. Always a single bite, always at night while he slept, but no longer on the hand. Wounds appeared on his arms and neck. Hour after hour he would lie awake keeping watch, but never heard nor saw the predator, nor felt pain when his skin was pierced. Though he knew he was losing blood at a dangerous rate, he gave up watching, caring only that his treasure was passing from death to life.

One night Walter woke suddenly, breathless and faint. He began to crawl from the cave when he heard a slight rustle in the leaves of the couch.

"I caught the vile thing," said a feeble voice in his mother tongue. "In the very act."

She was alive! She spoke! Walter dared not yield to his exultation lest he terrify her.

"What creature?" Walter whispered.

"The creature that was biting you."

"What was it?"

"A great white leech."

"How big?" he said, forcing himself to remain calm.

"Nearly a foot long ... "

"You have perhaps saved my life! How brave of you! But how could you touch the horrid thing?"

"I did," was all she answered.

"Where is it?"

"I shoved it into the river."

"Then it will come again, I fear," answered Walter, then adding in a comforting tone, "but we will kill it next time!"

Walter could say no more. He had grown faint, sought the open air, and collapsed just as he reached the cave's entrance. When he regained his senses, the sun was up.

The lady stood a little way off, looking grand and graceful in spite of the clumsy attire. He *had* heard that wondrous voice and seen those glorious eyes! She stood erect as a column, regarding him. Her pale cheek indicated no emotion but only questions.

Walter rose to approach her, then stopped. A strange smile had flickered over her beautiful face.

"Did you find me there?" she asked, pointing to the cave.

"No. I *brought* you there," Walter replied.

"You *brought* me?"

"Yes."

"From where?"

"From the forest."

"What have you done with my clothes and my jewels?"

"You had none when I found you."

"Then why did you not leave me?"

"Because I hoped you were not dead," said Walter, bewildered.

"Why should you have cared?"

"Because I wanted you to live."

"You kept me," she said with proud scorn, "and still would, for my beauty!"

Her words and look roused Walter's indignation. "There was no beauty left in you when I found you."

"Why then, once more, did you not leave me alone?"

"Because you are of my own kind."

"Of *your* kind?" she cried, in a tone of utter contempt.

"I thought so, but find now I was mistaken," Walter shot back.

"Doubtless you pitied me!"

"Never had a woman more claim on pity and less on any other feeling."

Pain-filled mortification and anger unutterable clouded her countenance. Silent hate crowded out all light from her starless eyes.

"Had you failed to rouse me, what would you have done?" she asked.

"Buried you."

"What? You would have buried *this*?" she exclaimed in fury. Her arms were thrown out and her eyes darted forks of cold lightning. Walter stared at her in wonder, a goddess incarnate. How could he have ever considered covering her over in sod?

Shaking his head clear he replied, "No! *That* is not what I was given. *That* took weary weeks of watching and tending ... but, I admit, had I seen the smallest sign of decay I would have buried you at once."

"Dog of a fool!" she cried, drawing herself up to her full height. "I was but in a trance! What a fate I have been dealt! Go and fetch the she-savage from whom you borrowed this hideous disguise."

"I myself made it for you. It is hideous, but I did my best. It took weeks on end ... "

"How long do you pretend I have lain unconscious!? Answer me at once."

"I cannot tell how long you had already lain when I found you, but there was nothing left of you save skin and bone. I tended you more than two months. Your hair was beautiful, nothing else."

"My poor hair!" she said, bringing a great armful of it round from behind her. "It will be more than a two months' care to bring *you* to life again! I suppose I must thank you, although I cannot say I am grateful."

"There is no need, madam. I would have done the same for any woman ... or for any man, for that matter."

"How is it my hair is not a tangled rat's nest?" she said, fondling it.

"It always drifted in the current."

"How? What do you mean?"

"I could not have brought you to life but by bathing you in the hot river every morning."

She gave a shudder of disgust, and stood for a while with her gaze fixed on the hurrying stream. She turned to Walter. "We must understand each other," she said cooly. "You have done me the two worst of wrongs: compelled me to live, and put me to shame. Neither of these can I pardon." She raised her right fist and jutted out a bare forearm as if to repel him. Something ice-cold struck him on the forehead.

When Walter came to, he was on the ground, wet and shivering.

25

FOR PITY'S SAKE

WALTER ROSE AND LOOKED AROUND HIM, dazed at heart. The lady was gone, and agonizing loneliness came crashing down. She whom he had brought back from the brink of the grave had accosted him and fled. Had he indeed done her a wrong in restoring her to life? If guilty, how could he ease the burden he had compelled her to take up again?

In the distance he caught sight of his lady walking swiftly over the grass, away from the river that had been her healing. Desperate hope surged in his veins and he plunged in and through the stream—bidding the loving waters good bye as he went. The warm font returned his thanks with a parting surge of restoration.

Strengthened, Walter pursued, but as he closed the gap her hating eyes haunted him. Her resentment was overwhelming. How could one so noble long for death? What soul-wound did she carry? How might he have furthered the injury? Why did she loathe him, the man who had healed her? He had labored, borne, and tended until all despairing hope faded to lowest ebb. Was ingratitude all that was to come his way? There must be some misunderstanding, some breech of her sense of modesty. Beauty *must* have a heart, however profoundly hidden, and Walter was determined to fight for the flowering of that loveliness.

Just ahead, the lady was ascending a gentle slope, walking straight and steady like one who knows where she is going. Not once did she looked behind. Walter quickened his pace and the gap was nearly closed when she turned on her heel in a graceful about-face. She showed no signs of fatigue or heat, nor the weakness that should accompany one recovered from the shadow of death. Her breathing was slow and deep. Her eyes gleamed like polished alabaster. In a tone sounding as if she had never seen him before, she demanded, "Why do you follow me?"

"I lived so long on the mere hope of your eyes … I must see them again."

"I command you," she replied, "to stop where you stand."

"I will not leave you until I see you to a place of safety," Walter countered.

"Then take the consequences," she said staring through him.

If beauty could kill, Walter would have been slain where he stood. He fell back against a large tree as if run through and pinned with a spear. Her irritant immobilized, the woman turned and resumed her journey.

"Have pity upon me!" Walter cried, then added in a whisper, "I am your slave."

She gave no heed. Despair reanimated Walter and he followed like a child whose mother has abandoned him. The sun climbed the sky, seemed to pause, and went down the other side. Not one moment did the lady relax her pace. Not one moment did Walter cease to follow.

When the night came she stopped and threw herself upon the soft grass. Walter knelt beside her and could see she was spent. Still sorrowing over the ferocious spurning, he gazed upon her and asked himself, "Do I love her? She is *not* good. Do I hate her? I *cannot* leave her." And he could not. No man could have.

"Begone! Do not dare touch me," she moaned in agony.

Her arms lay by her sides seemingly paralyzed, but in a flash they closed about his neck, rigid as those of the iron maiden. She drew down his face to hers. Her lips clung to his cheek. A sting of pain shot through him, and pulsed. He was paralyzed but gradually the throbbing ceased. Slumberous weariness and dreamy pleasure stole over him.

Then Walter knew nothing.

WHEN WALTER CAME AWAKE, the moon was a little way above the horizon but spread no radiance. She was but a bright disc set in blackness. His cheek, wet with blood, smarted. His neck, also wet, ached. He scanned with listless eyes and saw the woman standing not far off. She was surrounded in a shimmering mist, enshrined in a cloud illumined in the light that belonged to the moon. He rose and staggered towards her.

"Down!" she cried as if to a rebellious dog. "Follow me not another step!"

"I will!" Walter asserted, with an agonized effort.

"Set foot within the gates of my city and my people will stone you. They do not love beggars and that is all that you are."

Walter was deaf to her words, weak as water, half awake, and unaware he still moved towards her. She took a step back, raised her left arm again, and flung it out to repel. Walter fell like one struck with an iron hammer but this time, though wet and shivering, he did not black out.

The woman stood some yards away, her back towards him. He watched as she threw off her garments and, before he averted his eyes, her gleaming white body fell onto all fours and shot away, a streak of white in a swift-drawn line. In that same instant the moon recovered herself, shining out full and bright. Walter saw the streak to be a great white cat rushing in great bounds over the grass. Dark spots ran like footprints down its back.

Walter reawakened to the pain in his cheek and the wet sting of blood dripping down over the corner of his jaw. Without the bewitching eyes holding his thoughts captive, he saw through the farce of the giant leech.

"What have I done!" Walter cried. "Where is the terrible creature going? On whom will it next feed?" He imagined he could hear from afar a sudden, spreading, outcrying terror; as if the pale savage were bounding from house to house, rending and slaying.

While Walter gazed after the beast, a noiseless arrow flew past him from behind. A second large creature, pure white, set out in pursuit. Straight through the spot where the woman had fallen on all fours it sped into the night. Smaller and smaller it grew, the very embodiment of efficient speed.

Walter rushed forward as if to pursue. Reaching the place from where the first beast had sprung, he stopped, knowing there was no way to keep pace. At his feet the gift of homemade garments remained, discarded in a heap.

26

———

STRIKING STONE

ORRIBLE SUSPICIONS BEGAN TO AWAKEN in Walter as he set out, determined to somehow track his assailant. On towards midnight he stumbled forward. A cloud came over the moon allowing him to see very little beyond the next step ahead. Hour upon weary hour he traveled with pounding thoughts of regret until out from the gray dark sprang a shrouded figure. It was a woman, stooped by terror and anxiety. She ran right past him unaware, clasping a child to her bosom.

"She is being hunted!" thought Walter, and stepped up in between her and whatever pursued.

He stole a quick glanced behind to see which way she traveled and, in this moment of distraction, up over his head flew a swift, soft-footed rush. A sharp blow knocked him to the ground as it passed. He was up in an instant, but still only saw a glimpse of vanishing whiteness. Walter ran after, hastening his pace all the more when a shriek of despair tore the quivering night. Useless! Too late once again, he thought, squinting into the vapor-dusted moonlight. A white shape approached. Walter ducked away from the path and hid himself in the brush. Crawling and floundering in agony came a great catlike monster going on three legs, carrying its right fore-paw high from the ground. Dark, oval spots glimmered on shining white skin. Walter saw that something streamed from the uplifted paw with a low rushing sound.

"More blood," he said to himself. "Someone has wounded the beast."

Walter feared the creature—he loathed it—but a great pity seized him at the sight of its suffering. If he had been armed with axe and sword he could not have struck it. He watched as it passed in a broken succession of hobbling leaps and disappeared from sight. Its trail issued after, flowing back softly through the grass.

Walter retraced the feline's path hoping to find the fleeing woman. In the distance he soon saw her, seated under a tree, her child in her lap.

"Can I do anything for you?" he called out as he approached.

At the sound of his voice she jerked as one struck. She would have risen and fled but Walter went to his knees saying, "You need not be frightened. I am glad the beast is wounded. It bleeds profusely and will soon be dead."

"There is little hope of that!" she answered, trembling. "Do you not know whose beast she is?"

Walter knew but did not want to know. He shook his head. "Who saved you from it?"

"No one" she answered. "I pounded her foot with a stone— as hard as I could strike. Did you not hear her cry?"

"You are a brave woman!" Walter said. "I thought it was *you* who cried out."

"It was the leopardess."

"I never heard such a sound from the throat of an animal. It was like the scream of a woman in torture."

"Well, it was not me," said the woman. "My voice was gone. I could not have shrieked even to save my baby, but when I saw the horrid mouth at my darling's neck, I caught up a stone and smashed the great cat's lame foot."

"What ... who is this leopard?" Walter implored. "I am a stranger in this land."

"You will soon know about her, having come so close to the City on the Grassland." She groaned. "I can never go back now!"

"I am going to the city," Walter confessed, "and hope to gain audience with the princess."

"Have a care!" she blurted but checked herself mumbling, "but perhaps you are ... the princess is a very good, kind woman." Her voice trailed off flat and uninflected.

Clouds had by this time gathered so thick over the moon that Walter could not read the woman's expression. Fearing she would rise and run from him, he whispered, "You are in no danger of any sort from me. What oath would you like me to swear?"

"I know by your speech that you are not of the city," she breathed, then paused a long while. "I will trust you. In truth, I am not of the city either, and, it seems now, never was. Otherwise I could trust no one." The lady exhaled a long breath, rocked her sleeping infant, and spoke again. "If only I could see your face, sir, but I do like your voice—there, there, my darling is asleep. The foul beast, little one, will not hurt you." The woman caressed her child and continued, "It was my baby she was after, but the leopardess would have torn me to pieces for protecting her."

Walter nodded and said nothing as the woman went on. "Some say the princess has two white leopardesses, though I know only the one with spots. If her majesty hears of a baby, she sends the cat immediately. Afterward, the baby either dies or grows up malformed and dumb. I would have taken flight much sooner, but—since the princess was far from home—I thought I had more time to recover."

Walter trembled and nodded for her to go on.

"Her Highness must have taken her beast with her, and been on her way home just as I stole away. Not far from here I heard the great cat scenting the wind behind me and ran—oh, how I ran." The woman glanced down at her sleeping new born and murmured—

> *"My darling will not die*
> *There is no mark upon her*
> *The city is a lie*
> *Its fountains have no water."*

"Where are you taking your baby now?" Walter asked.

"Where no one ever tells."

Walter pressed her no further and changed the topic. "Why is the princess so cruel?"

"There is an old prophecy that says a child will be the death of her. They say this is why, besides sending the beast to hunt the offspring of others, she accepts no offer of marriage."

"But what will become of her country if she kills all the children?"

"Some say she is in league with the Shadow to put an end to our race."

Though Walter could not see her face, as she went on, "At

night we hear the spotted leopardess out upon her quest. We lie awake and shiver. The feline can tell at once the houses where a baby is coming and lies down at the door, watching to get in. There are words and prayers that have power to drive her away, only they do not always take effect."

The mother rose in haste. "But here I sit talking, giving the beast time to make it home and her mistress will send the other out after me!"

Walter rose as well, "I do not think the wounded cat will ever get home. Let me carry the baby for you." But when he reached to take the little girl, the mother withdrew, bidding him an abrupt farewell. Over her shoulder she warned, "You should not go near the city. There are sounds in it at night as if the dead were trying to shriek, but cannot open their mouths."

Walter's loneliness redoubled watching her leave. After listening to her footsteps die away over the soggy grass, he turned back and continued the way the spotted leopard had gone.

27

CITYSCAPE AND SHADOW

THE DARKNESS GREW THIN and the sun's pale aura lit up the silhouette of wall towers that appeared as old as time itself. Around the city were gardens separated from the nearby walls by heaps of gravel and refuse thrown from the battlements. Walter recognized none of the produce, and saw no cultivated flowers or domesticated beasts. Going up to the nearest gate, he found it half-closed and unsecured. No guard or sentinel stood watch; thin hinges were encased in thick rust.

Walter passed through the entrance and looked down a long, silent, ancient street only to turn and exit again. He resolved not to re-enter until some sign of activity occurred. He began to explore the perimeter. Toiling over dusty heaps along the crossroads, Walter found that each road led up to an empty gate. Circling the city aimlessly caused a questioning of purpose: Why had he come? What had he hoped to find? Why did he need to see once more the woman he had brought back to life? He did not desire her company and was no longer able to to deny the unspeakable horrors concerning her.

The city stirred. Walter moved forward with an uneasy feeling of responsibility. He had brought a source of evil back from the brink of death and was accountable for whatever misfortune might unfold. Most troubling was the fearful face of the fleeing mother that told Walter that the Dearlings were somehow in danger. He must find some way to protect them. The quest for such knowledge was reason enough to encounter temptation.

WALTER TURNED ASIDE into an alley and found a semblance of shelter in a small archway. Before he could sit and settle, a woman, thick and squat, came hurrying in after him. He pressed against the wall to give her room in their shared sanctuary. She turned trembling and looked out upon the courtyard. A few minutes passed in silence as they both saw a dappled leopard dart across.

The woman pressed close. Walter's heart filled with pity. He put his arm round her and promised, "If the brute comes here, I will lay hold of it and you must run."

"Thank you," she murmured.

"Why is the great cat allowed to run loose?" asked Walter.

"You are a stranger here then ..." the woman said haltingly. "Our princess keeps her in a cage, bound with a muzzle and chain, but still she escapes."

Walter wanted to ask why the cat was kept at all, but noted with alarm that the woman was great with child. Her face was pale with dark circles under eyes, while her belly bulged.

"It hunts and feeds on the blood of any child it can find," whispered the woman. Her voice crawled on in a droning monotone, tragic words disconnected from meaning. "Thankfully," she continued, "there are not many infants in our great city."

"Has she been hunting you long?" Walter asked, unable to take in the horror.

"Just tonight." The dam broke and the woman began to sob. "I wish I were at home! The princess returned only last night, and the leopardess is out hunting already! How am I to get into my house? She will be lying at my door, watching ... But I am a fool to talk to a stranger!"

"Not all strangers wish you ill," said Walter. "The beast shall not get to you until she is done with me. That may buy you time to get to safety."

"Get me home unhurt, and I will give you shelter from this terrible wind."

WORN AND WEARY, Walter and the woman of the city waited to see whether the feline menace would move on. In her nervousness the woman began to prattle on to him about commerce and citizenry, confirming what Mara had said the first night he had walked with her under the moon. Citizens of the City on the Grassland dug for gems within their cellars. All other work was viewed as disdainful. Wares and food were gained in trade, made by 'lesser sorts' in faraway towns.

"Why do not some of your citizens, those perhaps not good at finding gems, learn gardening and weaving, baking and milling, just for the sake of well-roundedness?" Walter asked.

"Do you think us *common*?" She curled her lip. "Such work is disgraceful."

When Walter asked about poverty, she balked as if he had broached a great impropriety.

"What will happen when you run out of gems?" Walter asked at last.

"There are so many, that day will never come."

"Suppose an enemy attacks and you are conquered. All your gems will be taken," he suggested.

"No nation would dare. Our princess is answerable to no one and makes all who surround us afraid. For thousands of years she has reigned. We are safe and free and rich."

Even while the woman's prideful words puffed from her lips, she glanced furtively about, clutching her belly. Stepping out, she led Walter edging through the shadows towards her house and Walter wondered that she trusted him at all.

He ventured one more query, cautious and curious. "It seems to me, kind lady, that you believe that strangers defile your city. How then can you take me into your house?"

"It is true that because we are more ancient and noble than any other nation, we must turn strangers out before moonrise. I am bending the law for I suspect you are somehow connected with rumors of a man who managed to cross the cursed burrows."

Walter creased his brow in puzzlement. The woman smiled knowingly, certain that she had uncovered a secret. "You are the one who traversed the haunted underground, unprotected yet unflinching."

Walter remembered his trudging ignorance, amazed that he had become, seemingly, a piece of folklore.

"Of course," she added, "You must be gone from my house before sunrise. Dignity is a delicate thing."

They made their way through lanes and narrow passages to a row of tall buildings. She put a finger to her lips, pointed upward, and began to climb the steep stair towards her door. Before they reached the top, however, her countenance became alarmed. She darted up the rest of the steps faster than he thought possible for a woman in her condition. He arrived just in time to have the door closed in his face. Shocked and confounded, he stood on the landing where he remembered Mara's words. "They are blind and believe themselves free and prosperous."

Walter found just enough space between apartment doors for a man to lie down. Weary, he took advantage of the shelter, poor as it was.

28

OF LEOPARDS AND LADIES

At the foot of the stair lay the moonlit street. Walter could hear the inhospitable wind blowing about below. He was just beginning to drift off when warm breath brushed his cheek. He opened one eye and found himself staring into the face of an oversized feline. Her front paws were upon the landing. Seeing him, she took a step backward. Walter sprang up and the great cat bolted. She tumbled backward having no room to turn, head over tail, only able to scramble to her feet at the bottom. He watched her go, noting her whiteness, pure as starlight. There was neither spot nor smudge on back or belly, undeniable proof that there were *two* leopards on the prowl.

Walter resolved to keep watch the rest of the night—not for the sake of the woman who had shut him out but for the life of her child. Just minutes after settling in as sentry, he heard the latch of the nearby apartment click open. The door swung half open but no one emerged. Rising softly, Walter slid into a barren front room where there was no light except moonbeams creeping in through high windows. Standing there was not the fearful woman of the streets or any of her kin, but Mara. Hidden beneath her scarf, she motioned for absolute silence. Walter bit his tongue, stifling a cry of shock.

Mara led Walter and bade him to lay down on a large loosely woven rug. It was warm and soft and he tried to sleep, but his ears would not rest. Doors opened and closed, water was brought to a whistling boil, and from a room beyond came the sounds of stifled moans. Then came the cry of a newborn, followed by a terrible shriek.

Walter sprang up and looked into the passage just in time to see the white leopardess carrying away the baby in her mouth as if it were a kitten of her own. He threw himself upon her and forced her to drop the child. The baby let out a piteous wail and from the inner room, Mara darted out. She stepped over both cat and man as they lay struggling and scooped up the infant. Walter, intent on keeping the great cat pinned, did not notice which way she ran. To his great surprise, Mara returned a moment later to the tussle. She lifted both man and leopardess, and put both out by their scruffs.

Walter, dismayed, had no time to lick the wounds of abandonment. Thrown to the lions quite literally, he sprang to his feet ready to renew the conflict. To gain room to maneuver he ran down the steep steps and turned, fearing at any moment the leopardess would leap upon his back. Ever watchful, the great white cat followed, taking one step at a time in her descent. Near the bottom, she sprang. Walter watched her arc over him, overwhelmed by the show of power. In a flash, the white blur crouched at his feet. He looked down and was shocked to see the great beast belly up and purring.

The white leopardess began to rub her whiskers against his bare feet. His heart melted. Not since the Dearlings had he received warm affection of any sort, and a well of tenderness sprang up. Surely the beast was a pawn, trained to obey her mistress through no fault of her own. He bent and petted, scratched and caressed, as the shining leopardess licked his hands and purred.

A SHADOW PASSED OVERHEAD. With no more warning than a low growl, the great cat took off in pursuit. Walter stood alone, awash once more in a sudden sense of abandonment. Chiding himself for the waste of precious time, he resolved to go straightway to the palace and demand to see Her Highness. He had spied her residence from the square—lofted above the heart of the city.

An hour later he reached the heights. The palace stood, surrounded by ramparts, a lonesome citadel. The inner perimeter was no better tended than the outer; it lay neglected, half in ruins. A great iron gate stood open, the drawbridge broken down. It was hard to believe any water had ever flowed in the moat underneath. Dispirited, Walter passed by the entrance and walked about the walls like an outcast dog. Coming to a recess with a stone bench, he lay down to spend the remainder of the night.

In the haziness of exhaustion, Walter dreamt that the leopardess with her rough tongue and bright teeth leapt upon him. He raised his chin, expecting to be bitten. Bedraggled and spent he yielded to what pain and loss might come, but the pang did not arrive. Instead, pleasant warmth diffused itself throughout his frozen body. The feline lay close to him and the heat of her frame slowly penetrated his. Her breath, which had nothing of the wild beast in it, swathed his head and face. Walter turned like a sleepy child, threw his arm over the animal, and sank into profound unconsciousness.

When the sun rose, he fancied he lay warm in his own soft bed. Was it possible he was again home? The well-known scents of the garden seemed to come crowding in. He rubbed his eyes and looked out to find he lay on bare stone in the heart of a hateful city. Sitting and stretching he wondered, disbelieving. Had he indeed had a leopardess for his bedfellow? The warmth of her body still lingered.

Reenergized, only one thing was clear—he must find the princess. Had he not saved her life? Might she not recognize her debt? These thoughts gave him courage for the coming encounter, whoever and whatever she might prove to be.

29

PALACE HOSPITALITY

WALTER APPROACHED THE INNER GATES. Like the outer ones, they stood yawning and unwatched. He crossed the moat that stretched over a rough ravine and found himself in a paved courtyard lined with trees akin to poplars. Between their trunks he glimpsed the royal residence. It was long and low with lofty towers at the corners, and one huge dome in the middle. The dome rose to half the height of the minarets and sat like a voluptuous hat on an over-burdened wearer. The main entrance, a low arch sloping up into a center point, stood wide open.

He proceeded unchallenged and was soon standing in the middle of the entrance hall. To his left in the farthest corner lay the spotted leopardess—caged, chained, muzzled, and huge. She stared out of wide-open eyes, her large head couched upon her front paws. Through crescent-shaped pupils surrounded by great green irises she watched, though not an eyeball, or claw, or whisker moved. Her tail stretched out behind her rigid as an iron bar. Walter stole a second glance trying to see her right front paw but her massive head blocked his view. He dared not look a third time.

Opposite the cage, one large door and two low passages led further in. Walter took the central one. It, in turn, branched out into many corridors, all narrow and irregular. The further he descended into the labyrinth, the more he wished for a ball of twine unwinding in his hand to guide him back.

At a narrow juncture, a palace page darted from around a corner. The pimple-faced lad ran straight into Walter and jumped back in terror. Sizing Walter up, he traded his initial fear for impudence. Puffing out his chest he demanded, "What is your business!"

"To see the princess," Walter answered.

"A likely thing!" the page retorted. "I have not seen Her Highness myself for days!"

Walter caught the young man by the back of his neck, tightened his grip, and through clenched teeth ground out a command. "Take me to her at once, or I will drag you along until I find her. She needs to be informed how her servants receive her visitors."

Tail tucked, the page acquiesced and began to lead Walter through the maze of servant entrances and exits until the two came to a spacious kitchen. There, among the pots and half-cooked meals, loitered several more servants. Half-hearted and half-asleep, most were just beginning a morning routine. Now outnumbered, Walter hid his wariness.

The group stared dumbly, statuesque and frozen. An egg was dropped with a crack-splash upon the dirty stone floor. All eyes stared at a singular point, just beyond Walter. He turned to see that not ten paces behind stood the pure white leopardess. Swallowing hard, he released his grip on his unwilling guide. The lad scampered off and out the farthest door, leaving it swinging on its squeaky, rusting hinges.

"Take me to the princess," Walter ordered, staring at a rugged unshaven man who seemed chief among the kitchen help.

"She has not yet left her room, Your Lordship."

"Then let Her Highness know that I am here and awaiting audience." All eyes still rested on the leopardess, now standing at Walter's side.

"Will Your Lordship please give me your name?" stammered the chief cook.

"Tell her that the one who knows the white leech desires to see her."

"She will kill me if I take such a message. I must not. I dare not."

Walter stared back at him in silence. The great cat, white as milk, nuzzled his hand.

The chef snapped his fingers and a servant girl scampered off.

The rest of the staff watched spellbound and terrified as the graceful feline stood on her hind legs, paws resting on Walter's shoulders as she licked each of his cheeks. One by one servants backed up and dashed out the squeaky exit as Walter took in the warm purring splendor. Several minutes passed before her ears pricked and all paws returned to the cold stone floor. The rumbling purr transformed into a low growl and she exited as quickly as she had appeared.

Walter turned to see that the original page boy had reappeared in the doorway trembling like one who had drawn the short straw. "Please come this way, my lord," he said, almost begging. The calming presence of the great cat gone, Walter's heart began to throb and he braced himself for the coming encounter.

After many dark passageways, twists and turns, Walter was at last shown into a room so large and so dark that the edges were not visible. A single spot in the center of the floor reflected back an oval-shaped luminosity emanating from the ceiling. Elsewhere all was black. Walter looked up. At a great height, through a space between the joints, a single beam of sunlight fell from the black marble dome to the slab below.

All at once, a radiant form stood in the center of the beam, flashing splendor on every side. Dark hair streamed like a waterfall over a robe of soft white, matching the shine and shade of the marble on which it fell. The eyes of the princess were a luminous blackness, her arms and feet like warm ivory. She greeted Walter with the innocent smile of a girl—but with the face, figure, and form of well-experienced womanhood. Her eyes flashed out of the dark straight into his, and Walter thought perhaps he may have overestimated his fortitude.

The woman he had rescued, the woman who had scorned his every tenderness, the woman who had spurned his cries for pity, moved to his side, smiling. "You have found me at last!" she exulted, laying her hand on his shoulder. "I knew you would!"

Walter quivered, attempting to analyze. He was attracted and repelled in equal measure. All power of logical thought ebbed away.

"You shiver!" she said. "This place is cold for you! Come."

She led him by the hand drawing him into the patch of light.

"Your skin is darker since last I saw you," she said.

"This is nearly the first roof I have been under since you left me," Walter replied.

"*Nearly?* Whose was the other?" she inquired.

"I do not know the woman's name."

"If you remember it," she purred, "please tell me. Hospitality is not a strong trait in my people and I want to reward her."

Again the princess led him by the hand. They moved

through the dark room, beyond a velvet black curtain, up a white stair, and into a beautiful chamber.

"How you must miss the hot flowing river," she said. "I've had a bath drawn there in the corner for you." With a half smile and a quick wink she added, "There are no white leeches in this font."

Walter gave a nervous laugh as she continued her show of cordiality. "At the foot of your couch you will find a garment. When you are refreshed, come down. I shall be in the room on the left at the foot of the stair."

She glided out. Walter, barely able to remain upright, could not take in the marvelous change. How was he to respond? Last he saw her, she sent him reeling with a blow. Now she received him like a long-lost hero. She behaved as if she had expected all along he would follow and find her. Could he believe her even in part? Which part? Could beauty and great wickedness exist in the same person? As to her hospitality, surely he had earned that and should stay simply to discern the situation.

30

____

THE TREMBLE OF ALABASTER

WATER SPARKLED CRYSTAL CLEAR IN THE DEEP WHITE BATH sunk into the marble floor. It was odd to see it flow in opulent abundance. Walter plunged in. As he immersed his bruised and battered body, an odor delicate and strange filled his nostrils, arousing fresh suspicion. Might the water be medicated or enchanted? He sprang out and dripped across the floor, almost slipping. Huddled and shivering, embarrassed by his fear, Walter tried to reason with himself—but neither the weight of logic, nor the draw of soothing pleasure could motivate him to re-enter the tub. He found and put on the robe laid out for him. Orchids dotted the hem in subtle embroidery, white on white slightly raised, barely noticeable except to the touch. Warmth infused him and down he went to the room at the foot of the stair.

Upon entering, he found himself in a round interior room built with walls of translucent alabaster. Soft, pearly shimmering light came through from all sides. Vague formless shadows flitted over the curved walls and low ceiling, like loose rain clouds over a grey-blue sky.

The princess stood waiting, robed also. On her garment, embroidered silver chainmail was woven tight, with spaces left for inlaid golden fish. Rings and discs shaped in diamond patterns fell unbroken from her neck down to where the hem hid her feet. Long open sleeves accentuated beautiful bare arms.

Beside her stood an ebony table covered in cakes and fruit and beverages. Near her stood a crystal jug of pale rose wine and a white loaf. The princess seated herself on an adjacent couch, and made a sign for Walter to sit beside her. She poured Walter out a bowl of milk, and, handing him the whole loaf said, "Take eat. Break off as much as you desire." As he chewed, she filled two silver goblets from the wine-jug.

"You have never drunk wine like this!" she said as she handed him a cup.

He drank, and could not disagree.

"Our natures are so different," she said softly, "but you have saved my life and I must try to make you understand me."

Walter nodded, already feeling intoxicated.

"Human men and women live only to die," she began. "I live on and on. Aging to you is a horror. For me it is sweet desire. Your maturation is a pathetic thing, coming too soon, and lasting a short span. One like me grows older and older and nearer and nearer to perfection. I have lived thousands of your years and have still not reached my summit."

Walter listened wide-eyed, unable to doubt words that rang so true.

"Many lovers have wooed me but I have loved none. Each sought but to capture me, like the men of my city digging for gems of high price. But when *you* found me, I was found by a real man."

Walter gulped and reddened.

"I put you to the test and you withstood it," she admitted

looking down, "and though your love is far from ideal, I cannot doubt that it is genuine."

Walter nodded, caught in the current of her words.

The princess continued her confession. "You showed love to me at first by your pity, but pity is not true love. What woman of *any* world would return love for pity? But, if you had first met me as I truly am, you would have loved me like the rest—to have and to hold on to.

"If I am to have love, I want the kind of love that overcomes hopelessness, prevails over indifference, conquers hate, and stands against scorn. This is why I feigned cruelty and ingratitude towards you. When I left you, I needed to make sure you were not following me out of pity. You had to see I no longer needed you. I needed to see if you had the kind of love that would follow, looking for nothing in return, not even gratitude. You have conquered. I yield the contest."

Soft and gentle was her countenance. Walter stared and she hid her face in her hands. His heart beat hard within his chest in glorious disbelief. And yet, just before her mouth and eyes were veiled, he caught a glimmer of a smirk, and checked his heart.

"Beautiful princess," Walter said, "Help me comprehend. When I found you, you were not your glorious self. How did you come so close to death?"

"There are things I cannot explain," she replied, "you will only understand when our love has grown perfect. There is so much experience in my many years that you may never be able to bear up under the weight, but since you ask so sweetly, I will try."

She smoothed her gown and continued. "A report had come to me that a part of my dominions had been taken over by a race of a savage dwarfs—strong and fierce, opposed to every kind of progress. I traveled alone to confront them as I had many times before, but these enemies to law and order had set a trap. When I bounded over the healing stream, what mortals would call a *spell* was activated. When my foot set on the opposite bank, an indescribable cold invaded me. Knowing it would only affect me temporarily, I dragged myself to a hidden place in the wood."

A shadow of embarrassment darkened her cheeks. Walter saw it, but held his face impassive as she went on. "I knew nothing more until I woke and saw you sleeping near me. The horrible worm was at your neck. After throwing the monster into the stream, I bent to kiss your wound. You began to stir, so I, being naked, buried myself again among the leaves."

The princess rose. Her eyes flashed in inhuman brightness as she threw out her arms towards her listener. "Oh Walter, you brought me back and I am yours! I will repay you as never a woman did for a man! My power, my beauty, my love are your own. Take them." She dropped to kneel beside him and looked up into his face.

Avoiding her hypnotic eyes, Walter looked down at her arms and noted for the first time her right hand was sheathed in a glove. He glanced at her left and it was as lovely as a hand could be. Walter remembered the wounded paw and in a flash recalled the hard-clenched hand, shut and bruised. Loathing welled up. He turned his eyes towards the ceiling and sat motionless.

The princess started to her feet. Walter sat second-guessing every discernment and decision. Aching loneliness began to whisper, "Perhaps to *me* she could be true." He turned his eyes at last downward to see entrancing loveliness staring past him, lost in a murmuring chant. The odor of the bath wafted into his nostrils, hypnotic and beguiling.

A frightful roar pierced the alabaster. The walls trembled as if they might shake into shards. The princess shuddered visibly.

Walter's heart bounded and rebound against the walls of his rib cage.

"My wine is too strong for you!" she said in a quavering voice. "I ought not to have let you take a full draught! You must sleep now. I will take you to your chamber ... come. When you awaken, ask me anything and I will open my heart to you." In one motion she was guiding him up the white staircase.

Another deep bellow emanated nearby. "The roars startle me too," the princess said in her gentlest voice yet. "It sounds as though she has escaped my cage, but it is quite impossible."

Walter knew that the roar did not come from the spotted cat chained in the foyer, but from one that wandered free, the one who had nuzzled his feet and the night before had kept him warm. The thundering bellow was meant for his ears, not for the princess, rattling him back to sober vigilance.

He walked with her in silence and she left him at the door to his room, saying goodnight with a winsome smile.

But as she turned, he read anxiety in her beautiful face.

31

A ROYAL CAT FIGHT

WALTER COLLAPSED INTO BED and began to turn over in his mind the tale told by the princess. She had been overconfident in her cleverness. He knew now from her choice of words that she had bounded over the stream as a leopardess. He also knew—having experienced the power of the healing stream first hand—the water had dissolved her self-enchantment. Lastly, her account of the race of dwarfs revealed a truth hard to stomach. He had saved the life of the mortal enemy of the ones he loved most.

Just as he was beginning to form thoughts concerning the gravity of his situation, Walter fell asleep. Not as one who drifts off in weariness, but like one pushed off a cliff. Down into a drugged stupor he plummeted. The lovely wine had been far from innocent. An hour before midnight, half conscious, he fought to open one eyelid. A suspended lamp swayed from the ceiling, casting a clear soft light throughout the chamber. He felt a strong sensation of floating. Delicious lethargy enfolded him.

A shot of sickening pain pierced Walter's chest. His hands

were useless, paralyzed as if tied down. He felt his body go limp. Seconds later the sharpness died away, but a weight of a profound depravity pressed down upon him. In utter agony, unable to assert any strength, he tensed in anticipation for the next wounding. Instead he felt a gentle hand lift his head back onto the pillow and a coverlet pulled over his quivering body and tucked beneath his chin. The weight on his chest subsided and he began to breathe freely again.

He fought towards consciousness, though his whole soul screamed for escape back to the oblivion of slumber. Refocusing his clouded vision, he saw the form of the princess over him. She stood upon the mattress, straddling his body, pinning down the covers, and staring out into the room with the air of one who dreamed. Her great eyes were clear and calm. Her mouth rested in satisfied passion. With the back of her hand she wiped a streak of red from her lips. Glancing down, she caught his gaze. A storm gathered in her countenance, like one intruded upon in a private intimacy. She bent down and grazed him with the edge of her bandaged hand. "How ... how could you?" she breathed, barely audible.

Walter felt a sharp claw draw across his eyes. For a moment he was struck blind. He heard the door close and found himself alone. Worse than his fear of further injury, more intense than his loathing of her evil presence, was the unbearableness of not knowing. Rising from bed, he dressed in haste and leapt down the stairs two at a time. He felt her everywhere, for she might be anywhere—even now waiting to pounce upon him. Only with her in full view did he feel he had a chance at self-defense and survival. As long as she was hidden he might become a human fountain for her thirst.

Toward the chamber of alabaster Walter rushed. In the pitch-dark, he groped his way along, at last feeling the plush black curtain. Pulling it aside, he entered the vast ebony hall. The moon sailed high and the space was lit eerily through the opening in the dome. She who had shown him favor in order to feed upon him was nowhere in view. Instead, he found a great muted assembly, a mass of shapes and mingled shadows possessing every square foot of the wide space. Through the dim confusion Walter somehow separated out familiar figures, glimpses of his wandering past. Shining eyes glanced out of encrusted skulls, wraiths armed with lances charged on skeleton horses, hideous burrowing phantasms writhed upon the marble floor.

Though nauseous and unsettled Walter remained honed in the singleness of his quest. He scanned high and low for any indication of the princess, but found none. Moving on he made his way through the silent shifting undulation. Neither figure nor form took the slightest notice of his presence.

Arms held stiffly in front of him, he cast about until he again found the outer wall of the great room. He dragged his hand along the surface as he groped along and, in time, detected an opening leading to the vestibule. Dim moonlight showed the cage of the spotted leopardess. Within was a silent desperate struggle between two vastly differing forms, human and bestial, entangled in confusion. Mingled bodies and limbs writhed and wrestled in close embrace, each struggling for dominance.

Walter averted his eyes from the hideous carnality and darted across the spacious room to escape out the wide front doors. The moon, halfway up the sky, shown round and clear. Her face wore a look of still expectation over the quiet city. Seconds later, a blur of rage passed Walter in the darkness. The great dappled leopardess tore straight on and out the open gate. Walter followed as fast as two legs can carry a man, but it was innate knowledge, rather than tracking, that brought him to his destination: the foot of the same apartment stair where he had kept watch two nights before.

Walter arrived just in time to see a body tumble down. At his feet lay the blackened, crushed, and barely recognizable corpse of the woman who had led him home and shut him out. In vain had Mara warned her to flee. He stood petrified, but before he could form a thought, out bounded the spotted leopardess from the open door above. The baby hung in her mouth. Walter stepped up between the iron banisters, intending somehow to seize the infant from the salivating jaws. Just as he came within arm's length another feline rushed in. Like a glowing bar of silver, the white leopardess shot through the moonlight, and, in a single powerful lunge, gripped her spotted foe by the neck. Walter caught the falling child and pressed himself against the cold hard wall below the stair.

The fight seemed an even match. Neither cat made a noise beyond a low hate-filled growl. As claws scrambled for foothold upon the pavement, Walter grew anxious. The spotted cat was bigger than the white, but the white held fast to the the neck of her enemy. At length, the spotted throat issued a howl of agony. In ever-quickening gradations the roar changed into the long-drawn crescendo of a woman's uttermost wail. The white one relaxed her jaws. The dappled one drew away and rose upright on her hind legs. Walter stared as her spots merged and flowed, fleeing into the refuge of her eyes. There they vanished, and upright in the moonlight stood the princess, a column of radiant whiteness erect in the midst of streaming ebony hair. From her throat, out of a small puncture, came a trickle of red. She turned and fled away towards her palace.

For the first time Walter gave thought to the infant in his care. As he glanced down to check the child's well-being, the white leopardess was upon him. She pulled the baby from his arms and flew with it out of the city gate.

32

UP A TREE

RELIEVED OF THE CHILD, WALTER CHASED after the woman, still unwilling to let Her Highness out of his sight. Back up the hill he tore and through the gate, reaching the entrance-hall just as the princess was throwing a robe around herself. She turned and saw him and flashed in anger, followed by an attempted smile.

"I have met with a small accident," she said. "The cat-woman came again to the city and I went down to send her away." Walter saw that she shook, and his fear and good judgement melted into compassion. Her words were lies, but her wounds were real. The weeks tending her in the cave flooded back.

The princess read his face, stepped towards him and caressed his cheek. "Always full of pity. You can once again heal my wounds, darling Walter."

Walter, still unwilling to lose sight of her, was led farther in. Together they entered the black hall where the phantom crowd was still present in the shifting illumination. Passing through,

Walter heard the mouthless musicians issue a macabre chorus that echoed against the dark walls—

> *Between burrows of demons ensconced underneath*
> *She crawls in the shadows in the mist of the heath.*
> *In the war of the woods where the dead writhe and moan*
> *"Ye are men!" she calls out, as bone shatters bone.*
> *Where the skull-headed dancers trod the leaf-covered floor*
> *Gloating enfleshed, she stands at the door.*

Walter could hardly compose himself. Their paths had crossed three times before he found her nearly dead and the revelation of his blindness thundered in his head. The princess touched his arm, "Come now," she said. "I will show you what I need you to do for me." In dazed compliance he followed her out into a courtyard.

The moon was near her zenith, and her silver seemed brighter than the gold of the absent sun. The princess brought Walter to the tallest tree in the center of the garden. Its branches drew their ends together at the top, resembling a pine-cone from beneath.

"On the summit of this tree grows a tiny blossom which would at once heal my scratches," the princess whispered. "If I had wings like a dove, I would fly up and fetch it for myself."

She adjured with one of her sweetest smiles, "Can you climb?" The smile vanished into a look of sadness and suffering, though the corners of her mouth barely turned. Her hand lightly touched the wounds on her neck.

Walter considered the tree and nodded. He moved to its base to begin, when the princess suddenly cried out, "Not with bare feet!"

"Princess," Walter's head was beginning to clear. "I have long gone unshod, both my feet are quite calloused."

He placed his hands upon the rough bark, eager for a task. She moved to stop him. "I cannot let you attempt it barefoot. The bark will cut you and a fall from the top would kill you. Please, oh please, Walter, wait a moment." She tore from her outer garment the two wide borders that met in front. Kneeling down, she bound both of his feet with thick embroidered strips.

Now shod, Walter turned to the tree, and began to climb. The trunk did not sway in spite of his weight and the strong evening wind, but every branch became more unsteady to the point of giving way. The higher he ascended, the colder it grew. When his head rose above the branches near the top, Walter expected to look about for a blossom in the moonlight. He found instead he was drenched from head to foot like one plunged into a stormy body of water. Flung about wildly, sinking and tossing, he rolled, gasped, and choked. Upended, he sank to a solid bottom.

"I told you so!" croaked a voice in his ear.

Up through troubled waters Walter saw a black bird clutching the edge of a stone basin. The Raven stood calmly looking down upon Walter who lay on his back under a few feet of water. The cold light of the dawn reflected from the bird's glossy plumage. Raising up on one elbow, Walter lifted his face above the surface, rubbed the water out of his eyes, and found himself in the bowl of the large fountain in the middle of his own lawn. Over him glimmered the thick pillar constructed by his father, a torrent shooting twenty feet upwards, rushing to form a spreading blossom of foam.

"You *told* me so? You told me nothing!" Walter retorted, spitting out water inadvertently taken in as he rushed to speak.

"I told you to never trust a person who has once deceived you and to never do anything such a person requests."

"You expect me, a mere mortal, to remember that?!"

"You will not soon forget the consequences," said Mr. Raven, whose human form stood leaning over the edge of the basin, stretching a hand out to assist. Walter took it and was immediately beside his guide on the lawn, dripping and puddling. The two walked towards the house, the door of which stood wide open.

"You must change your clothes at once," instructed Mr. Raven.

"I have not much to change," Walter said wryly, for he had flung aside his robe to climb the tree and was wearing very little. Food also came to mind along with a warm bed and the possibility of a good book. The house was asleep. Walter went to his room and dressed. Descending again, all seemed changed. He had seen too much and there would be no return to the Walter that was before.

As he entered the library, Mr. Raven was exiting the closet. Walter collapsed on a couch while Mr. Raven drew up a chair. For a minute or two neither spoke. "What does it all mean?" Walter finally asked.

"A good question, but what it means depends upon how you make use of it."

"I have made no use of anything yet."

"Not much. But you know of your uselessness, and self-awareness is something. At least you have not been without the *desire* to be of use."

"I did want to do something for the children—the Dearlings, I mean."

"You started the wrong way."

"I did not know the right way."

"Had you accepted our invitation to sleep, you would have

known the right way. When a man will not act where he is, he must go far to find his work."

"Indeed I have gone far, and got nowhere. I left the children to learn how to serve them and have only learned of the danger they are in."

"When you were *with* them, you were where you could serve them. Twice now you have left your work to go look for it."

"Do you mean, Sir, that I could have done something for the Dearlings by *staying* with them?"

"Could you teach them anything by *leaving* them?"

"What could I teach them? They were far ahead of me!"

"That is true in more than one sense, but you saw they were afraid of growing."

"But surely I had no power to make them grow!"

"You might have removed some of the hindrances."

"What hindrances? The lack of water?"

"Yes, which caused the lack of tears."

"I would not wish tears upon them!" stammered Walter.

"No doubt—relieving others from crying is the aim of all small-brained philanthropists. Why, Mr. Ludwell, no world is worth saving except that there is weeping in it."

Walter sat in stunned silence. Mr. Raven returned to simpler matters. "You are right to think it might be water the Dearlings needed. Why not dig them a well?"

"It never entered my mind."

"Not even when the sound of the waters under the earth entered your ears?"

"It did occur to me once perhaps, but I was afraid it would draw the attention of the Hoons."

Mr. Raven removed his spectacles and leaned in, "Walter, you nearly taught the noble little Dearlings to be afraid, not just of *becoming* like the Hoons but actually *of* the big stupid giants. While the Dearlings fed and comforted and admired you, you submitted yourself the whole time to be the slave of bestial men. You gave the Dearlings a seeming coward for their hero."

"I was concerned, Mr. Raven," returned Walter somewhat tersely, "that more knowledge might render them less innocent, less lovely. Is not a little knowledge a dangerous thing?"

"That is one of the pet falsehoods of your world. Is man's greatest knowledge more than a little? Is it therefore dangerous? It is illusion to think knowledge is, of itself, much of anything at all."

"I must insist, Mr. Raven, that it was for love of the Dearlings, not from cowardice that I served the Hoons."

"You ought to have served the little ones, not the giants. You muffed your chance with the Dearlings, Mr. Ludwell. You speculated about them instead of helping them."

Walter sat for a very long time, sullen and silent.

33

HERE KITTY KITTY

WHAT MR. RAVEN SAID WAS TRUE AND WALTER KNEW IT. He had not helped the Dearlings. In fact, he had prided himself in leaving no impact whatsoever.

The Raven was not finished. "If you had managed to show the least bit of bravery, by this time you might have made the Hoons cutters of wood and carriers of water for the little ones. In this you wronged the dull-witted Hoons as well. For them, slavery to the Dearlings would have been progress."

"I did not know the Hoons were cowards and could be so easily subdued," mumbled Walter.

"What difference does that make?" asked Mr. Raven. "The man who grounds his action on another's cowardice, is essentially a coward himself."

Walter reeled, cornered and silenced yet again. The only person he could look to for guidance on the mysterious path unfolding before him rebuffed and discouraged him at every turn.

Mr. Raven, himself dispirited, put his face in his hands. "By now the Dearlings might have been able to protect themselves from the princess. Instead, because of your relations with her …"

"I hate her!" Walter cried.

"Did you let her know you hated her?!" came Mr. Raven's abrupt reply.

Walter shook his head. Mr. Raven did the same. "Not even to *her* have you been faithful," he sighed."Duplicity is not limited to … " but the homily stopped before it began. The Sexton put a finger to his lips and lowered his voice. "We were followed, I fear, from the fountain."

Walter straightened and gazed out the window. He caught sight of a soggy, disreputable-looking cat bolting into the shrubbery beside the front entrance."What do you mean, Mr. Raven?" Walter whispered, a creeping fear wrapping round his throat.

"We shall see," said the Sexton. "I know a little about unmasking cats of several sorts. Please close all the exits to this room."

Walter did as instructed.

Mr. Raven went to the door of the closet and brought back the mutilated volume. Walter stared. The book, entire and sound, lay open in the Sexton's lap.

"Where has the other half of it been?" Walter gasped.

"Sticking out into my cottage library," Mr. Raven said.

A thousand questions came flooding into Walter's mind, but there was a more pressing matter at hand.

"Listen," said Mr. Raven, "I am going to read a stanza or two. She will not, I imagine, enjoy listening." He opened the vellum cover and turned a few discolored leaves. His eye roved over page after page for a certain passage in the midst of a continuous poem. Somewhere about the middle of the book he began to read aloud. A strange, repulsive caterwaul arose somewhere in the room. Walter started and stared about but could not find the source.

"I thought some foul thing was in the room," commented the Sexton, as calmly as a butler criticizing the housekeeping. He turned several pages and continued.

Again there was a cry of ugly feline pain. Again Walter looked, but saw neither shape nor motion. The Sexton cocked his head and again turned several more pages before resuming his reading.

Once more arose the bestial wail.

A leaf or two was turned and the Sexton read on.

With a fearsome yell and with clammy fur standing, tail thick as a cable, eyes flashing golden-green, distended claws entangling in the carpet, the cat floundered and made for the chimney. Quick as thought, the Sexton threw the manuscript between her and the hearth. She crouched instantly, her eyes fixed on the text. The Sexton's voice went on in an intoning chant, sounding in deep baritone four lines from memory.[1]

At this a howling, prolonged yell of agony burst from the cat. Both men stopped their ears. When the noise ceased, the Sexton walked to the fireplace and took up the book. Standing between the creature and the chimney, he pointed his finger at her for a moment. She lay still as stone, her large head couched upon her front paws. The Sexton took a half-burnt stick from the hearth and drew in charcoal some sign on the tile. He then crossed the floor, and put the manuscript back in its place. Returning to the crouching feline, the Sexton said in a still, solemn voice, "Lilith, when you came here on the way to enact your evil will, you had no idea into whose hands you were delivering yourself."

The Sexton turned and addressed Walter. "Mr. Ludwell, when God created man out of His own endless glory, He brought Adam an angelic splendor to be his wife. There she lies."

Walter had no desire to come for a closer look. He stood still, continuing to wonder how the strange world he left was now invading his own.

"Lilith believed marriage was beneath her and bearing children to be slavery. Still, one child was born. Instead of embracing motherhood, she considered herself equal to the Creator—one who gave being. She demanded her husband fall down and worship her. In short, Adam refused. She fled to the army of the Other and soon ensnared the heart of the great Shadow."

Statuesque and frozen, the cat watched the Sexton, but not an eyeball, not a claw, not a whisker moved. Her tail stretched out behind her rigid as an iron bar.

Sexton began to pace, ever watching the feline's beryl eyes fixed and flaming. "How far you have fallen, Lilith! How is it, having been created to rule the earth, to now be Queen of Hell?

"Walter, you know of Eve—not an angel, but a woman—she is light and humility when compared to this creature's darkness and pride."

The cat gave a horrible screech, and began to grow, enlarging and morphing into the shape of the spotted leopardess. A roar shook the house. Walter sprang to the far side of the room, but the Sexton did not flinch or blink.

"It is only her jealousy that speaks," the Sexton said, "foiled and fruitless. For here I am now, her master, a direct descendant of him whom she would not have for her husband! Beautiful Eve and many of her daughters live, hoping and repenting towards immortality. Lilith's hated child lives also, but beyond her grasp."

Walter could scarcely take in all he was hearing, privy to matters too marvelous for him. He began to shake. The

Sexton pressed on, "Adam repents and so do many of his sons. But the Queen of Hell refuses. Is the great Shadow beautiful, Lilith? How long will you remain beautiful? Answer if you know."

The leopardess reared and buckled, twisted and contorted, fell and rose until the shape of the princess stood radiant. "I AM beautiful—and immortal!" she cried. Walter thought she looked every bit the goddess she declared herself to be.

"As a bush that burns, and *is* consumed," answered the Sexton. "What is that under your right arm?"

Lilith's arm was pressed against her side. A swift pang contorted her beautiful face, then passed. "It is but a leopard-spot that lingers! It will quickly follow those I have dismissed," she retorted.

"You are beautiful because you were created beautiful, but you are a slave. Remove your arm from your side." Her arm rose obediently, but she looked at him with a fierceness that had no surrender.

The Sexton gazed a moment at the spot. "It is *not* of the leopard. It is of the woman!" he said. "It will not leave you until it has eaten to your heart." She showed no shadow of concern as he diagnosed her cancer. He looked in her eyes and added, "Your beauty flows away from you through the open wound." She gave a glance downward, and shivered.

"Lilith," his tone now changed to tender beseeching, "Hear me and repent. He who made you will cleanse you. The child that you fear is your destruction will one day be your salvation."

Her hand returned quivering to her side. Her face grew dark. She gave the cry of one from whom all hope has vanished. The cry passed into a howl. She lay writhing on the floor, once again a leopardess covered with spots.

The Sexton continued, "How will you fare when time has

vanished? Repent, I beg you. Repent, and be again an angel of God!"

She stood upright, a woman once more, and said smiling, "I will not repent and I will continue to drink the blood of your children."

Walter's eyes fastened on Lilith. The Sexton stood towering above her, his countenance altered, his voice terrible. "Down!" he cried, "or by the power given me I will melt thy very bones."

Lilith flung herself to the floor, dwindled and shrunk. Again she was a gray house cat. The Sexton caught her up by the nape, bore her to the closet, and threw her in. He drew the same figure upon the threshold that he had scrawled before the hearth. Closing the door, he locked it.

Sad and worn, Mr. Raven crossed the room and sat down at Walter's side upon the couch. Walter, trembling, handed him a handkerchief to wipe away his flood of tears.

34

THREE THROUGH THE LOOKING GLASS

"WE MUST BE ON OUR GUARD," said Mr. Raven, having recovered himself, "or she will again outwit us. She makes men fools upon the least sliver of pride."

"What is she after?" Walter asked.

"Lilith has come to this house as a pathway towards her daughter, whom she fears and therefore hates. The birth of children is, in her eyes, the death of their parents."

"How have the Dearlings survived within her territory so long?" asked Walter growing alarmed.

"She dare not cross the divine boundary of the stream. She did once and lay dying."

"Damn my pity and compassion!" cried Walter. "Worse yet, my meddling desire to play hero. Mr. Raven, does anyone ever discern and live by right motives?"

"If a man waits to act until his motives are pure, very little good would ever be done. It's pride, dear Walter, that undoes all virtue."

"Damn my pride then. What now? How ... "

"She has found another way. By your feet you have led her."

"My feet?"

"She had no right to enter this world, for she slew her own body that belonged to it. Only in personal contact with one attached to it could she re-enter. You provided the opportunity. With the lightest touch on one of your muffled feet, she clung as you climbed the tree. She is now watching to go in again, back to hunt, thinking herself wiser for having come and gone."

Walter shook his head in dismay. Into his mind flashed the countenance of the eldest Dearling. Superimposed upon upon the face of Lona was Lilith's cheek, chin, and nose. "Lona ... her daughter?"

"Hush, hush!" whispered the Sexton, with uplifted hand. "She can hear!"

The Sexton motioned Walter into the garden, but even there he spoke in a whisper. "The woman who hates mothering did indeed birth the mother of all the Dearlings. Lona has forgotten. She thinks she herself came from the woods, the first of the family."

Walter cut in. "What a fool I am! I saved the life of Lona's sworn enemy! Sir ... Father ... Sexton ... Lilith cannot know anything about the mirror!"

"You must go at once, and make your way to my cottage. I will stay and keep guard."

"Your cottage? I must go to the Dearlings!" Walter cried.

"Beware of your own plans, Mr. Ludwell. Go to my wife and do as she tells you."

Walter shook his head in wonderment. Why the hurry to delay? If not to protect the children, why go at all?"

"Tell me first, Mr. Raven," Walter insisted, "why, of all places, do you have Lilith shut up in the closet? It is a doorway to your house!"

"The closet is no nearer nor farther from our cottage than any other place."

"But the mutilated volume sticks into your library from mine!"

The Sexton led Walter back through the main doors, muttering to himself, "The dear boy. It is hard to be persuaded when one does not understand."

At the foot of the great stairway he turned and sighed. "Walter, you are constantly experiencing things you *do not* and also *cannot* understand. You have grown familiar with many wonders and are thereby not surprised at all by them." The Sexton was now walking backward up the stair punctuating each phrase with a sharp footfall. "You accept them, not because you understand them, but because they have unavoidable, every-day relations with you. The fact is, no man understands *anything*. I have now become quite certain I cannot help you understand, but I may, perhaps, help you a little to believe."

On the second landing the Sexton detoured into a sitting room with windows facing east. The hallowed space once belonged to Walter's grandmother, and the matron's prayer books and kneeler still sat between the sills. Between windows the hung a large icon of the Theotokos in the style of Kells.

The Sexton emitted a low bass note like that of byzantine chant and cocked his head listening. A moment after, Walter heard a soft whir of wings. He looked up and saw a white dove perched on the shelf below the icon where its fluttering knocked over neither taper nor sensor. The bird dropped to the Sexton's shoulder and lay its head against his cheek. By the motions of their two heads Walter could tell that they were talking together, though he heard nothing at all. He never averted his eyes yet suddenly the dove was not there. Without a word, the Sexton led him back out to the hallway and towards the second flight of stairs.

"Why did you sing the low bass drone?" Walter asked. "Surely sound here is not sound there."

"You are right," Mr. Raven answered. "I intoned that *you* might know that I called the dove, but now we must not waste more time with more talk about things that must be experienced rather than explained. And you must go."

"I will at once!" Walter replied, and moved towards the steps.

"You will sleep tonight at my chamber," the Sexton said— not as a question, but in a tone of tender authority.

"My heart is with the children," Walter asserted. "But if you insist ... "

"I do insist. Otherwise, you can affect nothing. I will go with you as far as the mirror and see you off."

As they reached the third floor, both felt a reverberation of the full weight of a leopardess throwing itself against the heavy closet door. Walter looked at his guide wide-eyed.

"She is terrified," Raven said and walked more briskly.

Before the two set foot on the wooden corkscrew to the attic, a howling roar shook the house. Its echo mingled with the scratch of great claws scoring the hard oak. Walter half turned.

"To think of her lying there alone with that terrible wound."

"Nothing will ever close that wound," the Sexton said, direct and terse. "It eats at her heart. She must live with it until she chooses otherwise."

Then came the sound of paws upon the stairwell.

"Could she have broken loose?!" Walter cried.

"Make haste!" the Sexton rejoined. "I shall face her the moment you are through and I have disarranged the mirror."

The two ran, reaching the wooden chamber breathless. Mr. Raven seized the chains and adjusted the shutters. He set the mirror at the proper angle and the mountain range emerged in the mist.

With the yell of a demon, the huge bulk of the spotted leopardess pushed the two men apart, and leapt through the glass. Away she went at a low, swift gallop. Walter sprang through to follow at a full run. The Sexton came afterward. "You need not exert yourself!" he called out after Walter. "We cannot overtake her! This is our way!" As he spoke, he turned in the opposite direction and added to himself, "She has more magic at her fingertips than I care to know."

"We must do what we can!" Walter said, and ran on in pursuit. Soon he stopped, puffing and clutching at his chest, watching the great cat dwindle in the distance.

He limped back towards the Sexton who answered him. "Mara has been warned and she will do her part. Your part is to sleep, and you have given me your word."

"Nor do I mean to break it, but surely sleep is not the first priority! In such an emergency, should not action take precedence over repose!"

"A man can do nothing he is not fit to do. See! Did I not tell you Mara would do her part?"

Walter looked in the direction the Sexton pointed and saw a white blur moving along the horizon.

"What a beauty!" the Sexton cried in delight. "The white leopardess will conquer."

"I have seen them fight," Walter said. "The combat did not appear one-sided."

"What can you discern, you who have never slept?" queried the Sexton, turning. "Come! Come! He who cannot act must make haste to sleep."

35

———

THE SEXTON'S WAR HORSE

WALTER STOOD AND WATCHED the last gleam of the white leopardess melt away, then turned shuffling to follow his guide the Sexton. What had he to do with sleep? Surely sleep served the same purpose in every world. The hour had come for brave deeds of live men! In the Sexton's chamber under the care of his cold and distant wife, how could he be certain of waking in time to make amends? Of waking at all? The sleepers in that house let morning glide into noon, and noon into night. Some *never* stirred! Walter murmured these things in his heart, but followed on, for he knew not what else to do.

The sun set and with it Walter's heart. In the air came the spreading cold of the Sexton's chamber. He hung back, in no hurry to keep stride with the lean, long-coated figure. At length he could no longer hear his swishing coattails through the heather and heard instead the slow-flapping wings of the Raven. It did not matter to Walter whether his guide was above or ahead, for he had ceased to watch, noting instead fireflies flickering and white moths rising into the rayless air.

As the moon appeared, slowly crossing the far horizon, the black bird with his frosted feathers about the neck alighted on a stone. "You are tired, are you not, Mr. Ludwell? You must make acquaintance with the horse that will carry you in the morning."

"One glad morning, he means," thought Walter gloomily.

The bird gave a strange whistle through his long black beak. A spot appeared on the face of the half-risen moon and the drumming of swift galloping hooves grew to a low thunder at the approach of a terrible steed. His mane flowed away behind him like the crest of a wind-fighting wave torn seaward in a hoary spray; nineteen hands high, huge of bone, tight of skin, hard of muscle. As he drew near, his speed slackened. His mane drifted about him, settling alongside the blinding whisk of his flowing tail. Even the moon regarded him with awe.

The sight of this mighty stallion awoke in Walter the passionate longing to possess. He reached and stroked muscle and bone under smooth hide. So shiny and supple was the horse's coat that the very shape of the moon was reflected in it. Walter fondled his sharp-pointed ears, whispered words in them, and kissed his velvet nostrils. The magnificent animal returned breath for breath and the bond was instant. The Raven, with wings half extended, approved. "Be friends with him," he croaked. "He will carry you all the better tomorrow, but now we must hurry home."

"May I mount him at once, Mr. Raven?!" Walter cried. His desire to ride had grown urgent.

"By all means," Raven said. "Mount, and ride him home."

The horse bent his head down lovingly. Walter twisted his hands in his mane and scrambled onto his back. "He could out-speed any leopardess in all creation!"

"Not that way while it is yet dark. The road is difficult.

Come, loss now will be gain later. To wait is harder than to run, but its results go deeper."

Walter heard neither proverb, nor the wisdom contained in them.

"Go on, my son," urged the Raven, raising his voice. "Straight to the cottage. I shall be there to greet you. My lady's heart will rejoice to see you, a son of hers on that particular horse."

Walter sat silent. The horse stood like a block of marble.

"Why do you linger?" asked the Raven.

"I long so much to ride after the leopardess that I can scarce restrain myself,"

"You have promised."

"My debt to the Dearlings appears a greater thing than my bond to you."

"Yield to this temptation and you will bring mischief upon them—and on yourself also."

"I do not care what happens to me. I love *them*, and love works no evil. I will go."

The Raven's eyes flashed through the darkness, and Walter knew that the Sexton now stood in full stature. Walter heard in his voice a repressed indignation barely contained. "Mr. Ludwell, do you not know *why* you have not yet done anything worth doing?"

"Because I have been a fool."

"Wherein?" the Sexton asked.

"In everything," Walter answered through gritted teeth.

"What do you think is your most indiscreet action?"

"Bringing the princess back to life. I ought to have left her to her just fate."

"No. You are talking nonsense. You could not have done otherwise than you did, being compassionate and not knowing she was evil. But you never brought anyone back to life. How could you, yourself, still dead?"

"I ... dead?" Walter cried.

"Yes," he said, "and you will be dead for so long as you refuse to die."

"Back to the old riddling!" Walter returned scornfully.

"Be persuaded, and go home with me," the Sexton continued, softening. "The most—nearly the *only*—foolish thing you did in this world was to run from our offer of sleep."

Walter pressed the horse's ribs and was off like a sudden wind. He gave the stallion a pat on the side of the neck, as he galloped into a sharp-driven curve, close to the ground, like a cat when wheeling after a mouse. Through the dark Walter heard the beat of wings. Five quick flaps and the Raven perched on the horse's head. The horse checked himself instantly and plowed up the ground with his feet, coming to a full stop.

"Mr. Ludwell," croaked the Raven. "Think of what you are doing. Twice already evil has befallen you: once from fear and once from heedlessness. Breach of word is far worse. It is a crime."

"The Dearlings are in peril, and I brought it upon them! But indeed, Mr. Raven, I will not break my word to you. After I have done them good, I will return. Then I will spend in your house however many nights—however many days—however many years you please."

"I tell you once more, Walter, you will do the Dearlings the opposite of good if you go tonight."

A false sense of power had been imbued by the stallion, rendering Walter too stupid to listen. Equine infatuation had overridden loyalty to the Sexton, even eclipsing all sober love for the little ones.

"Would you take from me my last chance of reparation?" Walter bellowed. "Do not ask me to shrink from my duty! I will no longer play the coward! I will go—if I perish for it, then I perish!"

"Go, then, foolish boy!" the Raven returned, with anger in his croak. "Take the horse, and ride to failure! May it be to humility."

Raven spread his wings and flew. Walter pressed the lean ribs under him and leaned forward whispering, "After the spotted leopardess." The stallion turned his head this way and that, snuffing the air. His first few paces were a slow, undecided walk. He quickened into a trot. Then came the gallop. His speed was tremendous and he seemed to see in the dark, never stumbling, never faltering, never hesitating. Walter felt under him the play of each individual muscle, every movement gliding into the next so that not once did the horse jar his rider.

Across the edge of the evil burrow they sped like a bolt from a crossbow. No monster lifted its head. All feared the hoofs that thundered above. Horse and rider rushed up the hills, shot down the farther slopes, and galloped unswerving over the chasms of the riverbed. The moon, halfway up the heaven, gazed with solemn trouble on her pale countenance.

Walter felt the pride of life as he rode like a king, his horse clearing channel after channel, sometimes two at once in his bounding stride. The moon reached the keystone of her arch and began to descend rolling faster and faster. Across the ravines came the howling of wolves. Ugly fear began to invade the hollow places of his heart and confidence began to wane.

The horse maintained his headlong swiftness, ears pricked forward, thirsty nostrils exulting in the wind. The moon jolted like an old chariot-wheel down the hill of heaven, with awful foreboding. She rolled at last over the horizon-edge and disappeared, carrying all her light with her.

The mighty steed was in the act of clearing a wide channel when he staggered, hobbled as one caught in the net of darkness. The sheer weight of his helpless bulk carried horse and rider across the ravine, but the beautiful steed fell in a heap on the edge of the opposite bank. Where he fell, he lay. Walter got up, kneeled beside him, and felt him all over. Not a muscle was torn, not a bone broken, but the horse was no more. The glowing coal in each blue-filmy eye had gone out.

Walter sat down upon the great body, and buried his face in his hands.

36

HIDE-N-SEEK

BITTERLY COLD GREW THE NIGHT. The horse's body froze where it fell. Atop sat its rider, no longer wild and free but crosslegged and cowed. The cry of the wolves came nearer. Walter heard their paws soft-padding on the rocky ground and saw their quick panting in the frosty air. Their glowing eyes contracted in a half-circle round him. Death had come and he hadn't even a stick to beat it off.

Dark throats gaped, eager to devour. Walter stood for a moment, but devastated by hopelessness sat back down, shoulders slumped to await his fate. Drawn by the smell of horse flesh, the wolves were puzzled by the hapless man. In their moment of hesitation came a sound of swift fluttering. A few yards beyond the wolf pack a murder of crows emerged from the forest. A cloud of black feathers crowded every surrounding tree branch, a flock of five hundred at least. The pack turned from its meal and snarled.

Walter ran from the midst of his foes. Minutes before, he had thought himself a man riding off to war. Now he fled, hoping and praying to be overlooked and forgotten. The wolves sped away to find a meal elsewhere, but the birds, ghastly and gaunt, came after, attacking Walter with beak and claw. Such a multitude clung to his body that he could not make his way in the darkness. He fought back, tearing them off, throttling them, flinging them away, and trampling. He thrust his fingers in their eyes, caught them in his jaws, but could not stop the onslaught.

In despair, Walter threw himself to the ground wherein a single crow, like an ominous ringleader, persisted in bloodying his scalp. He rose and continued running as the horde that accompanied him turned all their aggressive energy towards driving him on. When he fell, which was often, the murder gave him time to rise. When from fear of falling he slackened his pace, they flew afresh upon his legs.

All that miserable night the crows kept him running. When he could form a thought he noted that the path they drove him upon avoided the peaks and gully that beset the journey. How was it that hundreds of birds were organized into such a purpose? He hoped the goal was not to run him to his death.

When at length the morning came, Walter saw he was beyond the dry channels and on the verge of the orchard valley. So joyful was he to see friendly territory, he stopped and turned to offer thanks to his persecutors; but not a crow was to be seen. A single black feather floated down to the forest floor.

Walter lay himself on the moss, and fell fast asleep.

WALTER WAS AWAKENED BY A KICK, finding himself bound hand and foot and once more enslaved to the Hoons. "How fitting," he laughed in the triumph of self-disgust, "right were I belong." A second kick stopped all false merriment. He was dragged to his feet and put straight back to his old labors.

This time the Hoons were more wary than before and did

not leave him alone to his work. They stayed to watch him and made a game of pelting him with rocks. Walter comforted himself with the thought that the Dearlings would come that night. When the darkness came, his captors tied his hands and left him bound to the tree, and though he dreamed of lying in the heart of a great heap of children, all he found when he awoke was the reappearance of his enemies, full of hatred.

Not until noon, when he was failing from fatigue and hunger, did Walter hear a commotion in the brushwood. Then came the bursts of bell-like laughter so dear to his heart. He gave such a loud cry of delight that his captors started to their feet but were met with storm of sharp stones. The Hoons retreated over the hill, and in a flash, Walter's ropes were undone. Once again he was in the arms of the little ones.

The Dearlings set a watch and made the Good Giant sit down. Lona came and, without a word, fed him with the loveliest red and yellow fruits. When she was satisfied he was full, the whole assembly formed a file and began to lead Walter away. He yielded to their pleasure, happy that they were happy.

Traveling through the forest where the babies were found, Walter realized the woods stretched from the valley of the Hoons all the way up to the very borders of the hot stream. A tiny girl had leapt into his arms. After patting his cheeks and twirling his hair in her chubby hands, she promptly fell asleep in the crook of his elbow. After a short nap, she awoke and the whole procession hung on her every word.

"We make a wekwest to King," she said.

"What is it, my darling?" Walter asked, enthralled.

"Shut eyes one minute."

"Certainly I will! Here goes!"

He heard a soft scurry, a little rustle, and then a silence.

"Open eyes!" twenty voices a little way off shouted at once. Walter obeyed and saw he stood alone. Not a creature was visible. He knew the children were marvelously quick in getting out of the way—the Hoons had taught them that—but looking about the open shrub-less forest, he could see neither hand nor heel. He stared in blank astonishment.

Walter lay down on the forest floor to listen, sure if he left the hiders alone they would soon come out. Even though the sun was almost set and darkness was coming, a multitude of birds began to sing and grew into a little storm of chirps and tweets. He looked straight up into the arched arbor over him and spied a little motion among the leaves. Flesh-colored spots appeared in the dark foliage, the music died down. A gale of childish laughter rippled the air and Walter saw that the trees were full of Dearlings. In the wildest merriment they began to descend, some dropping from branch to branch so rapidly that he could scarce believe they had not fallen.

"How is it that I never heard you sing like the birds before?" Walter asked.

"Ah," said one of the wildest, "the bad giants tore up our hidey-places in the bushes so into the trees to build nests we went! Now we live like birds and sound like birds. Come and see my nest. It's not big enough for King, but it's big enough for King to see me in."

"I cannot climb in the dark," said Walter, "but I promise to see it first thing tomorrow."

And with that, up they all went. Walter heard no more of them until he was awakened the next morning with a kiss.

37

THE OTHER WOMAN

UNDER THE SHELTER OF A TREE near the center of the grove, Walter lay awake in spite of being bone tired. He felt strangely out of sorts, for Lona had not bid him goodnight. The moment he had seen her again he had been struck with her resemblance to Lilith. In Lona the dazzling beauty of the princess was softened by childlikeness and deepened by motherhood. She is occupied with an infant, he told himself.

Lona did come at last and sat down beside him. Taking his hand, she began to pour out all that had befallen the tribe since his departure. Walter watched her face in the moonlight as she talked. How such a daughter could have been born of such a mother was hard to understand. Then again, she had *two* parents, and her own free will had also formed her.

"Where have you been, dear King?" she asked softly. "Did you find what you were searching for?"

"Lona, you are not a child and should not call me 'King.'"

Lona looked puzzled. He could not tell if her befuddlement was the suggestion of her adulthood or his refusal of the royal title. "The littlest ones can address me as 'King' if they wish," he continued. "They will know in time that I am not, but you and I are equals. You have learned from motherhood just as much as I have learned from all my wanderings. In fact, I have it on very good authority that you have likely gained more wisdom from staying and doing the work at hand than I have from dashing about between worlds."

Lona's brow furrowed just a little, unsure of accepting the weight of what he said.

"Please call me Walter," he implored.

"Ok ... Wa-ter," she said, suddenly cheered. "You shall not hear 'King' from me again."

He shook his head and enunciated, "WAL-ter."

"I know, silly," Lona said with a wink and a smile.

Walter knew then that he had begun to love her.

"When you awaken tomorrow you can ask me anything, Lona. I will open my heart to you. For tonight, please continue telling me of you and the children."

"After you left our orchard valley, the giants believed a little more in our existence, awakening in them fear and hostility. Sometimes, from our hiding places, we would see them trampling furiously at some imagined sign of our presence. The little ones would stand by and laugh at their foolish rage. Then their animosity took a practical shape. They began to uproot and burn the dwarf trees from which we eat."

It was Walter's turn to furrow his brow. Lona patted his hand and her eyes sparkled with levity. "In reality, it was *you* they were after. They seemed to think you were lurking about, and might steal upon them in their sleep."

Walter relaxed a little at her lightness.

"We decided to move. That is a long story but the short of it is—here we are out of their reach, learning to live as birds."

"Amazingly adaptable, you and your children," Walter

murmured. Every word she spoke seemed to go straight to his heart and make it purer.

Lona laughed. "In a way, the littles are less afraid of the idea of growing up now that they live 'up.'" Her tone became more serious. "As for their safety, no giant ever seems to throw back his dull head to look skyward. The Hoons are certain we have completely left the country. Or they have gone back to believing we never existed in the first place." She sighed, "Change seems on the march, Walter. Have you noticed that many of the children are now grown?"

"I had not, but it makes sense, now that fear of 'up' has softened."

"There is something else," said Lona. "Another Good Giant has joined us."

Walter tilted his head with interest, trying to hide his alarm.

"One moonlit evening, out gathering fruit, we came upon a woman seated on the ground with a baby in her lap. The littles took her for a Bad Giantess with a stolen child. I do not know how vicious the fight would have become had not the woman kept her wits and quickly yielded the baby. The littles were pacified when I held the little girl in my arms and by how the woman hugged and kissed the baby before giving her up. In an instant they were persuaded she was good—like you—and our guest was brought food and shown every sort of Dearling hospitality."

Walter smiled at the memory of his first welcome, but grew serious again. "Does she intend to stay? I may have met her before ... " A flash of the leopard's smashed paw came flooding back.

"I *hope* you have, Walter," Lona said, "for there are times I do not know what to think of her. She seems of two minds about the city, missing her husband and talking of his riches, but also terrified at any mention of returning. Also, I do not understand her indifference to motherhood. She lets us care for her daughter without hesitation, rarely asking to see her baby. I try to understand, but I do not. Perhaps you will speak with her." Her voice trailed off.

"I will find her first thing tomorrow," assured Walter.

Lona was visibly lightened as she parted.

THE NEXT MORNING Walter went in search. He spied the woman sitting alone in the distance under a spreading tree, lost in thought. It was indeed the same woman who had clutched her child close the night that Lilith had left him. Now, empty-armed, she sat passive. The difference was disturbing. In their last meeting she had stared death in the face and wounded a fierce leopard. She had refused all help when he had offered to carry her child. Now, she paid no mind as her baby was passed around by children barely able to fend for themselves.

As Walter drew close, he pondered the place of her origin. There was no mothering in the City on the Grassland. The city's very air crushed the sacrificial endurance parenting required. Brief instinctual urges for survival was all the child-rearing this woman knew. In spite of her age, Lona and the other older girls were far beyond her. Even many of the boys seemed wiser in the ways of playful learning.

Walter called out a greeting and she stared at him until slow recognition dawned on her sleepy face. She held out her hand and gave her name: "Sylvia."

Walter extended his hand in return, welcoming but cautious. "I'm Walter. I believe we've met."

No small talk passed between the two. Both had survived the dangers of the City and witnessed the retreat of the great spotted leopardess. Sylvia seemed to know Walter had come to assess her.

"I must admit I am surprised, but glad to see you again."

"And I you," Walter returned. "It is good you found safe harbor among the Dearlings. Your daughter is in the best of hands."

"Safety is a fragile and temporary thing," Sylvia said, as Walter settled in the grass across from her. "I am sure you are well aware of the prophecy and know the reason the princess fears little ones."

"The prophecy has stood for a thousand of years. Why speak of it now?" hedged Walter, keeping his tone measured.

"Many of the citizens have seen the subtle deterioration of our princess's youth and beauty. Most sense her desperation in the face of a coming doom. Long have we noted the crumbling walls of our domain and yearn for improvement. We have been too fearful to arise against her, though we nourished secret hope for change. But no one dared to speak. Then you came and pursued her majesty into her lair, and emerged again whole and sound."

Walter was abashed that the citizens of the city had taken note of his private doings. He wondered at Sylvia's eagerness and questioned her further. "For what change exactly do you hope?"

"To speed the fulfillment of our glorious destiny, of course!" Sylvia said, impassioned. "The princess has ruled long enough. She sits stagnating on a crumbling throne. Fear of the future has invaded her heart making her weaker by the day. The city, half in ruins, will not fight to keep her." Sylvia smiled and stared straight into Walter's eyes. "I have never seen such brightness and bravery as the Dearlings possess under Lona's care. Their well-developed character makes sense now that I know *you,* the man who does not waver in his pursuit. You are in part responsible for their upbringing, are you not? Just imagine, Walter, if you, leading the Dearlings, entered through the broken gates. The citizens who appear to be cowards will find inspiration to rise to their higher potential."

Walter saw the flattery but did not care. He suspected her motive might be simply safe passage back to her husband, but what she said contained some truth. The shock of children, the city's *own* children, and a few well-aimed stones might overturn all. The Sexton himself had said that the Hoons were cowards. What were the folk of the city, but gentrified Hoons?

As he stood to leave Walter pondered the inescapable events: the growth in the Dearlings, the presence of Sylvia, and —underneath it all—the princess's waning power. And Walter knew something Sylvia did not: the white leopardess, a sworn enemy of Lilith, was on the move.

38

A LIFE OF ITS OWN

ALTER SAW THAT CHANGE WAS HAPPENING—had happened. The Dearlings were growing. Many had grown. A citizen from the city lived among them and two leopards were on the hunt.

The children reported having seen a spotted kitty, who liked to claw at the base of their trees. They took her presence with no more gravity than they did the presence of the Hoons. Besides, a second white kitty always seemed to chase her away before they could find out what Spotty wanted. Walter trembled wondering if the protective boundary of the healing stream had been nullified by Lilith's knowledge of doorways through his house.

It was not wise for them to sit and wait for tragedy to strike them in their beds, but what part should the innocent Dearlings take in deciding their own destiny? No good decision was ever made in haste. Then again indecision was itself a decision. *"A man must act where he is,"* came the Raven's voice into his selective conscience. Well, he was with the Dearlings now and meant to stay with them. This time they would not have a seeming coward for a hero.

Walter was determined to speak more openly with Lona, but also resolute that the younger children should stay protected from the wider world for as long as possible. However, moving through the forest grove he discovered, to his horror, that Sylvia had no such scruples or discretion. Children above, playing chase through branches, chattered about a wicked 'pwincess' in a gated city. His chest tightened for he knew they had not the least notion of what a city was. One lisped the words 'de-fence-wess' and 'bweach-in-the-wall,' and Walter's heart sorrowed; none of them knew what fortifications were or why they might exist in the first place.

Walter rushed about in search of Lona, but when he found her, she was not alone. She and Sylvia sat together under the trees, each holding a baby. "Walter," Lona began after kissing his cheek in greeting, "Sylvia tells me of the mourning women of the City on the Grassland, about their plight and great loss. It makes me wonder if their hearts would not turn towards their own children if only they had a chance to meet again. I cannot imagine a life without little ones."

"It is not the citizens that make me worry," said Walter. He wished he had caught her alone and sooner—days sooner.

Lona guessed his thoughts. "Sylvia has also told me of the princess, but she assures me that Her Highness is greatly weakened, and that *you* are to thank."

Walter shuddered. How could he explain to the simple purity of Lona all that had transpired? He murmured a denial of heroism, but the women only thought him modest.

Whether he willed it or not, the time of the prophecy seemed to be coming ripe. His simple presence among the Dearlings pressed it ever onward. Were not the little ones growing? Growing and *not* becoming Hoons! Might they not become a youthful people whose government and influence would be for righteousness? The city's great riches might be put to work for noble purposes.

Walter envisioned Lona on the throne instead of her mother. The fantasy was banished before it took root, but not before the thought wandered through his head, "Between the two of us, much good could be accomplished." Though unaware of it, Lona had grown into the full flower of womanhood. Often she would turn her eyes upon him with glowing gladness and this pierced him through with painful joy.

He told her nothing of her mother.

WALTER, burdened, could hardly sleep. What dreams he had were invaded by fragments of the Sexton's reproaches.

One morning, he found Lona and broached the idea that the finding of water might perhaps expedite the growth of the Dearlings. "Have you seen a well before?" he asked. He did his best to explain the concept, even offering to share with her the sound of the bubbling aquifer.

"I know very little of water and nothing at all of wells, but I do not doubt your wisdom. Dearest Walter," she said, laughing, "We are planning travels and the taking of a city. One expedition at a time!"

Walter dropped the topic of wells and aquifers, but was glad to find his conscience somewhat relieved. He had tried. Lona was right that immediate and practical preparations consumed their time. Walter spent every waking hour describing to eager little listeners the upcoming trip. He drew pictures of the city in the dirt to communicate the nature and size of the man-made structures, and even drilled little regiments in extra rounds of stone-throwing in case of unexpected trouble. Their skills were already formidable, but the mock-military exercises helped salve Walter's uneasiness.

Lona gave all her energies to the supplies that would have to travel with her large family. Sylvia looked on, above all the scurrying about, with a face of complete confidence. She announced more than once that she herself was, "ready with a good stick to take out any two men of the city," and that if the princess used magic, it would "prove powerless against the children."

The night before their planned departure, the three adults counseled together. Walter confessed to the women that he shrank from taking *all* the children into the face of the unknown. "Would it not be better, Sylvia," he pressed, "if you remained here in the forest with your baby and the smallest of the Dearlings?"

"Oh Walter, what thoughtful tenderness!" Sylvia said. "But our best weapon for the least amount of conflict is the sight of babies. What an impression they shall make on the women—especially the childless mothers. When they see the darlings, their hearts will be taken by storm."

Lona's eyes glowed at the thought of sharing her greatest joy with those who had not yet tasted of it. Sylvia smiled in triumph adding, "When we win the women, we win the city. The men lost their courage long ago, forfeiting all authority."

Both women saw the pang go through Walter's heart. Both moved to each side of him and touched a shoulder. Lona said, "We have explained our destination to the children, that we are going there to find their mothers."

"I have warned them of the risk," said Sylvia softly. "In fact, I told a group of older boys of the danger of the princess just an hour ago, and they claim to be ready to die."

"The children have promised to stay together and scurry

away if any but their own mother should touch them," added the guileless voice of Lona.

Walter quaked, but could find no footing for opposing two women of one mind.

Lona said, "I would give my life to have my mother. She might kill me if she liked. I would just kiss her and die."

Lona's declaration was a pearl poised to be tossed to a depraved boar. The stark contrast between mother and daughter shamed Walter into speechlessness. Looking into her glowing confident eyes, he knew that with her and for her, he would triumph or perish.

39

NESTS OF STONE

I T WAS AN EARLY MORNING when out between the blue sky and the green grass stepped the tribe of Dearlings—a gallant show upon the plain.

"Come along, boys!" cried a girl of medium height. "We're going to our mothers!"

"I'm not afraid of the wicked princess!" a young boy hollered in return. "She's afraid of babies!"

They traveled until midday and rested in the afternoon, rising in the short twilight to continue under the stars. Walter's plan was to arrive at the city on the fourth morning and be well inside the gates before they were discovered.

When the children first saw the City on the Grassland pressed against the horizon, the hulking walls appeared to them as a great mass of rock. Walter explained as best he could that the structure was full of nests of stone. Apprehension and dislike invaded his listeners' tender hearts. How were they to find mothers in such a place? But on they went bravely, trusting King Walter and Mother Lona.

The padding of small feet came through that city's archway.

Some of the Dearlings shivered, and all were silent as death. Girls held closer the infants they carried. On the countenance of Sylvia lay a dark anxiety, and Walter himself felt nearly crushed by the general dread. He had brought an army of children into the heart of an ancient enemy, supported by dreamy notions of a coming kingdom of little ones. Lona walked beside him—calm, silent, watchful, yet somehow still fearless.

The throng of Dearlings was halfway to the central square before any of the inhabitants became aware of their presence. Windows began to open, sleepy heads looking out from half-empty apartments. Every face wore a stare of astonishment, then unanimous consternation. The women noticed that their invaders were almost all children and came running into the streets. The men followed, keeping close to the houses, huddling under the eaves.

At length a boy of five, full of fantasies about motherhood, spied a woman in the crowd whose face he liked. Running, he threw himself upon her and clung about her neck. She warmly returned his embrace and kisses, but the hand of a man came over her shoulder. He seized the boy by the neck and began to shake him like a feral cat. Instantly, a Dearling girl ran and snatched the boy back.

Dismay clouded the face of Lona. "They are just a bunch of Hoons!" she cried, looking around with flashing eyes.

The citizens withdrew to cluster in doorways while the children marched quietly on to the main square. Hardly had they halted when two girls ran to Walter, consumed by anxiety. Two of the boys had been snatched after Sylvia, their guide, had disappeared with her baby. Walter took a deep breath and strained to think of some word of direction, but no one was looking to him. All had turned towards a narrow lane leading up to the palace. Bounding down the passageway, full speed, was the white leopardess.

The children froze in terror except for one—a small boy named Otis. Stepping from Walter's shadow, Otis ran headlong to meet the cat. Shocked, the leopardess pulled up short to avoid knocking him down. Head over tail she went tumbling. When she recovered her feet, Otis was perched upon her back. The citizens of the city, seeing an invading urchin child bestriding their fiercest foe, dispersed.

Walter and Lona used their retreat to conduct a house-to-house search for the two missing boys. In the end, one was recovered. For the other, it was too late. He was a lad of about ten and had wandered from the Dearlings' ranks into the arms of his chosen mother. Her Hoon of a husband feigned welcome, but behind closed doors he took hold of the boy's throat, shook him, and would not stop. Now the white leopardess locked the murderer's neck in her massive jaws and dragged him through the streets like a house cat with a rat. She shook the body of the dead man with such fierceness that windows were slammed and shuttered, and doors locked tight.

"Let us leave this horrid place," said Lona. "There are no mothers here." But immediate retreat was difficult. The children were exhausted and Lilith was still holed up in her palace. What might she do if they appeared to turn and run?

The Dearlings settled in to rest on the ancient pavement in the square. Walter, Lona, and the eldest boys kept watch as the sun set. When the whole wicked city appeared to sleep, Walter found Lona standing alone, holding an infant and staring at the moon. She did not look at him as he joined her, but took his hand. "What should the children call you now, Walter?" she whispered. "The childishness of 'King' is over and the innocence of 'Good Giant' is long past."

"I am so sorry, Lona, for the death of the boy," Walter said. "We shall bury him under his favorite fruit tree as soon as we get back to your orchard."

"Perhaps it was a severe mercy," Lona said, hardly listening. "He had been lately gnawing at green apples and was most likely lost to us anyway."

Walter saw through her brave words. Her heart was clearly broken. The death of a Dearling, even a doomed one, was a loss far too great. Lona turned to him in sorrowful confession, tears streaming down. "I was too easily fooled. Sylvia seemed like one of us in the forest." Clinging to his neck she sobbed. Walter held her in solemn silence until she pulled herself away and wiped her tears. "Walter. We must gather the children and leave as soon as the moon is high. I know you want to redeem this mad adventure, but this is no place for our children."

"What lesson would quick retreat teach our little ones in the long run?" Walter asked gravely, groping about to find meaning in his mounting list of mistakes.

"That we know how to repent," Lona answered.

Walter nodded. Her voice was that of the Sexton. He said, "Lona, there is something that you need to know, something I should have spoken of before we traveled. Once you know, I place in your hands whether we leave or stay, retreat or press on." He inhaled and sighed heavily. "Lilith, hiding in her palace, is afraid of our children. But there is someone she fears more."

Lona stared at him.

"The princess is afraid because of a prophecy, a prophecy which states her daughter will be her doom—the end of herself and her kingdom."

"Lilith is my mother," said Lona, understanding at once.

Walter trembled and began rambling. "I believe the sight of you might take her heart by storm, but she could grow violent. I will step between if ... "

Lona was no longer listening. The syllables "mo-ther" were forming silently on her lips in soft repetitions.

Still he prattled on. "I will strike her without pity if she so much as raises a hand ... doom can mean many things. It might simply mean that the *evil* in her is doomed. And by our arrival ..."

Lona spoke now, clear and sure. "Tomorrow I will accompany you to the palace." She placed the snoring infant in his arms, curled up at his feet, and, in seconds, was fast asleep.

Walter had never seen her sleep so soundly.

40

───────

A MOTHER AND CHILD REUNION

FROM THE TOP OF ONE OF THE PALACE TOWERS, Lilith had seen the army of children enter the sleeping city. The sight awoke in her an over-mastering terror. For weeks she had hunted them on four feet, clothed in spots, and had been foiled again and again, not just by the white she-cat but the children themselves. The Hoons' bumbling hatred had driven them out of her reach. Now they were upon her, and the prophecy screamed in her ears.

With halting steps her majesty descended to the black hall and seated herself under the elliptical opening. Perhaps here she could think. Opposite the throne a mirror was suspended, tilted to receive the beam of noontide sunlight soon to arrive. Lilith knew the resulting vision—the splendor of her self-rendered beauty—would renew her power and strength.

Shadowy figures fluttered about her in the darkened chamber. With her inner eye she located the presence of one she had once held in high regard, now to her but the wisp of an old inamorato. Self-occupied, she gave no acknowledgment of his silent, brooding power.

The sun at last arrived. For a few minutes she saw herself all glorious within its beams. Then the vision passed, and her citizens still cowered before little ones encamped below in the square. Even when the night came, she did not stir. Darkness clothed and filled the glass and gloom invaded every wing. All night long the princess remained, motionless and waiting. She must try again to think! But courage and will had grown weary of her, and fled.

As the tide of light came creeping again up the shore of the sky, Lilith felt the presence of two intruders ascending the steep avenue to the palace. The gate lay open, the palace door hanging limp on its hinges. All servants now hid in their quarters paralyzed in soulless dread.

Again the sun gazed in through the eye of the black marble roof and flashed upon the mirror within. Lilith looked with a half-smile, then sprang to her feet. The slow siren of a banshee passed through her half-parted lips. The spot upon her side had spread from shoulder to hip, black as the marble around her. She clutched her gossamer robe and fell back upon her throne as the great Shadow glided out unnoticed. He passed the spotted leopardess who lay as a lifeless heap within her cage. Her body heaved against its bindings as he went by, and the next instant fell supine and motionless.

Two visitors entered as the Shadow exited. Echoes of their footsteps on the stones of the courtyard came to Lilith's ears and she flinched, pressing her hand to her side harder. As they entered the hall she leaned back in her chair under the shaft of sunlight. One visitor she knew and disdained—the servile man always one step from his manhood. The other she knew and feared—the girl long time a woman.

Her daughter sprang towards her, bounding away from the man's attempts to stay and shield. "Mother! Mother!" The pure loving tones burned Lilith's ears and brain as they resonated throughout the dome. Lilith shivered, her face blackened with hate. She rose to her feet and faced the oncoming foe.

"Mother! Mother!" came the cry again, as hope and adoration bound in humility leapt up and flung her arms around stiff neck and bare shoulders.

AN INSTANT more and Walter would have reached the throne where the women stood intertwined. Given a moment, he could have prevented the horror that would unfold.

Mother Lilith ran her left hand swiftly along her only child's scalp, clutching Lona's tresses between white fingers and thumb. Like the compulsion to uproot a tick or crush a leech, she jerked back, snapping the young woman's neck. Lona's arms went limp and dropped. Her body convulsed and fell in a heap on the hard floor.

Lilith stepped back and took her seat again and smiled her sweetest smile, ready for Walter to spring upon her in a melee of fury and grief. He gave her no notice. To him, she was not there. Dropping to both knees he reached out to take up the body of Lona.

Lilith sat in disbelief. How could the disfigured dying waste upon her floor eclipse the magnificence upon the throne? She glanced again to the mirror. Before her eyes, youth and beauty was withering, wasting away, fast approaching what she had been the hour before Walter had come to her rescue. Over-mastering vanity shrank and groveled within her deepest heart. Her eyes tore around the room. The man she loathed had lifted the other woman's broken body to his bosom and was retreating back across the palace hall. Back to the mirror her eyes darted. She stood up in horror. Her eyes alone were alive, wickedly flaming. All else was that of a cadaver.

As he made his way out, Walter saw nothing but Lona. Lona saw nothing at all. A final whisper, "Mother," came in a dying breath, then all breathing ceased.

Lilith sat back down on her throne, as still as the body being carried from the room. She closed her eyes and felt the sunlight on her white skin. Grasping-for, hoping-for, willing-there-to-be a rejuvenating change, she opened her eyes to seek the mirror yet again. Instead of a glorious reflection, three faces stared down upon her.

A trio of Dearling boys had followed Walter and Lona unbidden. They raised their fists determined to finish what 'King' had left undone. But they restrained each others' trembling rage and bound the exhausted princess hand and foot.

They dragged their prisoner out through the courtyard, past the gaping servants, down the narrow streets, and towards the square. Not a muscle of her blanched white carcass moved save her eyes that rolled in their ghastly sockets.

WALTER CARRIED Lona out to where the sun shone upon her quiet face. Her head hung back in the crook of his arm. A pitiful shadow of a smile had formed with her final breath. He forgot the little ones waiting in the square. He forgot the murdering princess. He forgot who it was who lay in his arms, and wandered down the narrow street looking for his Lona. She alone could comfort him in this devastating loss.

The doors and windows were crowded with brute faces jeering, but none dared more than the screeching of epithets from behind thick panes, for the white leopardess followed, hanging her head close at Walter's heels.

When Walter reached the square, his little army was gone. The emptiness roused him to his senses. Where were the little ones? *Her* little ones? Had he lost her children as well? He staggered to the central pillar and sank upon its base. Finding no rest he arose again. Even the leopardess was gone now. Encumbered with his dead, he made his shuffling way down towards the gate he had entered by. He gave no notice to a trickling crowd, filling the street with hateful glances darting his way. Before he reached the gate, the rabble found courage and began, shoving and hustling, to block his progress. A man pushed against the sacred burden and Walter gave a kick that sent him howling, but still the crowd pressed without mercy. Walter freed his right hand and clutched Lona closer with his left, instinctively protecting one who was beyond all hurt. The crowd crushed, and Walter's desperation grew.

A commotion arose outside the throng. A way broke open and through it strode the three young Dearlings, dragging as their spoils of war the former queen of power, the dust of the city falling from their feet. Walter followed in their wake out of the evil place knowing in agony that his army of Dearlings had captured their tormentor and in doing so, had lost their beloved mother.

41

A REQUIEM

HE CHILDREN HAD ENCAMPED in a spacious place beneath the trees, a hundred yards or so beyond the city walls. A murmur of pleasure arose as they caught sight of Walter approaching with Lona in his arms. Close behind came the three young men, dragging their captive. A crowd ran to greet them, but all happy shouts died away and sobs broke over like billows. Walter carried grief into the camp and a haggard look came upon the childish faces. All pressed around him, holding out their arms, desiring to take his burden.

Walter found a spot beneath a beech where the grass grew soft and thick. There he laid Lona down and stepped back to let her children approach and grieve. The tender hopelessness of their smiles and the way in which they reverenced her brought fresh tears. In vain they sought to entice from her some recognition of their love. In vain they kissed and caressed her hands and feet in an attempt to wake her. As many as could crowd near put their arms around her body. Walter looked at Lona's face within the crowd. To his surprise, her countenance spoke comfort. "You shall see me alive. It is not me, but you who are lost. I will find you." Somewhere in the suffocating sorrow, Walter believed her.

The singer who had caused Walter his much earlier tears—eons ago it felt—was no longer little. Atop a stump he climbed and began to sing a noble requiem. His music sent arrows through every listener. Tears ran down every face—

Night is come
Our fight is done
Which way now is our home?
Dear Mother waiting for her grave
So very much alone
Have we chose best
To leave our nests?
Chase phantom yearnings in our breasts
Hearts cut down within the quest
So very much alone.

As the song continued, Walter caught sight of Lilith, bound and lain under an alder tree. She stared and trembled. Otis stood nearby and whispered, "I have seen that woman before!" His friend Lupe leaned in to listen as Otis pointed. "It was she who stared hungrily up at us in our nests in the trees, until White Kitty chased her away."

"Doofus!" said Lupe. "That was a wild beast. This is a woman!"

"Look at her eyes!" insisted Otis. "I know she is the evil princess, but she is a wild beast all the same."

Lupe took a step towards Lilith. Otis drew her back with a sharp pull.

"Don't stare!" he cried, shrinking away, yet fascinated too by the hate-filled longing in Lilith's eyes. "She would eat you up in a moment! She is the wicked princess. It was *her* shadow that passed through us when we were in the square."

"How can that be?" asked Lupe. "They said she was beautiful!"

"Wickedness has made her ugly."

Lilith heard and turned and it was a mercy that no child was looking in her eyes, aflame with venom.

"It was very wrong of me to run away from the square where we were told to sleep," said Otis thoughtfully.

"What made you run?" Lupe asked.

Otis did not reply at once. Several children had now gathered round, wanting words of explanation for the shared experience of terror. Walter paid close attention as well. Something dire had befallen the Dearlings in his absence

"A Shadow came down the hill from the palace," said Otis. "Not a human for he had no thick to him. He was nothing but blackness."

Otis looked up at Walter, took his hand, and continued. "We were frightened the moment we saw him, but we did not run away. We had been told to stay and we meant to. We stood still and watched him come straight on without a change in his steps, as if he would walk right over us."

All now crowded around Otis. Walter motioned to the eager listeners to give the boy some space, and nodded for him to go on.

"Before he reached us, the Shadow began to spread and spread, bigger and bigger until, at last, he was *so* big he was too big to see ... and then he was upon us!"

"What do you mean *upon* you?" asked Walter.

"He was all black through, between, around—we could not see each other. And then he was inside us."

The group nodded in solidarity, clinging to the words.

"How did you know he was *inside* you?" Walter asked his brows furrowed in consternation.

"He made me ... a different me. I felt bad. I was not Otis any more—not the Otis I knew. I wanted to tear Lupe to pieces!" He turned and hugged Lupe. "It wasn't me, Lupe," he sobbed, "really, deep down, it was Otis, loving you always!"

Lupe patted her friend reassuringly and let him blubber on. "I grew sick, and thought I must kill myself to get out of the black ... " Walter now took Otis into his arms. The boy continued with salt streaks encrusting his chubby cheeks. "Then came a horrible laugh. The Shadow had heard my think, and it set the air trembling about me." Brows furrowed on the face of every listening ear and Walter wished he could draw them all into his arms.

"That is when, I suppose, I ran away," said Otis. "I found myself running, fast as I could, and all the rest running too. We could not stop until we were out of the gate and tumbling into the green, soft grass." Otis bent and ran is fingers lovingly though the blades, and continued almost in a whisper. "When I felt the grass I knew that I was the Otis that loved Lupe and not the Shadow that wanted to be me—but wasn't."

Knowing looks passed between multiple companions in the crowd.

"And now I know that I ought not to have run. But I did not quite know what I was doing until it was done! My *legs* did it. *They* grew frightened, and forgot me. Naughty, naughty legs!" Otis finished his speech with a kick to each of his naughty members. Many small boys in the audience did the same.

"What became of the Shadow?" Walter asked quietly as the audience broke up into private conversations.

"I do not know," Otis answered. "I suppose he went into the night where there is no moon."

The children gathered in groups to lean against each other, falling quickly off to sleep. Walter relieved the sentinels, intending to walk the perimeter all night, himself keeping watch instead. But when the moon rose high, he caught sight of the white leopardess. She swept silently around the sleeping camp, and passed three times between the bound princess and the little ones. Assured that all was well-guarded, Walter stretched himself beside the body of Lona and whispered in her ear, "Where are you, Lona my love?" But her lips, neither cold nor stiff as yet, gave no answer. He kissed her cheek, turned from her, and fell asleep.

42

BLOOD AND BERRIES

IN THE MORNING THE WEARY ARMY WITHDREW from the City on the Grassland, leaving the ruin to collapse under the weight of its own delusions. Walter would allow no one else the burden of carrying Lona. He would take her to the Sexton in the hope that she would be given a couch in the chamber of prayer. If the Sexton would not accept her as a sleeper, seeing she had not come of her own volition, Walter would take her to the desert and watch over her until to dust she did return. But Walter believed Father Raven would take her. Surely she had died long ago, died in ways Walter had himself steadfastly refused.

He must take the princess to the Sexton also. Walter knew he had no power to make Lilith repent, no right to slay her, and even less a right to let her loose. He doubted it was his destiny to be her perpetual jailer either, though it could be argued he deserved such a fate.

Again and again on the way, Walter offered Lilith food. Again and again she answered only with a look of hungering hate. Her fiery eyes kept rolling to and fro, never closing. Not until they crossed the healing hot stream did the lids come down over the great orbs. They did not open again until the party reached its destination.

One morning, as everyone was waking, Walter saw Gracie, a little girl no more than four, carrying berries towards the bound princess. He rose in haste to prevent the attempt at kindness but before he could reach them, Gracie had put fruit to the lips of Lilith and drawn back with a cry of pain.

"Please, Father Wah-ter," she whimpered looking up, "kiss finger. Bad Giantess make hole in it!"

Walter kissed the tiny finger.

"Well now!" Gracie said, indignant. Still determined, she made a second attempt, this time wisely snatching her hand away. The mouth was greedy for other fare and the fruit fell to the ground, rejected.

On the second afternoon, the whole company ate grapes by the ivy-covered hall where Walter had watched the dancers. That night they crossed the hot stream and the third morning all arrived at the Dearlings' high village of nests.

Walter remained a single night. The little ones were quickly resettled. Lona still looked like one just dead so there was no need for haste for fear of decay on her account, but Lilith looked like one many days past repose. Walter felt the weighty burden of them both. A bitter repentance awaited him at the feet of the Sexton.

After the children were all softly snoring, Walter went to the princess and rolled up his sleeve and offered his bare left arm. She bit into it so fiercely that he cried out—then all went dark. He awoke just out beyond Lilith's reach with the moon's sad countenance shining down upon him. A warmth infused him head to toe, and he looked to see the white leopardess laying inches away, tailed curled round, keeping watch. Upon seeing his opened eyes, she stood, nuzzled his tender forearm, and strode quietly into the wood.

WHEN THE SUN peeped over the horizon, Walter made ready to depart. He asked for volunteer companions to travel alongside. A few of the biggest and strongest stepped forward, but also the most peace-loving and merry. Lilith was placed upon a litter and pulled. Lona was wrapped in a clean cloak and carried, as always, in Walter's arms.

Back across the warm stream to the desert house of Mara they headed. From her Walter hoped to learn how to best cross the rough river course and avoid the burrow of monsters. He thought it wise that they stay at Mara's house before approaching the Sexton's. It was needful for what little life remained in Lilith. It was needful for the pain of heart that was ever expanding in him.

Passing into the arid land between the two branches of the dead river, Walter chose a sheltered place between giant rocks to camp. Lilith, lain upon the sand seemed quite dead, her eyes tight shut. Walter lay a little way from her, out of reach, with the body of Lona on his other side. There he kept watch between the dead and the dangerous and did not doze until the pale thoughtful moon was sliding halfway down the western sky, mottling the desert with shadows. A gust blew up, eclipsing the moonlight in shadow and cloud. A translucent film covered her patient beauty. For a space, she sent forth no beams. The air turned cold with a burning sting, and Lilith was upon him. Her hands were still bound, but her teeth sank into the flesh of his shoulder. Walter lay as one paralyzed—life flowing from him into her.

Then Walter remembered the valor of Sylvia defending her

baby girl. With all the strength he could gather, he sent his fist down upon Lilith's closed right hand. She raised her head with a gurgling shriek and Walter was on his feet. She rose to her knees, rocking herself to and fro. A second blast of hot-stinging cold enveloped them both, but now the moon shone again, clear and white in her radiance. Lilith's face was gaunt and ghastly, smeared with red.

"Down, devil!" he cried.

"Where are you taking me!?" she demanded, crouching low, her voice like the dull echo from a sepulcher.

"To the Sexton's cottage."

"He will kill me!" she moaned.

"At least he will take you off my hands!" shouted Walter.

"Give me my daughter," she suddenly screamed, grinding her teeth.

"Never."

"Loose my hands. Have compassion," she groaned. "I am in torture. The cords are sunk in my flesh."

"I dare not," he said, putting his hand to his wounded shoulder. "Lie down!"

She threw herself on the ground like a fallen tree.

In the morning she again seemed like one dead.

43

─────────

BREAD AND WATER

THE NEXT AFTERNOON the troupe came in sight of Mara's cottage in the far distance.

A little one riding on Walter's shoulders leaned down to his ear, pointed, and whispered, "Please, Fadder Wahter, we not go to dat house."

"Indeed we are" Walter said. "It is where we will stay the night."

"Oh, no! Dat might be where da cat-lady lives."

Otis strode up to listen in so Walter addressed them both, "Listen you two—and please tell all the others—when you meet our hostess no one is to *ever* call her by that name."

"Father, I know about this lady," Otis said. "She has no face!"

"Who told you so?"

"I heard the Hoons speak of it more than once."

"It is not true, Otis. I saw her face when I spent a night at her house."

Otis looked at Walter in awe. "But they say she has claws in her toes! The Hoons had scratches to prove it. Perhaps, when you saw her, the claws were folded up inside their cushions."

Walter tussled Otis's unruly hair. "Perhaps you think that I have claws to *my* toes?"

"Oh, no. That can't be," said Otis shaking his head, "*You* are good."

"The Hoons did not think so."

"We should not believe what the Hoons say about *you!*"

"Are the Hoons good?"

"No. They love lying."

"Then why do you believe them about *her*?"

Otis, unable to answer, fell silent.

The other travelers had gathered round. Walter, seeing the consternation in their faces, said in his most assuring tone, "Dearlings, I would not take you to her house if I did not believe her good."

"We know you would not," they nodded.

"The white leopard frightens us sometimes," Lupe proposed, "but she never hurts us."

"When you see the woman in that cottage," Walter assured the group, "you will know that she is good. You may wonder about what she does, you may not understand her. You may even feel a bit frightened, but I promise, you will soon know that she is good."

Silence fell for spell until Walter said, "It is important that I take the princess to her."

"Why?" asked a chorus of little voices.

"Because she will be a friend to the princess."

"If she is a friend to the princess, how can she be good?" asked Otis with a hint of triumph in his little voice.

"Little Lupe is a friend of the princess," Walter said, "as is Gracie. I saw them both, more than once, try to feed her majesty fruit."

"Little Lupe is good! Gracie is very good!" agreed Otis.

"Will the leopard-lady—I mean the woman that isn't the cat-lady, and has no claws in her toes—give the princess grapes?" asked Gracie.

Walter shook his head. "She is more likely to give her scratches."

"Why? You say she is her friend!"

"A friend is one who gives us what we need," said Walter with a knowing sigh, "and the princess, like many of the Hoons, is sorely in need of a terrible scratching."

For some time there was nothing but the sound of feet crunching in the sod below.

"If any of you are afraid," Walter said, "I will arrange for you to go back home. I shall not stop you nor love you any less. But I cannot take someone with me who believes the Hoons' opinion rather than mine."

"There she is—in the door waiting for us!" cried one, and put his hands over his eyes.

"Please, Father Walter," said Lupe, "I'm so sorry and tired of being afraid!"

"My darling," Walter answered, "there is no harm in being afraid. The only harm is in doing what fear tells you."

"I don't like the leopard-lady! She is frightful!" said a tiny voice.

"You cannot like, and you ought not to dislike, what you have never seen. And I warn you again, I will be sore displeased if *any* of you call her leopard-lady!"

"What are we to call her then?" asked Gracie softly.

"Lady Mara."

"That is a pretty name. I will call her 'Lady Mara' and perhaps she will show me her beautiful face."

They were now within a hundred yards and Mara, muffled in white, was standing in the doorway to receive them.

"Welcome Sir Ludwell and Dearlings," Mara called out. "At last! Lilith's hour has come! Thousands of years I have waited—and now not in vain."

Walter bowed, releasing the treasure of Lona into Mara's waiting arms. She bore the young woman with great gentleness into her house, laying her in a newly-made-up room, and returned for Lilith. Lilith shuddered but gave no resistance. The Dearlings and Walter followed their hostess inside, all looking very grave. Mara lay Lilith on a rough-hewn pew at one side of the room, unbound her, and turned to her other guests.

While his companions shrank back a little, Otis went near and put his hand in the hand of their hostess. "Will you scratch her very deep?" he asked, jumping straight to the point of his deepest concern.

Mara caught him up in her arms, turned her back to the rest of the group, and drew the muffling down from her face. She held the boy at arms' length and he stared intently as if into a mirror. His little mouth opened and a divine wonder arose in his face, transforming in a flash to intense delight. Suspended in that moment, he gazed entranced. Mara set him down and for a minute more he stood looking up at her, lost in contemplation. Back to the Dearlings he ran, with the face of a prophet that knows a bliss he cannot tell.

Mara rearranged her scarf, turned back around, and set the bread of her house before them with a jug of cold water. "You must eat and drink before sleeping, you have a long journey ahead tomorrow."

Though the children had never seen bread, they ate it without any sign of distaste. They had never tasted such water before, but they drank without hesitation. One after the other each looked up from the jug with a face of glad astonishment.

Mara took the hand of the smallest and the rest went marching up after her to their beds in the attic.

All the while Walter watched Lilith, who, though unbound, did not move. Mara had made him a pallet under the stair, one wall away from Lona, but he could not rest knowing the coming ordeal. Their hostess must do what she could to lead Lilith to repentance. The princess would not yield to gentle measures, and harder ones would have their turn.

"May I sit with Lilith in her coming trial?" Walter inquired when Mara descended.

"You may sit, but since she loves no one, she cannot be *with* anyone."

"What if the Shadow should come, God forbid, to keep her company?"

"The great Shadow is *in* her, I fear, but is not company to anyone. She will know I am beside her, but that will not comfort her in the least."

44

WIND, WATER, AND FIRE

THE CHILDREN'S SLEEP WAS A TROUBLED ONE and they told a strange report of it the next day. They could not tell whether the fear in their sleep came out into their waking, or their waking fear had sunk with them into their dreams, but all spoke of the same sensations the next morning. All night something seemed to be going on in the house—something silent, something terrible, something they were not to know.

During the darkness, a frightful wind filled the cottage. It shook the plaster on the walls and passed their chamber as a soundless sob. Then all went still again and they all went back to sleep, only to be jolted awake once more. This time it appeared that the house was filling with the same water they had been drinking. Seeping in from below, it swelled until the attic was full to the very eaves. But it made no more sound than the earlier wind, and when it sank away, they all went back to sleep, dry and warm.

None of them woke again until the sun was rising. They

agreed with one accord that it was the silence, not the wind nor water, that was most terrifying.

Walter took no rest but remained to keep watch with Mara all through the night. He was no more able than the children to describe his experience the next morning. What he saw, what he felt, what his heart might have measured he did not possess language to recount.

While Mara had been bedding down the Dearlings, Walter had taken a seat by the hearth, farthest from where Lilith lay. He noted the white leopardess crouching in the east-most corner. The massive fur-covered body trembled, as if in mortal terror of what might come next. "That which is about to occur has happened in some way before," whispered Walter to himself. He felt an impending initiation. A lamp stood on the high mantelpiece throwing shadows. Seeing that the man intended to remain awake, the great cat crept across the room and into the alcove under the stair. She was neither seen nor heard from again until morning.

The princess lay in absolute stillness. It was a fearsome waiting and Walter felt something terrible was on its way. When Mara came down, she pulled the pew with Lilith upon it to the middle of the room, and sat down at the other side of the hearth, opposite Walter. Between them a small fire burned. A cloudy presence flickered and a silvery creature like a slow-worm came crawling out from between fitted stones adjacent to the cottage entrance. Crossing the clay floor, it slithered without hesitation straight into the flame.

The hours passed. Midnight drew nigh. Mara sat motionless as the *something* drew nearer. Not a sound broke the silence, neither hiss nor crackle came from the fire, not a creak from board or beam. Walter perceived no change except for, now and again, a sort of heave. Whether in the earth, or in the air, or in the waters, or under the earth—he knew not. Whether in his own body or soul—he could not tell. A dread sense of judgment pervaded, but he was not afraid. He had ceased to care about anything except the thing that must be done.

It was midnight. Mara rose, turned towards the pew, and methodically unwound the long swathes that hid her face. The cloth dropped on the ground and she stepped over it. Walter beheld her: lovely beyond speech, heart-and-soul sad, but not unhappy. Severe pity lined every expression and great tears ran down her cheeks. She wiped them away with her robe and her countenance grew very still.

The feet of Lilith were towards the hearth. Mara went to her head. She laid her hand on the Lilith's crown and brushed away the hair from her forehead. Mara stooped and breathed on the sallow brow and Lilith's body shuddered.

"Will you turn away from the wicked things you have been doing for so long?" asked Mara gently.

The princess did not answer. Mara repeated the question in the same soft, inviting tone.

Still there was no sign of hearing.

Mara spoke the words a third time.

The corpse opened its mouth and answered, framing words in something other than sound. "I will not. I will be myself and not another."

"You are another *now*, not yourself."

"I will be what I am now. I will act according to my nature."

"Your nature is good, and you do evil."

"I will do as my Self desires."

"You do as the Shadow, overshadowing your Self, inclines you."

"I will do what I will to do."

"Lilith, you have killed your daughter."

"I have killed thousands. She is my own!"

"She was never yours. But *you* are another's."

"I am not another's. I am my own. And my daughter also is mine."

"You are not the Self you imagine," breathed Mara. "If you were restored, would you make what amends you could for the misery you have caused?"

"I would not."

"Then, alas, your hour has come."

"I care not. I am what I am. No one can take from me my Self! What I choose to seem to myself makes me what I am. Another shall not make me!"

"But Another *has* made you, and you will not much longer be able to see yourself other than how He sees you. Lilith, you are quite aware of the coming change."

Lilith spat. "No one ever made me and I defy any Power to unmake me. You are His slave, and I defy you! You may be able to torture me, but you shall not compel me to do anything against my will!"

"There is no value in compulsion, but there is a Light that goes deeper than the will, a Light that lights up the darkness behind it. That Light alone can make your will truly your own and not another's—not the Shadow's."

"That Light shall not enter me. I hate it! Begone, slave!"

"I am no slave, for I love that Light. There is no slave but the creature that wills against its Creator. I join my will with the deeper will that created mine."

"You speak foolishness from a cowering heart!" spat Lilith. "You imagine me given over to you. I defy you! I hold myself against you! What I choose to be, you cannot change. I will not be what you think me—what you say I am!"

"I am sorry for the suffering you must now face," moaned Mara.

"I will be free!" hissed Lilith.

"She alone is free who makes others free. Every life, every

will, every heart that came within your grasp, you sought to subdue. You are the slave of every slave you have ever made—enchained and unaware."

Mara took her hand from the head of the princess, took two paces backward and cried, "See your own self!"

A soundless Presence as of roaring flame possessed the house.

45

JOINT AND MARROW

ALTER TURNED TOWARDS THE HEARTH. The fire remained a still, small, unflickering glow, but out from the flame crept the snakelike slowworm, white-hot, incandescent silver. Along the floor it crawled, so slow it seemed unwilling, towards the bench where Lilith lay. Walter rose and stole nearer. Mara stood motionless, as one who waits an event foreknown. The shining creature crawled up onto Lilith's bare bony foot, crept along her robe until it reached her rib cage, and disappeared among the folds.

The face of Lilith lay stonily calm, lids closed as over dead eyes. For some minutes nothing followed. Then the finest dew began to appear on her dry, parchment-like skin. A moment later the drops were as large as pearls and ran together, pouring down in streams.

Walter darted forward to find and snatch the worm away, intending to crush it with his foot, but Mara stepped between. She drew aside the closed edges of the robe to show that the creature had passed into the center of the black spot. It was piercing through the joints and marrow, into the thoughts and intents of the heart. Lilith gave one writhing, contorted shudder and the watchers knew the worm was in her secret chamber.

"She is seeing herself," said Mara. She laid her hand on Walter's arm and drew him three paces back from the pew.

Suddenly Lilith bent her body belly up into an unnatural arch, sprang to the floor, and stood erect. The horror in her face made Walter tremble. He feared her eyes would open and he would be overwhelmed. Her chest heaved and sank, but no breath issued. Her hair hung and dripped, then stood out from her head, then hung down again to pour the tortured sweat upon the floor. Walter would have thrown his arms about her, but Mara prevented him.

"You cannot go near her," she said. "She is far away from us in the hell of her self-consciousness. The fire of the universe is radiating into her the knowledge of good and evil. She sees at last the good she is not, and the evil she is. Do not fear for her. She is not forsaken. No gentler way to help her was left. Wait and watch."

Whether in five minutes or five years—Walter could not tell—Lilith at last flung herself facedown. Mara went and stood over her. Her large motherly tears fell on the woman who had never wept, and refused to weep. Mara said, "Her torment is that she is what she is, and has no idea that the Light of Life is in the heart of the exposing fire."

At length she asked, "Are you willing to change, Lilith?"

"Why did He make me thus?" gasped Lilith. "I would have made myself—oh, so different! I am glad it was He that made me and not I myself! He alone is to blame for what I am! Never would I have made such a worthless creature!"

"Unmake yourself, then," said Mara.

"I cannot and you know it! And mock me! How often have I wished and agonized to cease altogether, but the tyrant keeps me being! I curse him! Now let him kill me!" Her words came in jets as from a dying fountain.

"He did not make you such," said Mara, slow and measured. "You have made yourself what you are. But be of good cheer, He can remake you."

"I will not be remade!"

"He will not change who you are, Lilith. He will only begin anew what you were to be."

"I will not be anything at all of *His* making."

"Are you not willing to have set right that which you have set wrong?"

Lilith lay silent. Her suffering seemed to have lessened.

"If you are willing, lay yourself again upon the pew."

"I will not," Lilith answered, forcing the words through her clenched teeth.

A wind awoke inside the house, blowing without sound or impact. A water began to rise with no lap or ripple. Unseen and noiseless it came. Walter was not pushed about by its billows, but knew it was rising for he saw it lift Lilith and float her with tenderness towards the pew. She, unable to resist, was left awash like driftwood upon her bed. Out rushed the gentle swells as in ebb-tide.

The soul of Lilith lay naked to the torture of pure penetrating inward light. The strife of thought, accusing and excusing, began afresh in gathering fierceness. She moaned, she sighed, she murmured in conversation with her divided self. One moment she exulted over an enemy, the next she wept—writhing, then laughing, laughing then writhing.

Next Lilith began a tale—herself the central character—in language strange and shadowy. Walter could understand very little, but the story felt familiar. Its images belonged to dreams he knew, but refused to recall. Her words brushed prophetic poetry from the lips of Mara, and phrases from the tattered manuscript in the Sexton's closet. Lilith alluded to influences and forces, visages and vices, with which Walter knew he too was well acquainted. She ceased, and again came the horror in her hair. Curses and flowing tears alternated.

Walter sent a beseeching look to Mara.

"Those, alas, are not the tears of repentance," Mara answered. "Those are from self-loathing which is not the same as sorrow, but it does mark a step towards the way home. When the prodigal found himself again in his father's arms he forgot the self he loathed. It will be so for her."

Mara took a step towards Lilith and said, "Will you restore that which you have wrongfully taken?"

"I have taken nothing," said the princess, spitting words of spite and pain, "that I had not the right to take. My ability to take manifests my right."

Mara left her.

Walter's soul grew aware of an invisible darkness, a something more terrible than the wind and water—a horrible Nothingness. It barely brushed him before he watched it enfold the princess. She dashed herself from the pew to the floor with an exceeding great and bitter cry, recoiling from a creeping annihilation.

"You have no pity!" she shrieked. "Tear my heart out, but let me live!"

The perfect calm of a summer night fell upon all three within the chamber, crushing all remaining echoes of agony. Suffering had reached the brim of the cup of Lilith's being, and a hand had reached out and emptied it. Lilith lifted her head, half rose, and looked about. A moment more, and with the air of a conqueror, she stood erect. She had won the battle! She had dared to meet and defeat her foes.

Lilith raised her withered arm above her head and a song of unholy triumph arose in her throat—but her mouth was stopped and her eyes transfixed into a ghastly stare. Walter spun about to see. Before all three, cast from an unseen mirror, stood the reflection of Lilith's present self, and beside that reflection a form of splendent beauty. She trembled, and sank again onto the floor helpless. The second form was as *He* intended. The first what she had made herself.

The rest of the night Lilith lay motionless. Walter slumbered also like he had not done since leaving the world of his birth.

46

OUTER DARKNESS

ITH THE GRAY DAWN GROWING in the room, Lilith arose. She turned her face to Mara and said in mock humility, "You have conquered. Let me go into the wilderness and lament."

Mara saw her submission was neither feigned nor real. "Begin by setting right what you have wronged."

"I do not know how," Lilith said, but she had the look of one who knew what came next and feared it.

"Open your hand, and let that which is in it go."

A fierce refusal rose up, but the princess kept the outcry of protest imprisoned within.

"I cannot," was all she gave voice to. "I no longer have the power. Open it for me."

She held out the offending hand. It was more a paw than a hand, and it seemed plain to Walter that it was, indeed, unopenable.

Mara did not even look at it. "You must open it yourself," she said quietly.

"I have told you I cannot!"

"You can if you will. Not at once, but by persistent effort. What you have done, you do not yet wish undone."

"You think you know," said Lilith with a flash of insolence, "but *I* know that I cannot open my hand!"

"I know you better than you can possibly comprehend. You *can* open it. You have often opened it a little. If you wished, you could beat it open. Gather the strength of your will and open it wide."

"I will not try what I know impossible. I will not play a fool!"

"You have been playing the fool all your life. Will you not listen and learn!"

Defiance reappeared on the face of Lilith as she turned her back and retorted, "I know what you are about. You think you have succeeded, or shall soon succeed. But I am not so easily defeated, and will yet be mistress of myself. I am still what I have always been—queen of Hell, and mistress of two worlds!"

Then came an unimaginable fear, an indescribable nearness able to kill with terror. A Life-in-Death that Lilith had but glimpsed before, was now fully upon her. Mara retreated to the hearth, fearing to stand nearby, and Walter followed. Something began to depart from him. A sense of something he could not describe crept not *into*, but *out* of his being. The lamp of life, the eternal fire flickered. He felt he might be left with nothing but the awareness that he had once been alive.

Walter's heart went out to Lilith. He knew that neither Mara nor himself felt what she felt, but yet, each sensed something of her torment. Profound loss that only brushed their shoulders had taken her fully into its embrace. Lilith was in outer darkness. Only a reflex of her misery reached the two watchers as reflected pain. They were with her, but in timeless, spaceless, absolute separateness.

Something was gone from Lilith. And now, only by its

absence, did she understand that it had been with her every moment of her wicked years. The source of Life had withdrawn. All that was left to her conscious being was the dregs of her dead corruption. She had become what God could never have created. She had usurped beyond her share in self-creation, and her part had undone His.

Lilith stood rigid. Mara buried her head in her hands. Walter gazed on a face of one who knew existence, but not love —a face that knew not life, nor joy, nor good—a face of living death. Lilith could not unmake herself. She could not cease to be. She was as a conscious corpse whose coffin would never disintegrate. Within the suffering on Lilith's face, Walter read dismay. Anyone else, anyone who had not nursed her back from death's brink, would only have seen a livid gloom. Her bodily eyes stood wide open, gazing into the heart of her own indestructible will. Her right hand now clenched upon undestroyable nothing: her inheritance.

Without change of look, without sign of purpose, Lilith stepped towards Mara. Mara felt her coming, and went to meet her.

"I yield," said the princess. "I cannot hold out. I am defeated. But still, I cannot obey you and open my hand."

"Have you tried?"

"I am trying now with all my might."

"I will take you then to the Sexton."

"How can *he* help me?"

"By forgiving you."

"Ah, yes, 'forgiveness,'" Lilith murmured as if hearing a nonsense word bantered about by children. "I would rather he would help me cease to be! This is what I want most now and find I am incapable. I am powerless even over myself. I am a slave. Let me die."

"A slave you are most truly, but you shall one day be a

child," answered Mara. "Truly, you will die, Lilith, but not as you think. You shall die *out* of death *into* life."

Mara put her arms around Lilith, and kissed her on the forehead. The fiery-cold misery went out in her eyes and their fountains filled. Mara bore her to her own bed in a corner of the room, laid her softly upon the mattress, and closed her eyes with a caressing hand.

Lilith lay and wept. Mara went to the cottage door and opened it.

MORNING STOLE SOFTLY in with a gentle wind rustling Mara's garments, then turned and flowed around Lilith, rippling the unknown, up-waking sea of her life eternal. She who had been flotsam cast on the dry sandy shore to wither and fade, might, it now seemed, one day become an inlet of the everlasting ocean that wished to flow into her and ebb no more.

Lilith took in the morning wind as a reviving breath, and, though she did not open her eyes, she began to listen. In the skirts of the wind had come the rain, soft rain that heals the trampled saplings and withered grass. In the hush that lives between music and silence, the water bedewed the desert places around Mara's cottage. The arid sands of Lilith's heart heard and drank it in. When Mara returned to sit by her bed, she found the Princess of the great City on the Grassland fast asleep with yielding tears flowing softer than the raindrops.

47

PEACEFULLY UNAWARE

ARA MUFFLED HER FACE and went to call the children. Their sleep had indeed been troubled, but the moment her voice met their ears they sprang to their feet, fresh as if new-made. Merrily down the stair they tumbled.

One at time, each Dearling snuck close to see Lilith sleeping in the corner. Her tears flowed even as she slept on Lady Mara's bed. The rain drumming on the roof and misting through the pane-less windows also captured their hearts and fascinated their tender minds. Their faces grew glad then grave, then glad again as they looked from the princess out on the rain, then back at the princess.

"The sky is falling!" smiled Gracie.

"White juice is running out of the princess!" cried Lupe with an awed look.

"The rivers Father Walter told us about are coming," declared Otis, "water rushing about like a lot of Dearlings making loud noises."

"The waters of the sky are coming down to wake the waters

under the earth," Mara said. "Soon the rivers will be flowing everywhere, merry and loud, like thousands and thousands of happy Dearlings. Oh, how glad it will make you, little ones! You do not yet know how lovely the water can be."

"The glad of the sky kisses the glad of the ground because now the princess is grown good," offered Lupe.

Lilith was now awake, and listening with a sad smile.

"But her rivers are running so fast!" said Gracie, who stood by her side and seemed unable to take her eyes from Lilith's face.

"Those rivers make the whole world clean," said Mara.

Walter sat dozing by the fire, half-awake and half-listening. Rising, he said to his hostess, "We must make ready to leave, but I need to know, is there a way to avoid passing over the burrow?" He said no more, not wanting to alarm the little ones, and saw in Mara's eyes that she understood.

"There is a straighter way to the Sexton that I will show you," she answered, "but you must, I am afraid, pass over."

"I fear for the children," Walter admitted.

"Fear will not come upon them."

Walter led the Dearlings outside the cottage and instructed that Lona be shrouded and placed on the pallet that had before carried Lilith. Lilith would now travel in his arms.

When Mara came out, a cry of delight arose from the children. She was no longer veiled. All gazed upon her entrancing loveliness forgetting for several moments the tasks at hand.

Walter took up Lilith tenderly.

"Why does the princess need to go with us?" asked Lupe. "She would keep good if she stayed here with Lady Mara."

"She wants to go, and she does not want to go. We are helping her," answered Mara. "She would not keep good for very long by staying."

"What are you helping her to do?" Lupe persisted.

"To go where she will get more help—help to open her hand, which has been closed for a thousand years."

"For so long? She has learned to do without it. Why should she open it now?"

"Because it is shut upon something that is not hers."

With that, Lupe was satisfied.

"Please, Lady Mara, may we have some of your bread before we go?" asked Gracie.

Mara smiled, and brought out four loaves and a large jug of water.

WHEN THE GROUP SET OUT, Lady Mara walked with them and the white leopardess followed. Walter thought Mara meant only to put them on the best path, but joyfully discovered she meant to continue on. The children frolicked about her and the first leg of the journey was without incident.

Night was falling when they began to cross the hideous burrow of monsters. Lady Mara took the lead and when she stepped onto the plain, not a movement answered her tread. The moment Walter, carrying the princess, touched it with the sole of his foot however, the solid earth seemed to heave and boil. The whole dread brood contained in the hellish nest uprose on all sides, every neck at full length, every beak and claw outstretched, every mouth agape. Long-billed heads, serrated jaws, knotty tentacles innumerable, all went out after Lilith. She lay in an agony of fear. Walter held her close.

Walter called out to the children, "Be brave and they will not touch you!"

"What will not touch us?" they called back. And Walter knew then their complete unawareness.

"Never mind, only keep close."

In this crossing, Walter knew the monsters were no figments, but still, he regarded them all with unmoved heart. Mara continued in front, but the leopardess turned and stopped, watching the last of the party go by.

"She is remaining as our rearguard," Mara explained. "A beast is coming that makes no distinction between prey, for it belongs to the Shadow and has no fear of destruction." Motioning to Lilith she added, "It comes to reclaim one whom the darkness long held."

She quickened her pace. Walter with his burden and the short legs of the little ones had to strive hard to keep up. Mara's voice wavered now. "My faithful companion shall stay to face it. I fear it is her time." The Dearlings grew quite serious and drew closer, shivering often, for it was growing cold.

Even as the moon rose she seemed ready to drop into hopelessness. The arc the great light made was stunted. The ground to Walter's left began to heave, and a low wave of earth came slinking towards the huddled travelers. The leopardess tensed and crouched. Walter understood the peril.

He glanced back and saw the leopard stalking a writhing snake on whose head appeared the face of a corpse. Its mouth, full of doglike teeth, was half-open. The white cat sprang, but fell baffled beyond her intended mark. The monster dove down again and in a low wave of earth undulated ever nearer its intended prey. Up it rose again, between feline and children, darting in high fury, waving its long neck in anticipation of a kill. From behind upon its head crashed the full ferocious weight of the white leopardess.

Walter pressed the children over the final ridge to the opposite bank, turning back to see what had become of the great cat who made possible their escape. He stood aghast to see the tip of her elegant tail disappearing into the burrow, pulled head-first by her foe. All was still now across the wide expanse, deathly still.

A gentle hand touched his shoulder. A single tear streaked down Mara's ashen cheek. "I shall miss her sorely. Yet I would not have her live beyond her hour. She is good and wise. She has gone down with the wicked and will rise up with the righteous."

THEY TRAVELED for some time in total silence. Walter at last spoke, "Lady Mara. Our company is mostly children. How will they be received by the Sexton?"

"It is well with those that go to sleep young and willing," she answered. "Sooner or later all must become as little ones." Mara glanced at the burden in Walter's arms. "She is neither young nor quite willing, but it is well indeed that she has come. A couch is being prepared."

She said no more. Walter saw a light in the distance. The Sexton stood in the door, holding the candle to guide the coming travelers. Behind him on the table within lay bread and wine.

48

TRUST HER NOT HASTILY

THE SEXTON'S WELCOME WAS ALMOST MERRY. He set his candle on a shelf jutting from the eaves and it shone like a searchlight as he strode towards Walter. His arms stretched out to take the burden of Lilith, but before he could touch her, she pushed him aside and stood alone and erect.

She swayed at first but, in a moment, steadied herself. The shame of her gaunt uncomeliness clung to vestiges of eons-old pride; knowing but refusing to know, she stood before one given the power to bind and loose.

The Sexton's eyes shone in spite of their seeming severity. "We have long waited for you, Lilith."

Lilith gave no answer.

Lady Mara stood in the doorway. Walter knew now that she and the Sexton's wife were one and the same. He had perceived this oneness a great while, but was not sure how or when he had begun to be conscious of it.

Mara spoke, stepping out from under the eaves. "Father

Raven, our children are no longer in danger from the princess. She has turned away from evil."

"Trust her not hastily," said the Sexton. "She has deceived a multitude."

"She consents to open her hand and return all she has taken," said Mara. "With this repentance will not the great Father restore her to her inheritance?"

"I do not know Him!" murmured Lilith, in a voice of fear and doubt.

"Which is why you are miserable," said the Sexton.

"I will go back to where I came from!" Lilith cried, turning and wringing her hands to depart.

"That is indeed precisely where I would have you go—to Him from whom you came. In your agony, did you not not cry out for Him?"

"I cried out for Death—to escape Him and *you!*"

"Death is even now on his way to lead you to Him. You are weary, heavy-laden, and full of shame. Upon your very being you have brought corruption. Do you wish to live on eternally in that disgrace? Will you not be restored?"

Lilith stood silent but with bowed head.

Mara stepped forward and said to her, "I am dead, and would see you dead." She turned towards her husband and added, "Father Raven, take her in your arms, and carry her to her couch. There she will open her hand and die into life."

"I will walk," said the princess.

The Sexton turned and led the way, and Lilith slunk with shuffling steps into the cottage after him.

WALTER REMAINED OUTSIDE, freeing Lona from the litter. Mara came out to him, took the burden from his arms, and carried her in. Walter followed after with the children.

All partook of bread and wine except for Lilith. She stood apart, the Sexton never once leaving her side. When Mara returned from the inner chamber—having laid Lona to rest—she offered a portion to the princess.

"It is death I would have, not food." said Lilith, and turned away.

"This food will help you to die," said Mara, but Lilith would not taste of it.

"If you will neither eat nor drink, Lilith," the Sexton said, "come and see the place where you shall lie down and rest in peace."

He led the way through the door of death. Lilith submitted and followed but, when her first foot crossed the threshold, she drew it back. She pressed her closed hand to her heart, struck through with the cold immortal.

At that moment, a wild blast of beating wings fell roaring on the roof, screeching and striking the air as if a great swarm of leathery bats had descended to feed. The horrific tumult died away in a low lingering moan just as quickly as it had come. Lilith stood in silent terror.

The words "It is he!" formed on her lips but she made no sound.

"Who, princess?" Walter whispered, stepping towards her.

"The great Shadow," she answered, trembling like a small child.

"*Here* he cannot enter," assured the Sexton. "*Here* he cannot come."

"Are all the children safe inside the house?" asked Lilith; at that word of concern, the heart of Mara loved Lilith without reservation.

"Lady Mara," said the Sexton, "let us first put the children to bed, so Lilith may see that they are all safe."

While the Sexton occupied himself in the gathering of Dearlings, Lilith fell to her knees in front of Mara, clasped her around her feet, and said, "Beautiful lady, persuade your husband to kill me. To you he will listen! Please believe me when I tell you, I am not able to open my hand."

"You cannot die without opening it," said Mara. "No one kills but the Shadow. And those he kills never know they are dead. They only live to do his will, while thinking they are doing their own."

"Show me to my grave," said Lilith. "I am so weary I can live no longer. It is clear I must go to the Shadow, but, please know, I do not wish to." Lilith struggled to rise—she did not, *could* not understand—but fell again. Mara lifted her into her arms and carried her inward.

The Sexton and Dearlings came into the chamber of sleep, followed by Walter. As they passed ahead of Lady Mara with her burden, they heard Mara murmur, "You shall not go to the Shadow, dear Lilith. Even now his head is under my heel."

49

THE OFFENDING HAND

THE DIM LIGHT IN THE SEXTON'S HAND flickered upon the multitude of sleeping faces. As the group moved through the chamber, the darkness opened and closed behind them. Profoundest prayer-soaked sleep filled the wide place. The darkness, the cold, the silence, the stillness, and the faces of the lovely sleepers made the hearts of the children beat softly. Their little tongues spoke with low, hushed voices.

"What a curious place to sleep!"

"I would rather be in my nest!"

"It is SO cold!"

"Yes, it is cold," said the Sexton, "but you will not be cold in your sleep."

"Where are *our* nests?" asked more than one, looking round and seeing no couch unoccupied.

"Find places, and sleep where you choose," their host replied.

The Dearlings scattered, advancing beyond the light

without fear. Walter heard their gentle voices disappearing into the darkness, and it was plain they saw where he could not.

"Oh," cried one, "here is such a beautiful lady! May I sleep beside her? I will slip in quietly and not wake her."

"Yes, you may," called out the soft voice of Mara coming up from behind.

The dwindling group came upon a couch where Lupe was creeping softly under the sheet. She laid her head in the crook of a slumbering lady's arm, looking up at Walter and smiling slightly. Her eyelids fell and she was asleep.

A little farther and Otis climbed upon a bed and murmured, "Mother ... Mother." He bent over the sleeper, his face close to hers. "She's so cold, but I will soon make her warm." Snuggling in, he put his little arm over her and, in an instant, was asleep.

It was Gracie next who stood on tiptoe, leaning over the edge of a bed. "My own mother would not have me," she said. "Will you?" Receiving no reply, she looked up at Walter. He lifted her up and tucked the snowy covering back round them both.

One tiny boy chose Walter's father. Walter noted his father lay as before—arm uncovered and hand half closed—except much nearer to perfect peace. Just beyond, between two unoccupied couches, lay Lona.

Mara set Lilith down upon her own feet. The Sexton pointed to the vacant couch on Lona's right. "There, Lilith, is the bed prepared for you beside your daughter. You sent her into the loveliest sleep, but she was already a long time dead when you slew her. Now you shall sleep together."

Shuddering from head to foot, Lilith looked at her daughter lying before her, like a statue carved in semi-transparent alabaster.

"You will soon begin to find comfort ... " began the Sexton.

"Promises to the dying are easy," Lilith said.

"I send you where I have already been. I too have slept and arisen."

"I fear my child," she said, pointing to Lona. "She will rise and terrify me."

"She is now dreaming of love for you."

"But the Shadow!" she moaned. "I fear the Shadow! He will be cruel to me!"

"He dares not disturb one sleeper in this dream-filled, prayer-filled chamber."

"I shall dream?"

"You will dream."

"What dreams?"

"That I cannot tell, but none the Shadow can touch, much less enter into."

"How long shall I sleep?"

"You will be one of the last to wake in the great morning of the universe."

Lilith lay down, pulled the sheet over her, stretched herself out straight, but did not close her eyes.

Mara drew near.

"Lilith," she said. "You will not sleep, even if you lie there a thousand years, until you open your hand and yield that which is not yours either to give or to withhold."

"I cannot. I would if I could, and gladly, for I am weary and the shadows of death are gathering about me."

"Slumber will gather and gather, but it cannot infold you while yet your hand remains unopened. You may think you are dead, but it will be only a dream. You may think you have come awake, but it will still be only a dream. Open your hand, and you will sleep indeed—then wake indeed."

"The fingers have grown together and into my palm," answered Lilith. A tear formed in the corner of her eye.

"Put forth the strength of your will. For the love of life, draw together your forces and break its bonds!"

"I have struggled in vain. I can do no more. I am very weary, and sleep lies heavy upon my lids."

"The moment you open your hand, you will sleep. Open it, and make an end."

A tinge of color arose in Lilith's haggard face. The contorted hand trembled with agonized effort. Mara took Lilith's arm, and sought to aid her.

"Hold off, Lady Mara!" cried the Sexton. "Therein is danger!"

Lilith turned her eyes upon them both, beseechingly. "There was a sword I saw once in the second Adam's hands," she murmured. "I fled when I saw Him. I heard Him say it would divide whatever was not truly one."

"I know of the sword," said the Sexton. "The angel gave it to the new Adam when he burst open the way and the gate no longer needed guarding."

"Find it. Bring it," pleaded Lilith. "And cut off this hand that I may sleep."

"I will," the Sexton answered.

Father Raven gave the candle to Walter, and together they went. Lilith closed her eyes. Minutes later, the Sexton returned with the ancient weapon in his hand. The scabbard was leather grown dark with years, but the hilt shone like gold that nothing could tarnish. He drew out the blade. It flashed like the tail of the pale blue northern star. Its light made the princess reopen her eyes and tremble. But she held out her arm. The sword flashed once, there was a small gush of blood, and the severed hand was laid in Mara's lap.

On the Sexton's heels came Walter, candle trembling in one hand, a bit of wine-soaked bread in the other. He pressed it to Lilith's lips and she ate—a meal much finer than any before taken. She gave one moan and was fast asleep. Mara tucked her handless arm under the sheet, and the three turned away.

"Will you not dress the wound?" Walter asked.

"A wound from that sword," answered the Sexton, "needs no dressing, for the weapon heals what it hurts."

"She will wake with but one hand." whispered Walter growing pale.

"Better to awaken maimed," said Mara. "In the coming morning, there is nothing that cannot be restored."

As Walter strode beside Father Raven back towards the narthex, passing couch after couch, he marveled at his growing despondency. He had not been offered his own place to lie down.

Mara followed the two men a few paces behind, the hand of Lilith in the lap of her robe.

50

JUST PASSING THROUGH

WALTER NOTED A CANDLE STILL BURNED **on a three-legged** table in the middle of the front room. Was it the same one he had seen so many nights ago on his first visit? Did it never go out?

He turned to Mara. "Madam, one couch next to Lona is empty. I know I am unworthy, but may I sleep there tonight in your chamber with my friends? Will you pardon my cowardice and foolishness and take me in? I am sick of myself and desire to sleep the sleep."

"The couch next to Lona *is* the one already prepared for you," Mara answered, "but something waits to be done before you lay yourself down."

"I am ready," Walter replied.

"How do you know you can do it?" she asked with a smile.

"Because you require it," he answered.

She turned to the Sexton. "Is he forgiven, Father Raven?"

"From my heart."

"Then tell him what he has to do."

"Give me the hand, Mara."

She held it out in the corners of her apron. He took it tenderly.

The Sexton seated himself upon a bench and Walter stood before him.

"Think, Son," Father Raven began, "how, after leaving Mara's house, you came to a dry rock, bearing the marks of an ancient cataract. At its peak you leapt across a narrow crevasse."[1]

Walter nodded.

"Go back to that summit and walk deep into the desert. Every few steps, lie down and listen for the waters. If you hear the murmur beneath, go a little farther, and listen again. If you still hear the sound, you are in the right direction. If not, you must search for it. Follow the sound, and never retrace your steps. The rush of waters will grow ever louder. When it becomes a deafening roar—dig. Continue to dig until the moisture sogs the sand. There lay the hand of Lilith. Cover it up again to the level of the desert and then, with all speed, come back home."

Walter was intent upon every word that proceed from the Sexton's mouth.

Father Raven continued, "Give heed—carry the hand with care. Never lay it down. Let no one else touch it. Do not stop or turn aside or allow anything to slow your pace. Speak to no one. Answer no one. Never look behind."

"How soon shall I leave, Father?" asked Walter, his voice just above a whisper.

"Though it is dark and the morning hours far away, you must set out at once."

He gave Lilith's hand to Walter and raised his own in blessing. Walter bowed, and left.

BEFORE, in broad daylight the way had been difficult. Now, in the cold pitch-dark, Walter dreaded falling with every step. Just as he left the last hint of candle flame glowing outward from the Sexton's house, a pale light broke forth, darting about his knees. A fluttering prisnix, much softer and shyer than the previous beauty, began to show a step at a time where next to set his foot. Through the heather and the jagged rocks, not once did he stumble. All the creatures in the evil burrow lay soundless as he crossed. Time and space seemed to fold as each stride took him further than the last. When the moon began to throw beams to show the easiest way, the prisnix flitted away overhead and back towards the Sexton's abode.

It was still an hour before dawn and Walter had made great progress over the dry channels of the first branch of the riverbed. Minutes before sunrise he saw before him on the path a figure covered from head to foot in moonlit mist. He kept on his way as if he saw nothing even as the figure threw aside its veil.

"Have you forgotten me already?" the voice of Lilith asked quietly.

Walter neither hesitated nor answered but walked straight on.

"Surely you did not mean to leave me in that horrid sepulcher?" a more assertive voice cried out. "Do you not yet understand that where I please to be, there I am? Hold my hand, dear Walter, and we will travel together! I am as alive as you!"

"Give me your *right* hand, my dearest!" was the clever thought that bubbled up in Walter's pride, but he held his peace and continued a steady pace.

"Give me my hand or I will tear you in pieces!" she shrieked. "I drank your blood. I took it as my rightful meal more times than you know. And, in the end, you freely gave it to me. You are mine!"

Walter remembered all she had stolen and his blood seemed the least of his losses. A tear fell on his cheek but he pressed on, not faltering. She sprang catlike into the air, assailing her prey, but nothing touched him and he saw her no more.

WALTER CONTINUED some distance when something white in the underbrush to the right below a spreading tree caught his eye. Its form was vague in the shadow of the foliage, but as Walter drew nearer it appeared to be a body. "Yet *another* Lilith?" he wondered, but pressed on. He glanced again and saw it was no woman, but the body of the white leopardess, laying on its side, pierced and wounded. Her life blood trickled slowly out, soaking the ground. She was so gaunt that every rib could be counted, her beautiful yet terrible teeth showed between retracted lips. Her tongue lolled unseemly, touching the soil. How had she come there? How had she escaped the demonic burrow to be here dying? How could he leave her un-revived? Or, if need be, unburied? Brutal claws might yet come and toss her about, well before rain and dew would wash her body into the soil. Did he not owe her at least the service rendered to Lilith?

Walter called to mind the words of Mara, "She has gone down with the wicked and will rise with the righteous." He walked on.

THE MOON SANK to the horizon. In the deep shadow just ahead, Walter spied a second woman. She was seated where the path narrowed between crouching boulders, her face shrouded with a woolen scarf. "Ah, you are come at last!" she called out merrily. "I have waited here for you an hour or more. You have done well, Walter. Father Raven sent me to meet and give you a little respite along the way. Hand me your charge, and lay your head in my lap to rest until the sun rises. All is well. Submit to my caretaking."

The offer was a terrible temptation. Walter was weary and her words were likely true. It tore him to think that now, by slavish obedience to the letter of the Sexton's command, he would trample underfoot the kindness of Lady Mara. His heart grew faint and his stomach tightened. Walter steeled his will against vacillation, not allowing his steps to falter. He bit his tongue between his teeth lest he should accidentally answer her kindness. On he went, willing to step over her if need be to keep on his way.

"If the Sexton has sent her," he thought, "he will forgive me for not heeding, and Mother Mara will not love me less for the fact that even she was not able to turn me aside."

Just before he reached the seated woman, she pulled the covering from her pleading face. Great was her loveliness, but Walter knew Mara and the twinkling orbs in the beautiful countenance were not Mara's eyes. No lie could truly or for long imitate the windows of *that* soul. He advanced as if she were not there, and his foot found empty space when he placed it where she had appeared.

THEN CAME THE SHADOW ITSELF. In the path an empty helmet crowned a headless, eyeless, mouthless, soulless, heartless torso. Behind the great fleshlessness, in tight formation, stood all the armies of the Evil Wood. No longer did each fighter turn against his comrade. No longer did the Queen of Hell cry, "Ye are men! Arise and slay one another!" The Shadow had made one the strife-tormented multitude. Here stood a horde bent to do his darkest bidding.

Onward came the body of armed skeleton-wraiths, marching lockstep. In their midst Walter sensed the presence of one dearly loved, an old guide and companion, one for whom he long to call out. The space between the great platoon and Walter's bare feet closed, step by quickening step, heavy hulking boots approaching. Within one stride of collision, Walter closed his eyes and continued in unchanging pace.

A cold wind smote him, dank and sickening, repulsive as the air of a slow burning crematorium. Firmness forsook his joints, and his limbs trembled as if they would drop him into a helpless heap. The Shadow passed through him. Or did he pass through the Shadow? For a moment Walter was as one of the damned, but still he marched on, a single soldier passing through their midst. At last the path was empty before him again, but to his horror, Walter heard the formation turn. Stamping boots followed ringing in his ears, the tremor of their march biting his heels. But he cast no look behind, and, at last, the sound of their steps and the clash of their armor died away.

THEN BLESSED DAWN AROSE, and a wind like the first breath of a new-born spring greeted his mouth and nostrils as a soft kiss. Walter quashed the urge to turn around and see all he had overcome. The way led him past the door of Mara's cottage. It stood wide open, and upon the table he saw a loaf of bread and a pitcher of water waiting to refresh him. He pressed on. Soon he came to the precipice that testified to the vanished river. He climbed its worn face, and stepped out onto the desert. There he searched and listened, searched and listened, searched and listened in every direction until the water was heard. Keeping with the sound, never retracing his steps, it did indeed grow ever louder.

When Walter found the place of deafening roar, he began to dig. Tucking Lilith's hand within his tunic, he flung the sand, hour after hour. It was a long arduous labor, digging a large hole in loose soil. At length the handfuls he threw up were damp. There he laid down his burden. A little water seeped between the fingers. Walter sprang back and in went the dirt and sand. When the grave at last was level with the surrounding desert, Walter dropped beside it in utter fatigue and fell asleep.

51

NOW I LAY ME DOWN

WHEN WALTER AWOKE BESIDE THE GRAVE, the ground was moist about him. His tracks to Lilith's buried hand were dissolving into quicksand. The river was swelling into its ancient courses and soon it would be roaring down the precipice. One branch would slowly re-submerge the orchard valley, the other would drown the monster horde. Between them, the Evil Wood was soon to become an island.

Walter rose at once to return directly to the Sexton, but a peaceful permission wafted over him. He was invited to pause and refresh himself at Mara's cottage. When he reached the door, it was still open. The bread and the water were still on the table and a deep silence pervaded within and around. He called aloud through the threshold, not wanting to intrude, even though he knew the mistress was away.

"Hello," a voice called back.

Walter peeked around to see a small, gray-headed man sitting in the westernmost corner weeping.

"What ails you, sir?" Walter inquired. "Have you been abandoned?"

The old man raised his head from between his knees, tears streaming down the dozen ravines in the furrowed creases of his face, and answered, "I weep because they will not let me die. I have just come from the Sexton's house and, in spite of my years, he refuses me entrance. Intercede for me, young master, if you know him."

"Sir," Walter said in a soft tone, "that would not be wise of me. Father Raven refuses no one he is able to receive."

"How do *you* know this about him?" questioned the old man. "You have never sought death! You are much too young to desire it."

"Do I understand, sir, that if you could be young again, you would *not* desire to enter under the Sexton's roof?"

"Indeed I would not! How could *you*? Your whole life is before you!"

"I may not be old enough to desire to *die*, but I am young enough to desire to truly *live*. It seems you wish to die only because you do not care to live."

"You are rude to mock a friendless old man."

"Did Father Raven not tell you something of the same sort?"

"He did, but I do not care to listen to riddles and excuses."

"Forgive me if I presume to offer counsel, kind father. I am indeed young, but I have wept many tears. Wait here for the Lady Mara. Eat of this bread upon her table. When she appears, ask her counsel, for she is true and her wisdom is great."

The old gentleman fell to weeping afresh, and Walter left him, quite sure his advice would not be heeded. But Mara would find him and she would know best what to say and do.

WHEN WALTER REACHED the burrow of monsters, the sun was down, and the moon not yet risen. All was still as a stone until he began to pass over. Behind him he heard the coming noise of many waters and a great outcry in its wake. As in his outbound journey, he did not turn his head. The cold and darkness entered into his bones, bitter and dense; in the end the Sexton's candle shining from the window was all that remained to guide his final steps.

The door stood open when Walter arrived, but the cottage lay empty. He sat down in the place he had last seen the Sexton, despondent from sheer weariness. Duty discharged, there was no exulting and none with whom to share its fulfillment. All sense of triumph faded into a quiet knowing—he had done what ought to have been done and he was the one who ought to have done it. Walter was the man who had buried the mighty hand of Lilith. He was the man who caused the waters below to rise again. And now, in the midst of immense victory, he was the man who needed no one else to know.

Thousands were near, just beyond the coffin door, but every soul was separated from him. They might come to him but he could not go to them. He slid off the wooden bench, his knees hitting the clay floor, and a dull sound reverberated into the chamber beyond. If only Father Raven or Lady Mara would come to him and take him to his place of rest.

Walter heard something move, a dim far-off sound. His soul sprang into his ears knowing someone drew near. The door began to move with a low, soft creaking of its hinges. He stared expectant. It opened a little way, and a face came peeking round. It was Lona's.

Eyes still closed, she spoke. Her voice was a sleepy night-wind passing through high grass. "Are you coming Walter? I cannot rest until you are with me, gliding down the river to the great sea ... the sleep is full of lovely things. Come and see."

"Ah, my darling!" Walter cried, coming to his feet. "Had I known you were waiting I would have come at once."

She crossed the room, lay her head on his chest, and sighed, "Carry me back to my bed, darling. I want to sleep." He bore her into the chamber and made a straight line towards her couch, holding her tight lest she should dissolve out of his arms, pausing often to kiss her forehead.

"Lay me down and cover me," she said, pointing. "Your bed is there, next to mine." As soon as Walter had tucked her in, she returned to deepest slumber. He collapsed upon his own couch feeling more blessed than a man on the eve of his wedding.

"Come, Sleep," he said, "and quiet my overflowing heart."

Walter laid down but sat up again for there was a glimmer of light in the chamber. He looked about and saw the faces of the Sexton and Lady Mara approaching. The Sexton looked down with a questioning smile at Lona's couch, then greeted Walter. "We have been to the top of the hill to hear the waters filling their channels ... But why did you not await our return?"

"Lona could not sleep and came for me."

"She is fast asleep," came the Sexton's puzzled reply. "The sleep of martyrs is at a depth unknown to you and me ... but how ... "

"She was awake and I laid her back down."

"She was perhaps dreaming about you ... and came to you?"

"Perhaps ... I know so little. But why am I not sleepy, Father? I thought I should go to sleep like the Dearlings the moment I laid my head down."

"Your hour is not quite come," Mr. Raven said. "You are in need of food."

"Ah, and I ought not to have lain down without your permission. I will get up and come to dine at once," Walter struggled to stand.

"There is no need," answered the Sexton. "We will serve you here."

Together at Walter's couch, the three partook of bread and wine.

"You are good indeed, Father and Mother," breathed Walter, "to offer me sleep once more."

"We knew you would come again," answered Mara, "even when you ran from this chamber in terror."

"Every creature is meant to yield and lie down," added the Sexton. "None is meant to be left a slave."

"It will be late, I fear, before *all* souls have lain down," Walter answered with a yawn.

"There is no early or late here," said the Sexton. "True time begins for each when they lay themselves down."

All at once Walter became blissfully drowsy. He glanced at his father's sleeping form and his mother's empty bed.

"When you see your mother again," whispered the Sexton, "you will not at first know her. She is steadily growing younger until she reaches the perfection of her womanhood, a splendor unpredictable."

Walter nodded, half-listening. Mother Mara sang sweet and soft and low—

> *Night is come*
> *The fight is done*
> *The wayward have come home*
> *The dawn will break and night will flee*
> *You've never been alone.*

Walter heard as one in a dream. He felt them put on him the white garment of the dead and forgot everything. The night about him was pale with sleeping faces.

52

WHAT DREAMS MAY COME

COLD SOOTHED AWAY EVERY CARE, dissolved every pain. Walter grew aware of profound and infinite existence. Sorrow was swallowed up in the life drawing near, ready to restore every good and lovely thing a hundredfold. He lay at peace, full of quiet expectation, stretched out and still, less and less conscious of himself and more conscious of bliss unimaginable—a bliss that belonged to him by mere virtue of laying his will within the Will that made him.

Walter was Adam, waiting for God to breathe upon him, countenance to countenance. He was a child in the bosom of a mother in radiant blue. He was a youth on a white horse, leaping from cloud to cloud. He was in the center of a melting glacier amidst the wind and the tangle of an icy sea. The wind and the water and the peaceful moon sang, waiting for a redemption that drew nigh.

Across the cold rippled the troubling of his conscious bliss. All the wrongs he had ever done, from his earliest memory down to the present moment, were with him. All of them he confessed, renounced, and lamented, without excuse or minimization. With those that he had hurt or offended he made atonement. Each human soul he had ever caused a troubled thought grew unspeakably dear. With them he sought to humble himself, agonizing to remove from between them any clinging offense. He wept at the feet of the mother whose commands he had slighted. With bitter shame he confessed to his father that he had told him two lies and long ago forgotten them.

Countless services he planned to render to every injured soul. For one he would build such a house as had never grown from the ground. For another he would train such horses as had never yet been ridden in any world. For still another he would plant such a garden as had never bloomed—alive with running waters, dotted with reflective ponds. He would write songs to make hearts swell, and tales to make imaginations light up. He would turn the forces of the world into channels of invention making all laugh with joy and wonder. Love possessed him. Love was life. Love was all in all.

Walter found himself in a solid blackness, but his heart—which feared nothing and hoped infinitely—was full of peace. He lay back and imagined what the light would be like when it returned, and what new creation it might bring with it. Then, with no forethought, he found himself sitting straight up looking about the Sexton's chamber. The moon was peering in through low, horizontal windows. Her long light slanted across the great sea of couches. But they were empty. All of his companions were gone! Where were his fellow-sleepers? Had he only imagined their loveliness? The others were up and had gone into some eternal new day and he was left alone and forgotten. Walter stared horror-stricken, struggled to his feet, and staggered from the fearful place. Out he ran into the night.

A broad shimmer came from far over the flatland, as if the moon were raining light. His striding legs continued on until brought up short by a lovely lake. Here, where the burrow of monsters had once pulsed, lay the clearest, stillest, brightest body of water. A musical murmur filled the air hovering in the reeds and bushes around the edges. Its melody drew Walter in and he pursued the sweet sound round the border of the little lake, climbing the range of hills beyond. The expanse that had once been sand and heat, deep-scored by channels and ravines, was now alive with melodious streams. The moon flashed on the water and the water answered back.

As Walter stood gazing, the grand expanse of the watery dance made his heart exult in the small part he had played. Like a child he shouted, "Look at what I helped to do!"

A torrent ran swift and wide at the foot of the range. He rushed in and waded and found it neither pushed nor pulled nor laid ahold. He continued on, springing over coursing, falling, white foaming water. At last he dove in and swam. In the seaward rush he traveled, buoyed by the wondrous, ceaseless flash and flow. Exhausted and exhilarated, he climbed out and sat upon a precipice.

Lost in delight of the torrents flowing beneath, Walter felt a hand laid on his shoulder. He turned to see a man in the prime of his strength, beautiful and young like one who cannot grow old. Walter knew it was Father Raven, large and grand, clothed in a white robe The full moon framed his face and windswept hair.

"Father!" Walter turned and clung to the Sexton in the warm embrace of a child. "Where is Lona? Where are my companions? Is the great Resurrection come and gone? Where shall I go to find them?"

"You are mistaken, my son," Father Raven answered in a voice whose very breath was consolation. "You are still in the chamber of prayers, still upon your couch with all your companions around you."

"I dream? But how am I to tell? How am I to distinguish between actuality and vision when both alike seem real?"

"Do you not understand?" Father Raven said with a smile that might have slain all the sorrows of all his children. "You *cannot* perfectly distinguish between much at all yet. At this moment you must simply believe."

"I am trying hard to believe you, Father. I do indeed believe you, although I can neither see nor feel the truth of what you say."

"You are not to blame that you discern so little, but, because even in your doubts you believe me, I will help you. Put forth your left palm and close it gently."

Walter did.

"Do you feel the hand of Lona?"

Walter nodded and closed tight his eyes.

"Neither she nor you are yet in the fields of home, but to each other, each is alive."

Walter's heart was glad, but then came a sharp stinging doubt. "Father," he said, "forgive me, but how am I to know that her hand in mine is not also a part of a lovely dream and I am not fooling myself with wishfulness?"

"You doubt, dear Walter, because you love the truth. Be content for a while not to know for sure. The hour is coming when you will behold the very Truth, and doubt will forever be dead."

Walter nodded, leaned to kiss the hand he held, and confessed with cracking voice, "In my final task, on my way to bury the hand, Father, I sensed my grandfather. He was within the Enemy's battalion ... "

"Burying the hand was not your final task," sighed the Sexton.

"What? Is my struggle still not over?"

"Not until the great Resurrection."

"But about Grandpa ... what can be done? Or can anything be done for those we love?"

"Answers in this arena are deceptive," said Father Raven with great gravity. "On one hand there is a concocted optimism that says Arthur McVeigh will assuredly be rescued from the damned in the end; and on the other, there is the hard-bitten notion that all destinations are decided before a man is ever born. Both stances rob from your grandfather the universal gift to all souls—the freedom to choose."

"So he has a choice still?"

"We must pray as if he does."

"Father, you knew my grandfather. What do you think?" Walter pleaded.

"I think it is a good sign that you sensed him. But the bigger question is whether *he* sensed you."

"I think I see, Father. "I *think* I understand."

"Walter, it is a dangerous business to speak of the journey of another, but tell me, do you recall the old man in Mara's hut?"

"Yes, Father. Is Mara with him now? Will he receive her help?"

"I will not speak of his present state, for that is holy ground, but I will touch on what is in his past. It was not long ago that the old man fought in the Evil Wood."

Walter's eyes grew large and bright with hope. The Sexton motioned for calm and continued. "The man in the cottage fought his way out of the Shadow's battalion. He showed great courage and daring. He must now set aside the strength that allowed him his survival—all he counts as his virtues. He has come a great distance but seems to be faltering at the final steps. You understand well this faltering. Do you not?"

Walter nodded knowingly.

"Trials still await you, Walter. Remember the things you

have seen. Remember and hold onto the lessons that have cost you dearly."

"But I have laid myself down, Father. I have gone to sleep. Why more trials?" Walter turned, seeking the face of his teacher, and found himself alone. Straining his ears he heard nothing but the sounding silence of the swift-flowing waters. He stretched out his hands for the hand of Lona. Nothing was found to hold again but solitude.

Walter felt wide awake, but he believed with all his heart he was in the chamber of prayers because the Sexton had told him so. He went on, crossing channel after channel, and came to a wider space of rock. Weary, he laid upon the hard surface, and feeling about discovered the flat rock formed the edge of a pit, deep and dark, like that of an open grave. He remembered that in childhood dreams a fall would always awaken him. Desiring change, desiring to once again perceive the realness of the chamber and Lona, he rolled himself over the edge.

For a moment consciousness left him. When it returned, he stood in the attic of his own house, staring into the glass of the black eagle mirror at his own haggard reflection. No light came through the vent above except a sliver of moon and the twinkle of Orion. Walter had desired change, he had chosen change. Of his own free will he had left behind that holy world and the guidance given therein. And now Lona slept not one, but two worlds away.

53

———

A HIDDEN RITE OF PASSAGE

ALTER CREPT DOWN TO HIS BEDCHAMBER and passed a dreamless night. Upon rising he listlessly sought the library. On the way he met no one. The house was dead. He sat down with a book to await the noontide, but not a sentence could he understand. The mutilated manuscript offered itself from the closet door, but the sight of it sickened him.

The library window displayed a brilliant morning. The fountain shot high, and fell roaring back. The sun seemed seated upon the spray of its feathery top, but not a bird sang, not a creature flitted by. Walter took another book, sat down again, and went on with his waiting.

Noon came near, so up he went, stair upon stair. Under the quiet, shadowy roof, he closed behind him the door of the wooden chamber, and turned to open the mirror-door out of his dreary world. Minutes later he left with a heart of stone. All was fruitless. He had pulled the chain, adjusted and re-adjusted the mirror. No result had followed. He had waited and waited to give the vision time, but it would not come. Nothing lay in the glass's dim old depths but the wall opposite and his own ashen face.

Back he went to the library. Books he once loved were now hateful kindling. That night he lay awake from sunset to sunrise, and next day renewed his endeavors with the mystic door, but all was in vain. Sleeplessness did not bring weariness, only desolation.

The fourth day crept into the fourth night. Walter did not bother to ascend the stair at all, but remained below slumped upon the library couch. The lost-then-found volume concerning the city on the Bosphorus lay on his chest[1], spine creased backward. A bending beam of candlelight caught his eye as it flickered against the icon of St. Alban. He rose and crossed to the niche in the wall where the little shrine sunk in among the expanse of bookshelves. The glowing light brought out the image wonderfully and it seemed, once again, to respond to his look. Walter peered closely, inches away from the ancient brush strokes; as he leaned in his shin pressed against a shelf just below. A small click released a latch and he discovered another feature in the ancient library—more whimsy from his distant ancestors. The lowest shelf of the shrine was cloaked in the same manner as the closet door. The shallow ledge was no more than an inch deep, two feet wide, and eight inches tall. Old book spines were affixed to it. It folded down on silent hinges and revealed the padded cushion of a kneeler, soft and burgundy.

Walter did not read the humorous titles printed upon the spines. He did not look closely at the clever craftsmanship. He went to his knees. From his knees, Walter stared up into the face of the icon. "Dear St. Alban, my forefather and kin, it is good for me to ask one who is more advanced to lift up my petitions. My heart has died within me ..." Walter choked, unpracticed in humble intercession. "Pray what is good for me and great mercy," was all that sputtered out.

He arose, blew out the candle, and, in the manner done by his grandmother, crossed himself unaware. Upstairs he trod, undressed, and slipped like a small boy between the bed linens.

Walter slept as Lona had, the night before she met her mother. When he awoke, he awoke indeed.

WALTER OPENED HIS EYES. He knew, although all was pitch dark, that he lay again in the chamber of prayer. He had always been there since the moment he had taken the bread and wine and laid willingly down.

"At last I see again!" he said to his heart as it leapt for joy.

A soft glow appeared and Walter saw that Lona sat on her couch watching him. All was dark but *she* was not dark. She had never been lost to him except in his tortured imagination. Her eyes shone with the radiance of Lady Mara's. This same light issued from her face and dress, and filled her entire body. Walter got up and folded her in his arms, and knew he lived indeed.

"I woke first!" she said, with a wondering smile.

"You did, my love, and woke me!"

"I only looked at you and waited," she said. "Did you sleep well?"

"Not very," Walter answered, "but the waking is heavenly."

"It is but begun, we are both hardly yet awake."

Father Raven approached them both. He put one arm around Lona and the other around Walter and all three turned to see the approach of Lady Mara.

"We've come to bid you farewell, but I think we shall meet you two again before long," the Sexton said.

"Do we have to die again?" Walter asked.

"No, you die but once into life. Now you have only to live, and that you must, with all your blessed might."

"How is such life sustained?" Walter asked.

"You are a branch on the vine, a seed that has fallen into good ground and died ... " began the Sexton, but Mother Mara gave such a look of love that he fell silent. She then looked upon Walter as if to say, "We are mother and son and we understand each other."

She kissed his forehead as Walter said, "I know you. You are the image of the new Eve whose soul was pierced for the rising and falling of many."

Mara smiled as one would at a small school boy. "And who then are *you*, Walter?" she asked.

Walter said softly, "Father Raven serves in the image and likeness of the second Adam. I might serve too—given time."

"These things are to be treasured within the heart." Mara whispered back.

Walter turned to find his earthly father. The couch was empty. For an instant, a sense of desolation overshadowed, and he looked away.

"What is it, my love?" asked Lona.

"I had wished to bid him farewell."

"He was up and away long ago," said Father Raven. "He kissed you before he left and whispered, 'Come soon.'"

"And I neither felt nor heard ..." Walter murmured.

"How could you? You were far away in your dreary old house thinking yourself trapped in that place once more."

Walter looked up into Father Raven's eyes, grateful for the words of knowing.

"What is that flapping of wings I hear?" Walter asked, his head tilting towards the great vaulted ceiling.

"The Shadow is hovering," replied Father Raven. "There is one here whom he counts his own, though never again can she be his."

Lona's head tilted also towards the hideous reverberations. She strode straightway to the couch of Lilith. Bending, she blessed and kissed the mother who had slain her. The sound of beating wings retreated.

"That kiss not only drives him off, my Lona," said Father Raven, his eyes aglow, "but will draw her homeward!" He took Lona's hand and placed it in Walter's.

"Amen, glory to thee!" cried Father Raven and Lady Mara as one, and the words rang through the chamber.

At their AMEN—like doves arising on wings of silver—up sprang the Dearlings to their knees as if they had both seen and heard them in their dreams. Each bid goodbye to his sleeping bedfellows and sprang from the couches. Little companions fell into each others' arms, one by one assuring themselves that they were alive and quite awake. Seeing Lona, all came running, radiant with bliss to embrace her.

Otis next ran to Princess Lilith. "Wake up! Wake up!" he cried, and pushed and pulled. He turned to Walter with misty eyes. "She will not arise!" he said.

Walter went to the boy and lifted him into his arms. "When you picked fruit from your trees, did you take what was not yet ripe?"

Otis shook his head no.

"She is still busy forgetting, Otis. When she has forgotten enough and remembered enough, she will be ripe and awake. Let her sleep for now, darling, let her sleep."

Otis was comforted, and wiped his eyes. He and the others followed Mara to the entryway of the cottage where she offered neither food nor drink but only opened wide the door for their departure.

In silence all went out. Two horses and several ponies waited at the door.

One of them Walter knew quite well.

54

FARTHER UP AND IN

A WONDROUS CHANGE HAD PASSED UPON THE WORLD. Or was the difference a marvelous transformation within Walter? All his senses awoke—ever expanding, ever making room to receive. There was not much daylight as yet but every heather bush, every shrub, every blade of grass emitted light and nothing cast a shadow. The dark wind that had blown within Walter went out of him now as a sigh of thanksgiving.

He and Lona rode along leading their little troupe. Presently they came to the fearful burrow, now a lake of translucent depths. A whirlpool had swept out the soil in which the abortive monsters burrowed, and at the bottom lay visible the whole horrid brood. A dim green light pervaded the crystalline water, revealing every hideous form beneath it. Coiled in spires, folded in layers, knotted in on themselves, they writhed in heaps. Convulsing tentacles, tumid bulges, glaring orbs of dislocated deformity formed a swirling maelstrom. This incarnation of hatefulness which festered and fed on every unwholesome thought of mankind froze in the presence of innocence as Walter and Lona led the children past.

The land opened itself to them. Down came the children from the backs of the ponies to frolic after fluttering butterflies and darting dragonflies that shot hither and thither about their heads. A cloud of colors and flashes descended like a snowstorm. Channels, once dry and weary, ran and flashed and foamed with living water that shouted out great gladness. So joyful were the waves that the Dearlings gave up their merry chasing, plunged in, and swam.

Walter and Lona left their steeds to climb the heights. Grassy plains flowed deep, wide, and silent before the wind. The desert rejoiced and blossomed as the rose. The place of the buried hand was now untraceable, lost in the glory of the land's glad resurrection.

The children, dripping dry in the sunshine, rejoined Walter and Lona, and all continued on foot together. They came to a forest where grand trees formed live pillars upholding a roof of branches so thick with leaves and blossoms that hardly a sunbeam filtered through. Into the rafters of this aerial vault the children climbed, scrambling and leaping in a land abloom. There they chased chipmunks and squirrels until the little creatures allowed themselves to be caught, petted, and released. Then the merry game would begin all over again. Now and again beautifully plumed birds would alight upon a child and sing a song of what was coming next, and then just as quickly fly away.

Lona and Walter continued on foot below the branches until a great shout came from overhead. The children began dropping down from the foliage one by one. Lupe reported they had climbed to the top of a tree, taller than the rest, and had spied across the plain a curious structure on the side of a mountain.

"Maybe a city," Lupe said out of breath, "but this one cannot be full of Hoons."

Walter climbed to look. A great city, did indeed ascend into the clouds. It was impossible to distinguish its edges from the backdrop of mountains, or mountain from sky, sky from cloud. All mingled in a chaos of broken shadow and sunshine.

Walter descended and told Lona all. In one accord, the company picked up speed towards the mystery in the distance, growing ever merrier and never looking behind. By and by they spied the beautiful city among blue clouds. In the wide open space just ahead, a sweet rain began to fall. Without thunderclap or roll it filled the atmosphere with a caressing coolness. Clouds gathered thicker, rain fell in torrents, the children exulted, and it was all Walter and Lona could do to keep them in sight. A great silent wave from the river swept from its banks and radiated over the grass dotted with primroses and daisies, crocuses and periwinkles, pimpernels and buttercups. No turbid cloudiness accompanied the gentle flood and the starry multitude of bright blossoms shone through the brilliant water. Delicate petals shimmered from below awash in their dainty beds.

Drawing nearer to the mountain, Walter saw that the river came from its very peak, rushing in full volume out the main gate of the city. It descended all the way down to the foot of the heights over gradual winding steps cut deep and wide into purple gems.

The Dearlings ran ahead, straight up the mountain stair towards the open gate. Outside on the landing sat the porter, leaning his heavy brow on an idle hand. The children rushed upon him, covered him with caresses, and—before he understood—rushed passed him through the gate, and in. Up and onward in a merry dance they continued out of sight.

"Ah!" said the gatekeeper descending to meet Lona and

Walter, "little soldiers taking heaven itself by storm! We will have valiant work waiting for each of them." The scales of his armor flashed like flakes of lightning as he bowed with a kind smile. "Welcome home!"

Walter and Lona returned his bow and stood at the gate. The flowing water roared by in front of them and rivulets split off curving around the foundations. Lining the riverbed were sparkling, living stones. Barefoot and laughing and splashing like children, they lunged into a side-eddy whose beds wound outside the walls. Each gem under each step resonated with music.

Above the city, through many openings between rocks, the river billowed out from its source. Walter could dimly discern three or four great stair steps disappearing in a snow white cloud. Atop the steps he imagined he saw a grand old chair, like the throne for the Ancient of Days. Over and under and between those steps, plenteously, unceasingly new-born flowed the river of the water of life. Walter's heart beat with hope and desire. His fingers interlaced with Lona's, and together they began to climb. Soon the way became so steep, and the current so strong, that they found that the rocks must be climbed alone; both hands and feet were needed for the toilsome ascent. With much effort, the two drew near to the cloud hanging down the steps like the hem of a garment. Both passed at the same time through the fringe and entered the deep folds.

A hand, warm and strong, laid hold of Walter and drew him aside to a little door with a golden lock. It opened, and the hand pushed him gently through.

The fog cleared away and Walter found he again stood alone in his library.

AFTERWORD

All the Days of My Struggle

IN HIS HOME WORLD, Walter searched for but never found another Lona, though Mara was very much with him—from her he never stopped learning. He never again sought to travel through the attic mirror. The heavenly hand had sent him back and he would not go out again by his own will. All the days of this struggle he would wait for his renewal to come.

Now and then, when he sat among his books, they seemed to waver, as though a wind had rippled their solid mass and another world was about to break through. Sometimes when he traveled abroad similar things took place. The heavens and the earth, the trees and the grass would appear for a moment to shake as if about to pass away. Then they would settle again into their old familiarity. At times he heard whispering, as if those who loved him were talking of him, but when he strained to distinguish the words they ceased, and all became very still. Walter could never tell whether these things arose from within him, or entered from without. He never sought them, they simply came; he learned to let them come as they would, and then let them go.

A residing sadness remained in the mundane burden of every day aloneness. The rare gleam in a fellow traveler's eye brought momentary relief, serving as a reminder that perhaps he was not the only soul to know of worlds within worlds and doors that lead there. He found that most did not believe him when he attempted to tell them. He recalled the words of Mara: "These things are to be treasured within the heart."

Walter ceased to wonder: what is real and what is dream, and how many layers of reality overlap existence? Was his blessed awakening also just a dream? Is he still asleep in the Sexton's chamber under the watchful eye of his beloved? Or, did he in some way come awake too soon? Are the things that make his heart exult truly existent? In moments of doubt, he still questioned: Did God create the lovely things I dreamt?

Then always came the hope-filled answer: Where *else* could such dreams arise from? And Walter for a moment understood that to dream the dreams given by the Maker is not fool-hearted naivety. When a man dreams his *own* dream, he is at the mercy of those dreams, but when Another gives it to him, that Other is able to fulfill it.

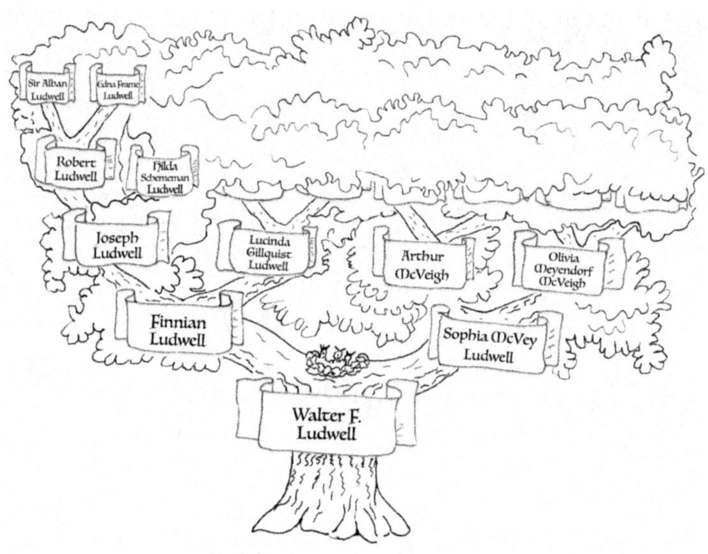

Sir Alban Ludwell
Edna Frame Ludwell
Robert Ludwell
Hilda Schememan Ludwell
Joseph Ludwell
Lucinda Gillquist Ludwell
Arthur McVeigh
Olivia Meyendorf McVeigh
Finnian Ludwell
Sophia McVey Ludwell
Walter F. Ludwell

NOTES

Preface

1. Michael Phillips, *George MacDonald: A Biography of Scotland's Beloved Storyteller*, p. 332

3. A Mirror in the Highest Attic

1. This initial conversation with the Raven might remind readers of Lewis Carroll's *Alice in Wonderland*. Carroll and MacDonald were lifelong friends and would often talk of literature, metaphysics, and the spiritual life. Quoting another author in that era was considered a compliment. *Wonderland* was actually published after *Lilith* and at MacDonald's urging.

33. Here Kitty Kitty

1. *Far more than rubies, worthy thou, O noble wife*
   Can offer no more than her one son's only life
   A widow well before thy temples turned gray
   Heart sore and silent while they mocked and betrayed

50. Just Passing Through

1. If the reader cannot think and remember, it is told of back in Chapter 19, *Leaf and Stem*

53. A Hidden Rite of Passage

1. see Chapter 3